Praise for

A+ for *Freshman Year*! Truly a class act!

The refreshingly composed journey of Tiara Johnson is captivating, credible, and relatable. Bravo to the Websters for their collaboration on this account. As a product of the DC metropolitan area's public and private school systems, this literary time machine escorted me back to the raw emotions I experienced during my transition to, and embracement by, the area's cliquish and exclusive precollegiate society.

—Bryn Phillips, author and editor

I read *Freshman Year* twice.

The story is beautifully written. The authors' creativity and flare for words make this story one which would appeal to a range of ages. It seems to reach two generations of readers. Preteens through late teenagers will enjoy and relate to the book's content. As an adult, I can read with enjoyment and understanding what a teenager encounters in the day-to-day school operation, extracurricular activities, and the relationships among teenage girls and boys.

A good book will hold the reader's interest and make the reader want more. That is exactly what this book, *Freshman Year*, does. I look forward to its publication so I can purchase a copy for that special teenager in my life and myself!

—Diane McFarland, retired teacher and elementary school principal

FRESHMAN YEAR

It has been more than twenty-five years since I was a high school freshman. Within the first few pages of this book, I felt as though I were there again. Like Tiara (the main character), I too was forced to move to a different state and school in my high school years. Therefore, I could relate to her experience. The scenes and interactions are very real to a modern-day high school experience.

As a mother and aunt, I loved this book. The content is relevant and clean for a high schooler. From a parent's perspective, it is appropriately presented. Preteens, teenagers, young adults, educators, and parents are just a few who will appreciate this book.

I strongly recommend this book!

—Teresa Hodge

Freshman Year
BULLIES BEWARE!

Kesia Ryan-Webster
and
Anita Ryan-Webster

Freshman Year: Bullies Beware!

Copyright © 2014 Kesia Ryan-Webster and Anita Ryan-Webster. All rights reserved. No part of this book may be reproduced or retransmitted in any form or by any means without the written permission of the publisher.

Published by Wheatmark®
1760 East River Road, Suite 145
Tucson, Arizona 85718
U.S.A.

www.wheatmark.com

ISBN: 978-1-62787-071-9 (paperback)
ISBN: 978-1-62787-072-6 (ebook)
LCCN: 2013952391

Prologue

"Tiara... Tiara... You've got to come with me! Coach Alice needs you right away," Mya panted, all out of breath from her sprint across the field to the clubhouse, where Tiara had just finished using the bathroom.

Tiara continued washing her hands. "What's wrong? Where's the fire?"

Mya Ingram's cute, coffee-colored face was flushed from her race across the athletic field. Mya was hyper, very easily excited, and Tiara was not in the least bit alarmed to see her come flying into the locker room as if the devil himself were chasing her.

"You have to hurry. Ebony did something to her ankle. They think she broke it. The ambulance is taking her away, and we need someone to run her race," Mya rambled on, still out of breath.

"Are you crazy? I've never even run the hurdles!"

"Coach Alice told me to bring you back to the track, pronto! She's already signed you up. If we don't get someone to fill in for Ebony, the entire team will be disqualified." Mya broke into a run, and Tiara sprinted after her. Together they headed across the field where the Boston regional track and field meet was taking place.

Tiara Johnson was tall for an eighth-grader. At five feet, seven inches, she was taller than all the other girls in her class and some of the boys, for that matter. As she ran alongside Mya, her caramel-colored skin started to take on a glow. Tiara loved running. Actually, she just loved moving quickly. That's probably the reason she and Mya had been best friends since first grade—they both had a lot of excess energy to burn.

Both girls were very pretty, but in different ways. Mya hated spending time on her hair, so her mom had allowed her to cut it short and keep it in a curly Afro. Tiara also hated fussing with her thick shoulder-length natural hair, but her mother had simply refused to let her cut it short. Instead, Tiara kept it together by getting it braided once a month at the Hair Gallery. That way, she didn't have to mess with it too often—just wash it, gather it up in a ponytail, tie it with a scrunchie, and that was that.

The two girls looked great in their navy blue track-and-field gym shorts and matching white tops with navy trim. Tiara and Mya were both eighth-graders at Boston Middle School in Newton, Massachusetts, a suburb just outside of Boston. They were both athletes, participating on almost all of their school teams. As a result, everyone knew them, and they were part of the popular crowd.

Today was the annual regional track and field meet. All the public schools in Massachusetts had been invited to participate. Boston Middle School had been doing great. So far, they were in first place. Tiara had already completed her two events. She'd taken first place in the hundred-yard dash and had helped her teammates get to first place by running anchor in the relay race.

Tiara had seen her mom and dad sitting in the bleachers, cheering her on as she'd zipped around the track during both of her events. She'd been thrilled to know that both of her parents, who were very busy professionals, had still managed to find time to attend her track meet.

Tiara's mom, Lisa Slade-Johnson, was a dynamic criminal defense attorney who worked for the Roxbury public defender's office in downtown Roxbury, Massachusetts. Roxbury was in the heart of the ghetto. Tiara's mom had been working there for the last eight years, defending some really hard-core criminals. Tiara knew her mom was a great attorney. Everyone said so, and anyway, her name was always showing up in the *Boston Globe* newspaper.

Tiara's parents had met each other when her mom was only a freshman in college and her dad was completing his last year at Harvard Medical School. Lisa Slade and Blake Spencer Johnson dated for the next three years until Tiara's mom completed her undergraduate studies at Boston College. Tiara's parents were married two weeks after Lisa graduated from college. Tiara was born two years later while her mom was in her second year at Harvard Law School. Tiara's dad was fond of saying that Tiara was an "on time" baby since she'd been patient enough to wait until two days after the semester had ended before making her grand debut. June fourth had been the special day.

Tiara's mom had continued at Harvard, even after Tiara's arrival. While Lisa attended her last year of law school, Tiara's dad had become her primary daytime caregiver. When Lisa returned from class in the evening, Blake would leave for his job at the Peter Brent Brigham Hospital, where he was on staff in the anesthesiology department. Because they worked as a team, Lisa had been able to complete her final year of law school on schedule right along with the rest of her classmates. And because of all the time she'd spent with her dad, Tiara and Blake Johnson had become extremely close.

For the first three years after graduating from law school, Lisa worked at a private high-powered law firm. However, things changed when Tiara's younger brother, Spencer Jr., was born. Working at a high-powered law firm with two small children was too much to handle. Lisa finally relinquished her position at Bennet and O'Brien and accepted a position at the public defender's office. There, she had a lot more leeway and flexibility to take time off when emergencies came up with either Tiara or Spencer Jr.

Lisa Johnson was Tiara's champion. Mother and daughter did everything together. Lisa attended all of her children's special activities. Blake also tried, but unfortunately, more often than not, he'd have to cancel at the last minute when an accident or some other emergency was rushed to the hospital. Today was definitely special for Tiara because both of her parents were attending her track meet.

Completely out of breath, Tiara and Mya arrived at the center of the field at the same time. "Coach Alice," Tiara puffed out. "You wanted to see me?"

"Tiara . . . great . . . great! I assume Mya's filled you in?"

"Yeah, but, I've never run the hurdles. I don't even know how to do it. I can't do it!"

"You have to. If you don't, the entire team will be disqualified."

"I can't!"

"There's no can't about this," Coach Alice commanded. "You don't have to win. You simply have to be an entry."

"Coach Alice . . . "

"Think about your teammates. You can't let them down."

Tiara looked around, taking in the faces of the rest of her classmates, who had circled around to hear the conversation. Coach Alice didn't say why she'd chosen Tiara to run this race. She didn't have to. Tiara was the best runner on the team. Still, jumping hurdles was totally different from running. There was a technique, and it wasn't easy to master. What if she knocked all the bars down, or worse yet, what if she fell flat on her face?

All of her teammates were staring at her, pleading with their eyes. She had no choice.

"All right. I'll do it, but you'll have to show me how."

"Yeah! Yeah!" A chorus of cheers went up from the others.

"Okay, Tiara," Coach Alice said, pulling her to the side of the track. "There are eight hurdles. You'll begin at the start line in a crouch position. When the gun goes off, you start running. Make a fast break, if you can. Now, everything about the hurdles is in the rhythm. As you approach the first hurdle, you want to jump over with your right leg and pull your left leg over behind you. You'll sprint to the next hurdle. Jump over that one with your right leg and again, pull your left leg over. Keep the rhythm going in your head . . . run, jump, pull over . . . run, jump, pull over. You'll do that until you've cleared all eight. When you've jumped the last one, make a break for it and run as fast as you can to the finish line. Do you have that?"

"Yes," Tiara hesitantly replied. "Jump with my right, pull over with my left. Jump with my right, pull over with my left."

"That's right. Now don't worry about placing. We just need you to run so the team won't be disqualified . . . got that?"

"Yes," Tiara said. Coach Alice walked her over to the start line to join the girls from the competing teams. Eight girls were competing. Tiara was the third one in from the edge of the inside field.

Tiara took a quick glance at the bleachers and saw the surprised look on her parents' faces. They knew the hurdle wasn't one of her events. She was sure they were wondering what the heck she was doing at the starting line. Tiara had no time to think about any of that right now. She could hear the head coach calling out the start of the race.

"On you mark . . . get set . . . " *Bang!*

The handgun went off, sending all the runners down the track. Her long individual braids, which she had pulled back into a high ponytail early this morning, flared out straight behind her like a horse's mane.

From a distance, Tiara could hear her teammates chanting. "Tiara... Tiara... She's our man... If she can't do it... No one can."

Over and over, Tiara heard the chant as her teammates cheered her on. Tiara flew. She arrived at the first hurdle, jumped, and pulled her leg over. She took a quick glance to her left. No one was next to her on that side. She kept going. The next hurdle was coming up.

Jump, pull it over.

Again, Tiara quickly glanced to her right. No one was next to her on that side either. Where is everyone else, she wondered.

"Go, Tiara, go!"

"Go, Tiara, go!"

She heard the chants. She kept moving. She was pumping her legs as fast as they would go.

Jump, pull it over.

This is fun, Tiara thought. All the while, her feet kept moving, barely touching the ground. She was running on her toes, her heels never making it back down. It took too much time to do that, and one thing Tiara didn't have right now was time.

Jump, pull it over.

Where is everyone else, she wondered again.

Jump, pull it over.

Tiara turned to her right and then to her left. No one was on either side of her.

Jump, pull it over.

Tiara looked over her shoulder. All the other runners were behind her... far behind her.

"Go, Tiara, go!"

"Go, Tiara, go!"

Jump, pull it over. Tiara couldn't believe it. She was out in first place. Jump, pull it over. That was the last hurdle.

"Run, Tiara, run!"

"Run, Tiara, run!"

Tiara ran like a bat out of hell. She was flying, way out in front of everyone else. She was coming up to the finish line by herself.

"Ti . . . ar . . . ra. Ti . . . ar . . . ra."

The entire bleacher had gone wild. Everyone was chanting. They were all calling out her name. Tiara crossed the finish line. Boston Middle School had just won the regional track and field meet. Everyone was at the final line: Coach Alice, all her teammates, Mom and Dad. This had to be the best day of her life.

Tiara came out of the locker room, five or six of her teammates tagging along beside her. The school bus had driven the team back to Boston Middle School, where the entire student body had met them in the parking lot to cheer for them. Now, forty-five minutes later, Tiara was again crossing the parking lot to meet her parents. She spotted them leaning against the family's dark green Volvo SUV. They were chatting with some other parents while they waited for her. As Tiara approached the car, Lisa pushed herself off the vehicle with one smooth movement, holding out her arms to pull her daughter into them. Lisa's hug was tight as she kissed her baby girl on the cheek.

"You were great, Tiara," Lisa said. Tiara stepped out of her arms and turned toward her dad. Blake Johnson gathered her up and gave his daughter a fierce hug.

"Great job, baby girl. You were fantastic!" He planted a kiss on her cheek. "You're definitely a champion." He opened the back door to allow Tiara to jump inside. Spencer Jr. was already sitting on the backseat, as usual, reading one of his science fiction books.

"I hear you did a good job today," Spencer Jr. said as Tiara got in and sat down beside him. He grinned. "I guess you were just lucky."

"Right!" Tiara agreed, giving him a playful smack on the arm. "Just luck." She smiled back at her brother. Even though they were three years apart, they got along pretty well . . . for a brother and sister, that is.

Blake started the car and drove the vehicle out of the parking lot. Lisa twisted around to look at Tiara. "What made you decide to do the hurdles?" she asked.

"They were desperate! Ebony did something to her ankle, and we would have been disqualified if someone hadn't taken her place. I was the only one they could send in."

"Well, you did that!" Blake said, not even trying to conceal his pride. Tiara thought he was going to burst. "We definitely have to celebrate. Let's go out for dinner. And we're going to let the champion choose where we eat tonight."

"Great!" Tiara replied. "Let's go to Legal Seafood."

"Legal Seafood it is," Blake said. He made a left, heading to the mall in Newton Center. "What happened to Ebony's ankle?"

"They think she may have broken it, but no one really knows for certain," Tiara replied. "They took her to the hospital for X-rays, so I guess we'll find out later tonight."

"It may only be a bad sprain," Blake said. "Sometimes a really bad sprain can feel just as bad as a break."

"Did her parents attend the meet today?" Lisa said.

"No, they couldn't make it... as usual." Tiara muttered the last part of her statement under her breath. Ebony's parents never made it to any of her school activities, or anything else for that matter. They were always too busy, or so they said. Tiara was sure glad they weren't her parents.

A short while later, the family pulled into the underground parking lot at Newton Mall. Although it was only six thirty, the lot was crowded with Friday-night patrons ready to get an early start on the weekend. Blake found a parking space at the far end of the lot. He slid out of the front seat, walked around the hood of the car to the passenger side, and held the door open for his wife before reaching back to open the door for Tiara. Spencer Jr. had already jumped out of the backseat, slamming the door of the Volvo shut. Blake reached for his suit jacket, which Lisa had been holding on her lap. Once he put it on, he joined the others and they all trouped inside the air-conditioned building.

As usual, the mall was packed. Legal Seafood was

located at the far end of the corridor on the first floor. The owner was a good friend of Blake and Lisa's. As was their routine, the family walked around to the side of the restaurant and entered by the employee entrance. They were greeted by Leonard Saul, one of the headwaiters, and were soon escorted to one of the booths in the nonsmoking section of the restaurant.

Tiara loved their New England clam chowder. She ordered a large bowl whenever they came to the restaurant. Spencer Jr. chose the fish and chips special, while both of their parents ordered the stuffed trout.

"Make sure the heads are cut off, please," Tiara reminded the waitress before she walked off. Tiara hated looking at fish heads when they were served up on the dinner plate. She often wondered about the fish . . . what had it been thinking just before it was scooped out of the water and shipped off to be turned into a meal? She wondered if it had a family, and if so, whether they too were also being eaten at that moment.

"Tiara?"

Tiara woke up from her mini-reverie. "Yes?"

"Your father and I have some wonderful news."

"What is it?" Tiara asked, looking at her parents with interest.

"Your father has been offered a position to head the anesthesiology department starting in July . . . at a brand-new hospital."

"That's super, Daddy!" Tiara said. "Congratulations!"

"Wow, Daddy! That's really great," Spencer Jr. said. "Which hospital is it?"

Tiara's parents exchanged a quick glance. Was something wrong?

"The hospital is called the Greater Northeast Hospital," Lisa said.

"Where is it?" Tiara asked.

Washington, DC," Blake said.

"Washington, DC!" Spencer Jr. shouted.

"Washington, DC!" Tiara echoed.

"Yes," Blake replied. "The managing director of the hospital has been in touch with me several times over the last three or four months. They'd been asking me to come down to take a look at the place. Last month, I finally took a tour. It's absolutely incredible! Everything is state of the art.

"I'd only intended to look around, but after touring the building and seeing the equipment they had, I really had to think about it when they made me an offer. Your mom and I have been discussing it for the last few weeks. It was an offer I couldn't refuse. Yesterday, I accepted the position."

"Daddy, you didn't!" Tiara cried out. "I don't want to move to Washington, DC. I don't want to leave my school! I don't want to leave my friends! I love it here. All my friends are here. I don't want to go!"

"Tiara, calm down," Lisa whispered loudly. "Don't make a scene."

"But I don't want to leave Boston," Tiara wailed. "Spencer, do you want to leave?"

Always the little diplomat, Spencer Jr. looked from his parents to Tiara and back to his parents again. "Couldn't we stay in Boston, Daddy? Maybe you can move to DC for a few months and come back after that."

Tiara looked at her brother in total disgust. "It's a permanent job, idiot."

"Tiara! Don't call your brother an idiot," Lisa said. "We might as well tell you the rest. An old friend of mine from law school contacted me two weeks ago. His firm needs to add several criminal attorneys to their staff. He offered me a position. It's a real prestigious law firm . . . McKenzie, Kennedy, and McKenzie. I gave up private practice when you were younger because it was too time-consuming, but now that both of you are older, I'd really like to work at a private firm again."

"What are you saying, Mom?" Tiara asked, trying unsuccessfully to hide her irritation.

"What I'm saying is that I've accepted the offer."

This was too much. Her mom and dad were making all their decisions without consulting any of the "little people" in the household. It just wasn't fair.

"Well, what about us?" Tiara cried out.

Several customers from the surrounding tables turned to look and listen in.

"What about Spencer and me? I'll be starting high school in the fall. I'm going to be a freshman next year. What about all my friends? I don't know anyone in DC."

"Tiara, trust us! It's going to be fine," Lisa said. "Alex McKenzie introduced us to his friend who teaches at one of the prep schools in DC. The friend told us about two openings for the fall at two of the really good private schools. One is for a seventh-grader at St. Paul's Prep, an all-boys school, and the other is for a ninth-grader at Skidmore Prep.

"Mom, you don't understand. I love Boston. I love Boston Middle School. I don't want to leave!"

"Princess, it's going to be all right," Blake said.

Whenever her dad called her princess she knew he was trying to soften her up. "How can you say that, Daddy?"

"Washington, DC, is not that far away," he said. "Mya and Ebony and all your other friends can come and visit. You'll really love it when you get there. Trust me, Tiara! Freshman year at Skidmore Prep is going to be wonderful. Trust me . . . you'll see."

Chapter 1

Washington, DC
Friday, September 4

September in Washington, DC, was a butt-kicker. Even though it was just eight o'clock in the morning, it felt like noon in the middle of summer. The humidity reached out and grabbed Tiara the minute she and her mom stepped out of Lisa's air-conditioned BMW in the underground garage of the law firm of McKenzie, Kennedy, and McKenzie.

Lisa glanced at Tiara as they waited for the elevator doors to slide shut. She pressed the fifth-floor button before turning to speak to Tiara. "We're only going to be at the office for an hour or two."

Tiara still hadn't gotten over the family's move to Washington, DC. She also hadn't forgiven her parents for making what she considered a very one-sided decision.

Now, instead of ranting and raving as she'd previously been doing, Tiara was simply subjecting her parents to the silent treatment, which she had really become good at. She spoke only when spoken to.

"After the meeting we'll go shopping for your clothes and school supplies," Lisa said.

Tiara nodded but still didn't say anything. Spencer Jr. and their dad were also spending the day getting the necessary items for back to school.

The elevator came to a smooth stop, the doors slid open, and Tiara followed her mother into the hallway. The huge mahogany doors facing them were emblazoned with the firm's name: McKenzie, Kennedy, and McKenzie.

Tiara was familiar with the firm. She'd already visited with her mom several times since their move to Washington, DC, two months before. Stepping through the double doors ahead of Lisa, Tiara took in the luxurious surroundings of the prestigious legal empire. Several burgundy wing-backed chairs were evenly spaced throughout the reception area, positioned around some brightly polished antique mahogany end tables. The furniture blended in well with the plush hunter-green wall-to-wall carpeting that was deep enough to sink into.

Ellen, the daytime administrative assistant, was seated behind the huge mahogany receptionist alcove, which took up a third of the receiving area.

"Good morning," Ellen said. Ellen had the prettiest blue eyes Tiara had ever seen. Her light brown hair was cut in a short bob that framed her petite face. Tiara immediately liked her the first day they'd met.

"Hi, Ellen," Tiara replied.

"Good morning," Lisa echoed. "How is everything going?"

"Just fine, Ms. Johnson." Ellen came out from behind the desk and walked with Tiara and Lisa to Lisa's office. "It's still fairly quiet on the home front right now, but then again, it's still early. Most of the other attorneys haven't arrived yet. They'll probably be drifting in shortly. I left a few phone messages on your desk. Can I get you something to drink?" Ellen asked, looking from Lisa to Tiara.

Lisa had picked up her messages and was glancing through them. "I'll have a cup of coffee, please. I'm headed to the conference room now, so if you don't mind, I'll take it in there. I can probably answer a few of these calls before the others arrive." Lisa gathered a few of the files from her inbox. "Tiara, do you want something to drink?"

"I'll have a glass of juice, please," Tiara replied, looking back at Ellen.

"Coming right up."

Lisa turned to look at her daughter seated in front of her in the large maroon chair. She imagined Tiara was pretending to be a great criminal defense attorney preparing for a big trial. Lisa was really proud of her daughter. Not only was Tiara a bright student, but she was extremely popular as well. She made friends easily. Lisa knew the main reason for that was Tiara's sweet, kindhearted disposition.

Lisa knew this move had been hard on her daughter. Tiara had spent the majority of the last two months working on the distant learning classes she was taking through Johns Hopkins University. Both Tiara and Spencer were part of the gifted and talented program. Aside from playing tennis at the Arthur Ashe Tennis Club down the block from their new home at the edge of Rock Creek Park, Tiara hadn't ventured too far around the city. She had yet to make any friends in their new neighborhood. Although this worried Lisa somewhat, she'd managed to put it out of her mind for the time being. She was sure everything would be fine once school started and Tiara made some new friends at Skidmore Prep.

"Would you like to wait here in my office, or would you prefer to join me in the conference room?" she asked, interrupting Tiara's daydream.

"Oh, ahh . . . I'll be all right in here," Tiara replied with a quick smile. "I brought along the last book on my summer reading list."

"Okay." Lisa walked over to the floor-to-ceiling bookshelves stacked high with heavy volumes of legal texts. Selecting one, she placed it under her arm.

"I'll be in the conference room. If you need anything, just give Ellen a buzz," she said, pointing to the intercom on her desk.

"I'll be fine, Mom. You can leave," Tiara said, trying her best to hurry her mother out of the room.

"All right, sweetie. I'll see you in a bit." Lisa walked out the door.

Tiara swiveled around in her chair and gazed out of the fifth-floor window. She'd hated the move to Washington, DC, although she sure did love her mother's new law firm. On the surface, it appeared to be extremely formal and highbrow, but the people she'd been introduced to seemed down-to-earth and really sincere.

Tiara swiveled the chair around as she heard Ellen reenter the office.

"Here you go." Ellen placed a tray with a glass of ice and a can of mango juice on the desk. Tiara had been given a glass of mango juice on her last visit to the office. She'd told Ellen then that she loved the fresh taste of the tropical fruit drink, so she wasn't surprised to see that Ellen had brought her some more.

"Can I get you anything else?" Ellen asked.

"No, I'm good," Tiara responded. "But I was wondering about the firm. How old is it? Has it been around a long time?"

"Kind of, sort of," Ellen replied with a smile, taking the seat nearest to the desk. "McKenzie, Kennedy, and McKenzie was initially established here in Washington, DC, almost one hundred years ago by Adam Alexander McKenzie Jr., the grandfather of Mr. Adam McKenzie, one of our senior partners and the great-grandfather of Mr. Alex McKenzie.

"Back then, Mr. McKenzie Jr. was a solo practitioner. Everyone was going through the Great Depression, but financially, Adam McKenzie Jr. was one of the few who didn't suffer in the least. He was a criminal law specialist. Some very high-profile cases landed in his lap, and he did a great job with them. Soon he was the attorney everyone wanted to hire. As a result, he became a very wealthy man.

"Within a short time, Mr. McKenzie Jr. expanded the practice by inviting one of his good friends, James Kennedy, to join the firm as his partner. When Mr. McKenzie Jr.'s son Adam graduated from Harvard Law School, he too joined the DC firm after spending a few years practicing in California," Ellen explained.

"Adam's son, Alex McKenzie, also started out at the firm right after graduating from Harvard Law School. Alex, as you already know, is now one of the senior partners in the criminal department. I believe he and your mom attended Harvard Law School together.

"McKenzie, Kennedy, and McKenzie is now one of the busiest and most sought-after law firms, not only in DC, but nationwide," Ellen proudly explained. "We're growing rapidly and we still have to hire more attorneys to keep up with all the work we're getting. That's why we were so excited that your mom could come and join us."

"Wow," said Tiara. "That's pretty impressive. My mom told me a little about the firm before she accepted the offer, but not all that. My mom's cousin also works here—Justin Kramer."

"Mr. Kramer...of course." Ellen nodded. "Mr. Kramer is one of our partners. He heads our entertainment division."

Glancing at her watch, Ellen seemed shocked at the length of time she'd spent talking to Tiara. "Well," she said, standing up and heading toward the office door, "I have to go. If you need anything, just give me a buzz."

"I will." If everyone else at the firm was as friendly as Ellen, Tiara knew her mom was going to enjoy working at McKenzie, Kennedy, and McKenzie.

Chapter 2

Lisa pushed open the door at the end of the hall and entered the room. Several men and one woman were seated at a conference table.

"Lisa, so glad to see you," Alex McKenzie said as he walked over and gave his newest associate and old law school friend a hug. For the last two months, Alex and some of the other attorneys had been out of town working on a major international case. This was their first Monday-morning meeting since Lisa's arrival at the firm.

"Thank you," Lisa replied. "I'm really happy to be here."

"Lisa!" The joyful shout came from the good-looking guy on the other side of the room. Justin Kramer III walked over and planted a kiss on Lisa's cheek. "You look wonderful."

"Thanks, cuz. So do you."

Justin and Lisa went back a long way. Justin's mother, Elaine Kramer, and Lisa's mother, Candace Slade, were sisters, born and raised in Boston. After high school, Candace traveled down to Washington, DC, to attend Howard University. Two years later, her younger sister, Elaine, joined her there. Elaine remained in DC while Candace returned to Boston after completing college. A year after graduation, Candace married Nicholas Slade, Lisa's father. Shortly after her graduation from college, Elaine met and married Justin Kramer Jr., Justin's dad, who was now a judge at the US District Court in Washington, DC.

Although Justin was two years younger than Lisa, they were still very close. Lisa sometimes thought of him as a brother. Justin used to have a brother—an identical twin who had died at the age of three, leaving Justin to be raised as an only child. During summer vacations, Justin would often come to Boston with his parents and spend time with Lisa and her younger brother, Nicholas Jr.

Lisa's friends had all had a crush on Justin. That was understandable since he'd always been so good-looking. Glancing at him now in the crowded conference room, Lisa realized that Justin had grown up and become a gorgeous man. No less than six feet, two inches tall and muscular, Justin looked like a poster boy for the US Army. Lisa knew that physique came from the years he'd attended West Point and the two years he'd served in the air force before completing a combined business and law degree in Atlanta at Morehouse University.

Justin's black hair was cut close to his head, military style. His nose was aquiline in shape, but his most striking feature against his sable-colored skin was his piercing golden eyes. As Lisa looked over at him, she realized that her cousin had simply improved with age.

"Let me introduce you to everyone," Justin said. "This young man is Joel Cohen. Joel has been with the firm for almost four years now, and he does a lot of work with Alex in our criminal law division. Joel is a Harvard graduate, but we don't hold that against him." He chuckled, knowing that Lisa was also a Harvard grad.

"Nice to meet you, Joel," Lisa said with a laugh, taking in his age. He was young, probably only around twenty-seven or twenty-eight years old.

"Nice to meet you too, Lisa," Joel replied. "It's great to have you onboard. We really need someone with your years of expertise. We have a ton of cases and more coming in every day."

"This is our newest associate, Paige Singleton," Justin continued. Lisa reached over to shake hands with the only other woman in the room.

"Welcome," Paige greeted her.

"Thank you." Lisa smiled back at the lovely African American woman standing in front of her. Paige was a tall, toffee-colored beauty, elegantly dressed in a cream pantsuit.

"It's going to be great having another woman here," Paige said.

"Again, thank you," Lisa answered.

"These young men over here are two of our junior associates," Justin continued. "They'll assist you with any of the overflow. This is Robert Brown." Justin gestured to a young Caucasian man. "Robert recently graduated from Boston College Law School. And this is Julius Johnson," Justin continued, gesturing toward the African American, another recent graduate. "Julius attended Columbia Law School in New York."

Lisa nodded at the two junior associates, shaking hands with each one before taking a seat at the conference table. Ellen entered the room and joined the group around the table, prepared to take notes.

"We generally spend our Monday-morning meetings assigning new cases and discussing the progress on current cases," Alex explained. "We heard that in our absence you jumped right in and have taken on several of our really tough cases."

"Well, since I was already settled in at home, I decided to get right to work, and I'm really glad I did. I've accepted the Davis case."

"Yes, we heard," Justin said, his admiration obvious. The Davis case looks like its going to be extremely difficult. "How is it going, by the way?"

"Actually, not too bad. I've been to DC Jail several times and met with Ms. Davis. She's in protective custody."

"How is she holding up?" Alex asked.

"As well as can be expected under the circumstances."

The Davis case was one of the firm's extremely high-profile cases. Kyra Davis, a twenty-one-year-old white college student from Howard University, was being held at DC Jail on a second-degree murder charge. She'd been arrested for allegedly driving the getaway car belonging to members of the Heats street gang. Apparently members of the gang had opened fire on a rival drug dealer last March, killing Tony Linwood, an uninvolved bystander. Kyra Davis was the only daughter of Senator Davis from Florida. Ms. Davis would serve a life sentence if Lisa's defense team was unsuccessful.

The Davis family had a lot of clout and a lot of cash. They'd retained the services of McKenzie, Kennedy, and McKenzie, the most prestigious law firm in DC, to get their daughter out of this madness. Lisa, with her exceptional credentials, had taken the case and was now the lead counsel.

"I intend to meet with her again on Tuesday, right after the Labor Day holiday," Lisa explained. "She was just starting to open up during our last visit. I'm sure by the time we meet again I'll really be able to get things rolling."

"Sounds great," Alex agreed. "Have you settled into the house yet?"

"Yes, we're all moved in."

Alex McKenzie had been instrumental in helping Lisa and Blake locate their new home. In fact, Alex had been the one to inform the Johnsons that the property next to his had just been placed on the market. Lisa and Blake had flown to DC the first week in April to take a look. They'd fallen in love with the huge house on Kennedy Street and immediately contacted the broker. Seconds after walking through the last room, they'd agreed to buy it.

Lisa listened intently as the other attorneys presented their ongoing cases. The legal group was a very friendly mixture of personalities. Lisa knew she'd made the right decision in coming to work for the firm.

Chapter 3

Tiara glanced up from *Jane Eyre*—one of the required classics on the ninth-grade reading list—and swiveled around on her mom's cushioned chair, turning to gaze out the window directly behind her. There was a great view from the fifth floor. Traffic was moving rapidly up and down K Street. But Tiara didn't really see any of it; her mind was focused on other things totally unrelated to the traffic below. Her thoughts wandered back to her last week in Boston.

Their house in Newton sold the very first day it was listed in April. The new family was frantic to move in by the first of July, so six days after school ended, Tiara and the rest of the Johnsons had loaded their last suitcases into the family Volvo and begun their eight-hour drive to Washington, DC.

The trip had not been pleasant. Tiara definitely made sure of that, sulking the entire eight hours. With her headphones blasting away, she had completely tuned out her parents' conversation from the front seat and her brother's snores next to her on the backseat. Already, she missed her friends. Yes, her parents had promised to invite them to DC for visits, but Tiara knew their friendships would never be the same. It was inevitable that Mya and Ebony would both find new best friends, possibly each other, and she would be left with no one.

They arrived in Washington, DC, late that evening and checked into the Hyatt Regency Hotel on Connecticut Avenue. Lisa had made reservations for them to stay there while the new house was being renovated. Tiara didn't care where they stayed.

Marilyn Goodly, their housekeeper for the last fifteen years, had driven down a week earlier to help the decorators get everything in place. Tiara hadn't been interested in any of the relocation plans. All she'd wanted to do was get the heck out of DC and back to Boston with her friends. That, she knew, was never going to happen.

The family checked into a suite on the third floor of the downtown hotel. No denying it, the place was dynamite, but Tiara was too tired after the long trip to enjoy any of the luxuries at her disposal. She'd fallen into bed in one of the smaller rooms in the huge suite and instantly gone to sleep. She woke the next morning feeling excited but not knowing why. Oh yeah, that was the day they'd finally get a chance to see the new house.

Tiara was the first one up and dressed. As she walked into the living room, it dawned on her that she had the run of the entire place. Flipping on the TV and turning the volume down low, Tiara started surfing the stations.

During the night, she had made a decision to end her tantrums. Realistically, ranting and raving at her parents wasn't getting her anywhere. The deed was done. Lisa and Blake Johnson had made this life-changing move and, for what it was worth, they simply expected her to go along with it. Well, she wasn't going to . . . and that was that.

The door to the other small bedroom opened slowly. Spencer Jr. walked out still wearing his pj's.

"Hi," he greeted his sister. "Why you up so early?"

"Couldn't sleep any longer."

"Excited about the new house?"

"A little," Tiara admitted. There really was no point in lying. She definitely was excited about seeing where they were going to live.

"Me too." Catching sight of the menu in her hand, he asked, "Can we order room service?" He smiled, hoping he'd be able to order whatever he wanted while their parents were still asleep.

"Why not?" Tiara replied with a chuckle. French toast, bacon and eggs, cereal, milk, and juice. They'd feasted like kings, watching cable television while they waited for their parents to wake up.

"This is the life," Spencer Jr. pronounced during one of the commercial breaks as he'd stretched out further on the sofa. Silently, Tiara nodded in agreement.

Tiara returned to the present and glanced around her mother's office. The clock on the desk indicated that it was almost twelve noon. The meeting had been going on for almost four hours. Even so, she wasn't bored. She enjoyed being in her mother's office, pretending to be one of the firm's brilliant attorneys, working on a serious case.

Noticing her mom's state-of-the-art telephone system, Tiara recalled the fun she and Spencer Jr. had talking to each other from all parts of the family's new house through the elaborate intercom system. Tiara hated to admit that she was sort of starting to like the new place, and having Alex McKenzie as a next-door neighbor was also a nice touch. Although he'd been away all summer, Tiara was happy that she would at least know one of their new neighbors.

The first day after arriving in DC, Blake had taken the scenic route to their new home. Leaving the Hyatt Regency Hotel, he'd taken a shortcut through Rock Creek Parkway to get to the upper northwest section of town.

Washington, DC, was an easy city to get around in, at least for a newcomer who took the time to figure it out. The nation's capital had been carefully laid out when it was first designed back in the late seventeen hundreds by Major Pierre Charles L'Enfant, a French engineer and architect. The city was divided into four unequal quadrants with the Capitol building located at the center. North Capitol Street, East Capitol Street, South Capitol Street, and the Mall were the four lines dividing the city's sections. It was also easy to tell the locals from the tourists because no one who resided in DC ever said the full name of any of the four sections. Locals always referred to the quadrants as Northwest (NW), Northeast (NE), Southwest (SW), and Southeast (SE). Not only did the thousands of year-round visitors who were forever coming to the nation's capital not know the abbreviated names, but those that didn't take the time to learn the system were forever getting lost going from one section to the other.

Tiara knew their new home was located in the northwest section of town, and no one had to tell her that the Northwest was the heart of Washington, DC—the undisputed avant-garde district of DC, Downtown Northwest was where all the most important government buildings, monuments, museums, and other tourist attractions were located. The city's main shopping district was also located in the area, north of Pennsylvania Avenue between the White House and the Capitol building.

Some of DC's nicest neighborhoods were in Northwest. Embassy Row extending along Massachusetts Avenue around DuPont Circle and over to Sixteenth Street contained some handsome consulates and embassies. Georgetown, the oldest section of the city, lay west of Rock Creek Park. It had been carefully preserved, and many of its townhouses, which were over two hundred years old, had been restored and were now great examples of early American architecture.

Blake had left the downtown hotel parking lot and driven past the Capitol building, allowing them to get a quick tour of the city before arriving at Rock Creek Parkway.

Parks were scattered throughout DC, but Rock Creek Park was the largest. It ran the length of a small creek, which was where it got the name Rock Creek. It continued all the way through the northwest section of DC right into Maryland in one direction and straight down into Virginia in the opposite direction. Tiara loved it. It was like having your own private forest right in the heart of the city.

Okay, Tiara admitted to herself, so there were one or two things she did like about Washington, DC, but still, she didn't want to stay. She definitely wanted to return to Boston.

Blake had driven through Rock Creek Park, passing the picnic tables scattered throughout. Down a littler further, they drove by the Washington National Zoo, which had been built in the middle of the natural woodland. Blake had parked outside the Carter Barron, a huge athletic facility that also housed an elegant performing arts center. He'd pointed out the Washington Tennis and Education Foundation, which was located on the premises. Lisa had been ecstatic when she'd spotted the tennis center. She'd already preregistered Tiara and Spencer Jr. for lessons but hadn't realized just how close the facility was to their new house.

Less than three minutes after leaving the athletic field, Blake had turned the corner to Sixteenth and Kennedy Street, the section of town commonly known as the "Gold Coast." Many of the city's elite—doctors, lawyers, high-level government officials, and other wannabes—resided in the area.

Blake parked the car in front of a huge redbrick Victorian sitting behind a black iron fence. Tiara's jaw dropped. The house was literally a mansion. In comparison, their home in Boston looked like a dollhouse. Lisa gave them a history of the place before they climbed out of the car.

Apparently the house had been built by some well-known architect in the early nineteen hundreds. Initially, this guy had built the house for himself, but once it was completed, he'd continued and built two identical ones alongside for each of his two daughters. Tiara had glanced over on either side of their new home and saw two identical structures. Lisa's colleague, Alex McKenzie, lived in the one on the right with his new wife, Kathleen, a famous author who wrote under a male pseudonym—a dignified man's name: Spencer Wright.

Lisa informed them that a judge, his wife, and two teenage children lived in the house on the left. The entire family was supposed to be spending the summer in Louisiana.

Blake had opened the front door to a blast of cold air . . . a big difference from the ninety-degree temperature they'd been standing in.

"Thank goodness," Lisa exclaimed as she'd walked inside, commenting on the new central air conditioning she'd instructed the workers to install. Tiara's parents had hired a team of architects to completely renovate the four levels of the hundred-year-old house, retaining the Victorian look but adding all the modern conveniences. Air conditioning had definitely been a priority.

Tiara didn't want to admit it, but the new house was really to die for. It had four different levels and a total of eleven huge bedrooms. Tiara and Spencer Jr. had the entire third floor to themselves while their mom and dad had the fourth floor. The second floor had two formal living rooms, a guest bedroom, a kitchen, and a formal dining room. As far as Tiara was concerned, the basement had to be the best part of the house. This area really was going to belong to Tiara and Spencer Jr. It contained a library for their books only and a large recreation room with a large flat-screen TV. They even had their own computer room with four desktops and a printer set up and ready for use. Tiara had toured the basement, admiring the three additional guest bedrooms and laundry room that were also down there.

Tiara had really wanted to hate the new house but hadn't been able to. Although she'd managed to conceal her glee, Spencer Jr.'s delight over their new digs had more than made up for her silence.

Tiara swiveled around in her mom's chair to face the desk. A glance at the clock told her that it was now twelve thirty. Tiara had finished reading her novel and drinking her juice ages ago. Ellen had returned to the office twice in the last four hours to make sure Tiara didn't need anything. There hadn't been a need then, but now Tiara was definitely hungry. Just as she began to wonder if she should get up and head for the reception area, the office door opened and Lisa entered.

"Everything all right?" Lisa asked, walking over to deposit the files and the yellow legal pad she'd used to take notes onto her massive desk.

"Sure . . . everything's fine. I finished *Jane Eyre*," Tiara replied, so relieved to have company that she completely forgot that she wasn't speaking to her mother. "Are we ready to leave?"

"Just let me get some of the files I'll need over the weekend and we'll be ready," Lisa replied.

Tiara loved shopping at Staples. They always had such high-tech gadgets to look at and all the latest electronic equipment to play with. She'd found all the supplies on the list Skidmore Prep had sent to their incoming students.

Tiara and Lisa had stopped at Chipotle's on Connecticut Avenue and eaten a late lunch before coming to Staples. They sat at one of the outside tables and watched the tourists as they strolled past. Tiara had ordered a veggie burger with fries and an ice-cold glass of lemonade. Lisa had ordered a large chicken salad and an icy Diet Coke.

While they ate, Tiara scribbled out a list of the clothes she wanted. Skidmore Prep didn't require a uniform. Students were actually allowed to wear whatever they wanted, as long as it was "socially acceptable." Tiara didn't need a definition of the term "socially acceptable." She already knew that whatever she wore, Lisa was certainly not going to allow her to walk out the door unless it was acceptable to her.

They'd bought some really cool outfits from Old Navy, Tiara's favorite store. They'd also purchased shoes, several new tops, jeans, and a few skirts. If nothing else, Tiara was really pleased with the "neat stuff" (as her mom described it) she'd been able to get.

By the time they left Staples and loaded everything into the trunk of the BMW, Tiara was on a cheap high. She wished she wasn't still putting her mom through the silent treatment because she really wanted her mom to help her decide which items she should wear with what.

Tiara glanced at her mother's profile as Lisa drove through upper Northwest. On impulse, Tiara placed her anger on hold for a moment and whispered, "Thanks, Mom."

Lisa was stopped at a red light. She turned to look at Tiara, completely caught off guard. "What did you say?" she asked.

"I said thank you," Tiara repeated. "Thanks for taking me shopping."

"Well, you're welcome," Lisa replied, trying hard to conceal her joy at finally having her daughter speak to her again. Lisa and Tiara had always been close and Tiara's silent treatment had really been bothering her.

"It still doesn't change anything," Tiara continued. "I'm still not happy about the move."

Lisa tried hard not to laugh out loud as she pulled up in front of their new house. Tiara climbed out of the car just as the front door to their new home opened. Simultaneously, the door to the neighbor's house on the left opened as well. As Spencer Jr. came flying out of their house and down the steps with Blake following behind at a slower pace, Tiara's eyes shifted to the neighbors' house.

"You should see all the cool stuff we bought," Spencer shouted as Blake walked over to help his wife out of the car. Spencer Jr. was already beside the trunk of the BMW lifting out bag after bag and peering inside each one to see if Lisa had bought anything else for him.

Tiara ignored all of them, staring instead at the two young people who had walked out of their neighbors' house.

Noticing Tiara, the light chocolate African American girl waved, walked down the porch steps, and came to stand by the fence separating the two properties. "Hi! My name's Kamilla," she said.

"Hi," Tiara responded. "I'm Tiara Johnson. That's my brother, Spencer, and my parents."

"Nice to meet you. My mom and dad aren't home right now, but that's my brother over there," she said, pointing to the young man checking his phone on the porch. "His name is Landon."

Tiara looked beyond Kamilla and got a look—a really good look—at Kamilla's brother. The young man now walking down the steps had to be around seventeen years old. He looked like a confident high school junior. He had to be at least six feet tall with the same light chocolate complexion as his sister and thick black hair that fell in waves. Tiara's eyes lowered to take in the broad expanse of chest and the wide shoulders outlined beneath his pale blue polo knit shirt. Below the hem of his short sleeves, his lightly haired forearms tapered down to slim wrists and long fingers, which rested loosely on his hips, touching his conservative black leather belt. The jeans he wore were perfect, not too low but not too high.

Coming to stand by his sister, Landon's dark brown eyes crinkled at the edges as he smiled back at Tiara before turning to Spencer Jr., Lisa, and Blake Johnson.

"Hello," he said, making eye contact with each of

them in turn. Beautiful white teeth, Tiara noticed. Unlike herself, Landon didn't have a set of braces on his to distort his smile.

Landon brought his gaze back to meet Tiara's. "Welcome to the neighborhood," he said with a smile.

She returned the smile. Maybe this move wasn't going to be so bad after all.

Chapter 4

"Mom, you don't have to come in with me! I'm not a kid!"

"Tiara, I'm not going to drop you off at the front door of the place and drive away. Do you want these people to think you're an orphan or something?"

Tiara and Lisa were sitting in the BMW outside the entrance to Skidmore Prep. It was Tuesday morning, the day after the Labor Day weekend, the first day of class. Tiara was determined that her mom was not going to follow her inside the administration building like she was some kind of infant on her first day of pre-k.

Tiara had gotten up at five-thirty that morning. Now that the day had finally arrived, she couldn't hide the fact that she was excited about starting school. She'd jumped into the shower before Spencer Jr. could beat her to it, returning to her bedroom a short while later to get dressed. She'd changed into one of her older pairs of jeans that was already well broken in and pulled on a brand-new white Ralph Lauren polo before racing downstairs to the kitchen.

Marilyn had already made breakfast. Lisa and Blake

sat at the table talking and finishing their eggs and toast. Tiara sat down and poured some raisin bran into a bowl as Spencer Jr. made his appearance, plopping down in the seat next to her.

"Good morning, princess . . . Spencer," Blake addressed each of his kids.

"Good morning," they said in unison.

"Who's driving me to school?" Spencer asked.

"I am," Blake said. "I want to have a quick talk with your headmaster before I leave you there." He turned to Tiara. "Your mom will take you to Skidmore."

An hour later, here they were parked in front of her school. Lisa stepped out of the car and walked around to the passenger door, her presence there forcing Tiara to get out. "Mom, you're illegally parked!" Tiara whined. "The sign right here says no parking." Tiara took a quick glance around the beautifully landscaped courtyard.

She was overwhelmed by the size and sheer beauty of the school. Skidmore Prep was located right in the heart of Northwest Washington, DC. Although it was smack in the middle of the city, you'd never guess it. The main building was at least a mile away from the gated front entrance. It was designed in the Southern tradition of the old antebellum homes. A formal façade was symmetrically graced with columns, balanced windows, and dormers. It was a modern building on the inside with an old-world look on the outside.

"Good morning."

Tiara's quick glance took in the older woman who had just walked out of the front door. As she approached the car, her piercing blue eyes gave Tiara a once over before coming to rest on Lisa standing by the side of the BMW.

"I'm Ms. Block, the headmistress at Skidmore Prep. You must be Ms. Johnson and Tiara Johnson," she said, smiling warmly.

Tiara wondered how she knew that. There had to be other new students starting today.

"Yes, we are," Lisa replied with a smile, stepping forward to shake her hand.

"Wonderful... wonderful. It's so good to meet you, Ms. Johnson, and I'm sure we'll see you this week at the parent–teacher social. Now, I know you probably have to rush off to work so I'll just take Tiara and show her to her homeroom class."

"Well, actually, I thought I would come in..." Lisa trailed off, not wanting to leave her baby girl just like that.

"Oh, that won't be necessary. We have everything under control. Have a good day, Ms. Johnson."

"See you, Mom," Tiara said, a big grin on her face.

Ms. Block put a hand on Tiara's shoulder and the two turned and walked back to the main building.

Déjà vu hit Lisa like a ton of bricks. She was instantly transported back to Tiara's first day at nursery school. Tiara had simply walked away with the nursery school teacher, leaving Lisa standing at the front door near tears. Tiara had strutted through the front door of the nursery school happily waving good-bye to Lisa... just as she was doing now.

"Well!" Lisa returned to the driver's side of her BMW and climbed in. I guess I'm not needed here, she thought as she turned the key in the ignition. She followed the circular driveway back onto Wisconsin Avenue and into the flow of traffic. Circling the block, she headed downtown to the law firm, still thinking about her daughter but actually visualizing a two-year-old Tiara on her first day of nursery school. God, how time flies, Lisa thought as she joined the flow of heavy traffic heading toward downtown Washington, DC.

Tiara walked alongside Ms. Block. They'd exited the main building by a side door and entered a very modern four-story structure about one hundred feet from the administrative building. Ms. Block informed her that this section was Skidmore's high school. The middle school was housed in a separate building one block away while the lower school was situated on a completely separate campus.

They were now standing in front of Tiara's new homeroom, room 401. "The freshman homerooms are located on the top floor of the building," Ms. Block explained. "The sophomores are on the third floor, the juniors on the second, while the seniors have the privilege of being on the first floor." Ms. Block opened the door of the classroom and nodded for Tiara to join her.

This was it, Tiara realized as she followed Ms. Block into the classroom. She knew that from this point on, any move she made would designate her status on the social map of Skidmore. She wasn't worried about the academic side of the school. Not that she believed she was some sort of genius or anything. It was just that academics were always exactly what they seemed to be. An A was always an A; a B would always be a B. Even an F would be, along with shameful, an F. But the social map was inarguably different. A smile was not always a smile, a frown not always a frown. This went for any other facial expression or gestures.

"This must be Tiara!"

Tiara had taken a moment to check out the room, but at the mention of her name she quickly snapped to attention. "Hi," she said, turning to the tan woman standing in front of her. The woman, Tiara's homeroom teacher, or so she assumed, had light blond shoulder-length hair. Although she wasn't definitively pretty, she looked like she could be a model—one of those models that made you think, "Hey, maybe I could be a model too." She wasn't ugly either, of course, but there was just something about her—her nose, maybe her eyes were too far apart, maybe too close—that made you think, Close, but no cigar.

"Hi, Tiara," the woman said.

"This is Mrs. Donovan," Ms. Block explained. "She will be your homeroom teacher for this year. If you have any questions, she's the perfect person to ask."

"Okay," Tiara said. All she was thinking though was, So, Mrs. Donovan is married. Tiara quickly checked out the ring on her finger. It wasn't amazing—gold band, medium-sized diamond—mostly unremarkable and a lot like Mrs. Donovan herself.

"You arrived a little early today, which is fine," Ms. Block continued. "This will give you some time to get acquainted with the classroom. The other students will be here soon."

Tiara took a quick glance around the room as she walked to the center row third desk, which Mrs. Donovan had assigned to her. There was no doubt about it, the classroom was state of the art. Three rows each with five new desks and chairs were the centerpiece of the room. One complete wall was taken up with five computer stations each containing a brand-new flat-screen desktop computer.

The back of the classroom was lined with built-in bookshelves, each loaded with books and other supplies. Tiara was surprised to see three comfortable chairs and a loveseat positioned next to the shelves as if inviting the students to take a seat and relax for a moment or two.

Seated at her desk, Tiara started to unpack her new book bag, placing her school supplies in strategic places on the inside. As she arranged each item, she listened to the conversation between Mrs. Donovan and Ms. Block.

"Oh, it looks like another student has arrived," Mrs. Donovan announced, glancing at the doorway.

From where Tiara was seated, she couldn't see who was standing there.

"Is this room 401?" a girl asked.

"Yes, it is. Come in," Mrs. Donovan said in a syrupy voice.

Tiara watched the girl walk in. She had assumed from the sound of the voice that the girl was white and she was correct. The student was about Tiara's height, maybe a little taller. She too was wearing a shirt from Ralph Lauren, but hers was a button-down, not a polo.

"And what is your name?" Mrs. Donovan asked.

"Brooke," the girl replied. "Brooke Duncan. I'm pretty sure I'm in this homeroom." She glanced at the schedule in her hand.

"Yes," Mrs. Donovan said, checking a sheet of paper on her desk. "You are. I'm Mrs. Donovan, your homeroom teacher for this year. And as you probably already know, this is Ms. Block, the headmistress."

"Hello, Brooke." Ms. Block reached out her hand for a brief handshake. "Welcome to Skidmore Prep."

"Thank you," Brooke replied with a smile. "I know I'm a little early, but my dad had to drive me here on his way to work and today he had to be at his office before eight o'clock."

"That's all right, Brooke," Ms. Block cheerfully replied. "Skidmore Prep opens at seven o'clock each morning, so arriving early is never a problem. Feel free to come anytime after seven o'clock if that's more convenient for your family. Just remember that the first bell rings at seven fifty-five."

"I'll definitely let my dad know that."

"You're not the only new student in this homeroom either." Ms. Block turned to look at Tiara.

"Brooke Duncan, meet Tiara Johnson," Mrs. Donovan said, leaving Brooke to make her way to the middle of the classroom where Tiara was seated.

The two girls shook hands, then Brooke made her way to her desk and sat down.

Seeing they were settled in, Ms. Block turned to Mrs. Donovan. "I probably won't be in my office very much today, but call me if there's any confusion about schedules or anything else."

"Okay, thanks."

There were a few moments of silence as Tiara returned to looking around the classroom. She stole a glance at Mrs. Donovan, who had taken a seat behind her desk. Tiara turned to face the new girl. She had taken the desk on Tiara's left and started to unpack her book bag.

"So," Tiara said, "you're a new Skidmore student."

"Yeah," Brooke replied.

"I just moved to DC from Boston. I'm still getting used to it. Are you from DC?"

"Yup. Born and raised."

"Cool."

Tiara struggled to think of something to say to keep the conversation going. Luckily, another figure appeared in the doorway, grabbing both girls' attention. This girl was taller than Tiara and Brooke by a couple of inches, with long black hair worn in a ponytail. She walked purposefully up to Mrs. Donovan's desk and said something to her. Mrs. Donovan gestured to both girls. Tiara glanced at Brooke but she just shrugged. The dark-haired girl then left the room.

"Who was that, Mrs. Donovan?" Brooke asked. Tiara was glad Brooke had asked because Tiara wouldn't have even though she very much wanted to know.

"That was Amanda Carter," Mrs. Donovan said. "She's going to be a buddy to both of you."

A few moments later Amanda returned. "They were in the teachers' lounge," she said, holding up some nametags.

Amanda walked over to Tiara and Brooke and gave one

to each of them. She took a Sharpie out of her pocket and handed it to Tiara.

"Hey, guys, I'm Amanda. I'm going to be your buddy, which means that we're going to be in the same classes together. If either of you gets lost or needs anything and Mrs. Donovan isn't around, then you can ask me. I'm basically your private tour guide," she said with a smile.

"That sounds helpful," Tiara said. She quickly wrote her name on the nametag and handed the Sharpie to Brooke, who wrote her name on hers and returned the Sharpie to Amanda.

"I hope so," Amanda said. She walked over to the desk in the first row directly across the aisle from Tiara and sat down, turning around in her chair to face Tiara and Brooke. "Why don't I give you a little history about Skidmore Prep," she said.

"Sure," both girls replied in unison.

"What's to know?" Brooke asked.

"Well, Skidmore is one of the oldest prep schools in the country and the oldest on the east coast. It's referred to as the Harvard of prep schools. As a result, it's almost impossible to get in here."

"Really?" Brooke asked, intrigued by this information.

"Yes, really. Not just anyone gets accepted here. There are two basic criteria for gaining admission."

"Those being?" Tiara asked, knowing that was exactly what Amanda wanted her to do.

"One, you definitely have to be smart to get into Skidmore. Two, you'd better know someone!"

Chapter 5

"So, are you guys excited about coming to Skidmore?" Amanda asked as the other students flowed in and noisily took their seats. She sounded very excited herself; either that or she was doing a great job of faking it. Tiara recognized the question as a social trick. If she admitted that she was excited—and she *was* a little excited—then Amanda would see her as some overenthusiastic newbie. However, if Tiara said that she wasn't excited, then the question would arise: Why was she there, then? To not be excited would practically be the same thing as not wanting to be there at all.

"The first day of school is always an exciting one," Tiara said, hoping that would cover all bases. She was as excited as she would be on any first day of school, at any school.

"Yeah . . . and that's especially true at Skidmore. It's like you're back at school and you get to see everybody, but it's still relaxed like summer, so you can take everything in. The real work doesn't start until tomorrow."

"Then what will we be doing all day?" Brooke asked. Tiara blinked at her. The candidness of the question, the blatant "I have no idea what's going on" of it shocked Tiara. Not that Tiara had a clue what was going to happen, but she knew better than to admit it.

"Oh, you know," Amanda said, waving her hand. "Regular old first-day-of-school stuff. Basically we're just going to travel around from classroom to classroom, meeting our teachers. They'll tell you about the curriculum and stuff like that."

"Oh," Brooke said, rolling her eyes. "That sounds pretty boring to me."

Tiara was starting to question Brooke's sanity. What was she trying to prove by insulting the school's schedule? That she didn't like the place? That she didn't want to be there? Tiara could practically hear Amanda saying, "Well, if you don't want to be here, then why don't you just leave?" As if parents didn't exist—as though the answer weren't obvious.

"Oh, I guess it would be if you didn't know anybody," was what Amanda said instead. "But by the time lunch hits, you'll know tons of people."

If Tiara had been Brooke, she would have pointed out that knowing people was not the same thing as being friends with them or even liking them. Brooke herself might have pointed this out if they had not been interrupted by a blaring bell.

"That's the five-minute bell. Everyone should be here by now." Amanda glanced around the room, noticing for the first time that all of the previously empty desks were now filled with other freshmen who obviously also belonged in the section.

"Do you know all these people?" Brooke asked Amanda, raising her voice over the loud chatter that was building in the room.

"Yes. The girl at the first desk closest to the computers is Megan Burke. She's been at Skidmore Prep since pre-k."

Tiara and Brooke both took a good long look at the girl in question. Megan Burke was short with ash-blond hair. She wasn't ugly but she certainly wasn't pretty either. She was a little on the fat side, but that could have been weight gain from a very laid-back summer.

"The boy behind Megan is Jonathan Meyers. He's also been at Skidmore since pre-k."

Jonathan was also kind of short with jet-black hair and pale blue eyes hidden behind a pair of Harry Potter horn-rimmed glasses. "Jonathan's kind of a dork but not actually a loser," Amanda whispered. "He has some real corny jokes, but everyone likes him for his entertaining presence, not because he's cool."

"Who's that guy?" Brooke whispered, pointing to the boy sitting directly in front of Tiara.

"Maxwell Blackstone," Amanda whispered back.

The tall young man was actually kind of cute with his dark brown hair and gray eyes.

"He's really nice. Unfortunately, he's related to Alicia Blackstone—and she's not nice at all. In fact, I have a couple of names I could call her, but I won't."

"What's the relationship?" Tiara asked. "Brother and sister?"

"No, they're cousins. The two guys sitting behind you, Brooke, are Patrick Simpson and Michael Richards. The two sitting on Michael's right are Sean Blaine and Jessica Harden."

For the most part, the incoming students ignored Tiara, Brooke, and Amanda, only giving Amanda a slight wave. Amanda was getting ready to provide a little history about the last four students she had mentioned when another guy and girl approached them.

"Hey, Amanda," the girl said. "Where've you been hiding?"

"Europe," Amanda responded with a laugh. "I literally just got back a couple of days ago. Would have called you, but my mom was seriously like, get ready for school now."

"Well, that sounds fun," the boy said, "even though you ditched us for the entire summer."

Tiara thought about this as they continued talking. Europe! And her entire summer! Tiara had not assumed Amanda was rich. Her outfit was basic, a pink tank top that Tiara recognized from Old Navy. Her jean capris had the American Eagle logo on the back and couldn't have cost more than forty dollars. Looks could be deceiving, Tiara reasoned.

"Oh yeah," Amanda said, giving her head a light smack. "This is Brooke Duncan and Tiara Johnson. They're new this year."

"Hi," Tiara said. Brooke only nodded.

"And this is Karen Samuels and Aaron Peters."

"Hi," Karen replied.

Tiara noticed that she was on the short side. Her long nearly black hair was caught up in a ponytail and held back with a scrunchie. She had sky-blue eyes and was cute in a Punky Brewster kind of way. Aaron simply smiled.

It was obvious that Karen and he were good friends. It was also apparent that between the two of them, Karen was the talker.

"Karen and Aaron are 'lifers,'" Amanda said.

"They're what?" Brooke asked.

Tiara was a little annoyed by Brooke's inability to figure things out for herself. In all honesty, Tiara hadn't heard the word "lifer" before, but it didn't take much cranium to figure it out.

"Lifer," Karen began with a grin. "Noun. A person who has been going to this school for his or her entire life. He, she, or it is a lifer."

"*It?*" Brooke asked.

"Yeah," Karen said, smirking. Pointing to Aaron, she continued, "He is a lifer, right?"

"Right..." Brooke said.

Unlike Brooke, Tiara could already see where this was going.

"She is a lifer," Karen said, pointing to herself. She then pointed to Amanda. "It is a lifer."

Tiara couldn't help smiling, not only at the joke itself, but at the fact that she had been able to predict it.

"Karen, one...Amanda, zero," Aaron said before sitting down at the desk behind Tiara.

Amanda opened her mouth to say something, but before she had a chance, three other female students approached, coming to a halt directly in front of Amanda, almost knocking Karen aside in their attempt to get close.

"Hi, Amanda," said a girl with a long pale face that looked like it hadn't seen the sun all summer. "Who are the newbies?"

"Hi, Alicia. Meet Tiara Johnson and Brooke Duncan. They're both new to Skidmore. Girls, meet Alicia Blackstone, Molly McKnight, and Brittany Jones," Amanda introduced the three girls who had surrounded the small group.

"Hi," Tiara and Brooke replied in unison. It was no mystery who the leader of the trio was. Alicia stood in front of them with the authority of the Queen of England; Molly McKnight and Brittany Jones were obviously her ladies in waiting.

Alicia acted as if she were holding court. Her long light brown hair was combed into a French braid that went halfway down her back. Her light gray eyes were extremely pretty and appeared not to miss a single thing. They darted from Amanda to Brooke and finally lingered on Tiara. Tiara returned the look before glancing over at the two ladies in waiting standing on either side of Queen Alicia.

Brittany was extremely short with mousy brown hair, average skin tone and complexion. Nothing spectacular. Molly McKnight, however, was another story. No doubt about it, she could easily pass for the identical twin sister of Olive Oyl from the Popeye cartoon. Molly had to be at least five feet, ten inches. Tall for a freshman. Tall even for a senior. She was also as straight as a stick. Her black hair was shoulder length and what else... straight. Her dark brown eyes never wavered but stared straight back at Tiara.

"You're new here, aren't you?" Molly asked.

Oh, this one is really bright, Tiara thought. "Yes, I am. I transferred from Boston . . . Massachusetts," she added.

"I have cousins who live in Massachusetts," Alicia piped up.

Great, thought Tiara. Then there was a good chance that she would know where Massachusetts was.

"They live in Chestnut Hill. You probably wouldn't know where that is, though. The black people in Boston all live in Roxbury . . . in the ghetto, you know. Is that where you're from?" she asked with a smirk.

Tiara knew a put-down when she heard one and Alicia was now definitely hitting way below the belt. It took everything for Tiara not to hit back. That definitely would not be a cool move for a new student to make. Instead, Tiara pulled out her "I'm speaking to an infant" voice and responded in her most polite tone.

"No, Alicia. I didn't live in Roxbury. We actually lived in Newton . . . you know, the town adjacent to Chestnut Hill?"

"Oh!" Alicia replied, her voice as smooth as silk. "I didn't know people like you lived so close to Chestnut Hill. It's really a very exclusive area, you know . . . Go figure!" Her smirk grew, knowing that all the students within earshot had heard her not-so-subtle insult.

Tiara didn't get a chance to make a reply. Mrs. Donovan had moved to the front of the room and clapped her hands three times to get everyone's attention.

"Okay, class. Will everyone take a seat so we can get started? Welcome to ninth grade and to my advisory. My name is Mrs. Donovan and I'll be your homeroom teacher for the next year."

As Mrs. Donovan's syrupy voice droned on, Tiara stole a peek at the other students as they made a grab for their seats. Because she was sitting in the middle of the classroom, she could see most of them without being obvious. She then turned to Mrs. Donovan, who was now surveying the room. At that point, a scary thought hit Tiara. What if Mrs. Donovan introduced Brooke and her to the class, like they did in the movies and on TV? Would she have to stand up, talk about herself—her hobbies, her favorite ice cream flavor—pretending that anyone in the class might actually care?

Mrs. Donovan moved over to stand closer to the doorway before continuing to address the class. "I don't want to burden you by discussing all, and there are quite a few, rules of the school or even this classroom. A lot of other teachers will be doing that as you travel from class to class today. I look forward to getting to know each of you this year and that starts with learning your names. Seeing as you guys are probably eagerly anticipating your schedules, I'll call you up to get them now. This will also give me a chance to get to know you."

She began calling out names, most of which Tiara didn't catch. What she did catch was a good sight of the other students in her class. Of course, after the first three or so, they all started to blend together. There was a total of fifteen students in the advisory, Tiara noted. She already knew they were all freshmen. Her mom had explained to her that the freshman advisories only had freshmen whereas sophomores, juniors, and seniors were mixed together.

"Tiara Johnson," Mrs. Donovan called. Tiara stood up cautiously, making sure not to trip or anything. She walked quickly, but not too quickly, to Mrs. Donovan's desk and got her schedule. As she took her seat, Brooke reached across, tapped her on the shoulder, and held out her hand.

"This?" Tiara asked, holding up her schedule. Brooke nodded. Tiara passed it to her, watched her quickly scan the page, nod, and pass it back. As Tiara accepted the sheet she wondered what Brooke had nodded at.

"Now the first-period bell should be ringing at any moment. Monday and Friday are the only days when we have a long advisory meeting. On Mondays it's at the beginning of the day and on Fridays it's at the end."

The bell rang. Tiara was so happy she could have started dancing right then and there. Mrs. Donovan hadn't called her and Brooke out.

"Mrs. Donovan . . ." Amanda said, gesturing to Tiara and Brooke.

Oh no! Tiara thought.

"And, of course, I almost forgot," Mrs. Donovan said. "We have two new students in this advisory. Make sure to say hello." She walked over to the door and opened it as the students got up, preparing to walk to their first class of the new school year.

"You two don't have to worry about where to go," Amanda said when Tiara and Brooke were out in the hallway. "We have the same classes, at least for the first semester."

"Why?" Brooke asked.

What kind of question is that, Tiara wondered. Because we're new and she's not.

"Well, because you guys are new," Amanda said. Tiara really wanted to add the "duh" to the end of the sentence but refrained.

The rest of the morning flew by. Tiara, Brooke, and Amanda sat next to each other in their next two classes—math and English. There were no surprises. Tiara knew math was going to be a breeze since they would be covering algebra I, the same course she'd taken last year in her accelerated math class at Boston Middle School.

English was also going to be fun. Tiara had always enjoyed English, and the reading list Ms. Tanner had passed out looked pretty interesting. The only downside to her two classes was the fact that Queen Alicia and her clique had followed right behind Tiara, Brooke, and Amanda, talking in undertones as they made their way to each new class. It was apparent that Alicia had decided that her quest in life was to torture the new student in class, namely Tiara. The funny thing was that Alicia didn't seem to be interested in Brooke. Her total focus was on Tiara and how she could make her life miserable.

Tuning back in to Ms. Tanner's monologue, Tiara listened as she announced the homework assignment for the next day.

Wow! Tiara thought. No playing around here. These teachers at Skidmore Prep were really serious. Usually the first week of school was all about play, getting to know your classmates, things like that. Apparently not here at Skidmore. These people meant business... serious business.

"Pssst!"

Tiara looked across the aisle as Amanda passed a note over to her. Opening it up, Tiara quickly scanned the contents.

"Be ready to cut out of here as soon as the bell rings. The cafeteria fills up quickly and the best seats will be taken if we don't hurry. Pass this on to Brooke."

Tiara reached over to her left and surreptitiously passed the note to Brooke. After giving it a quick glance, Brooke nodded her head and mouthed *okay*.

The lunch bell rang a short while later. All three girls made a dash for the doorway. The rest of the class did the same.

"Walk!" Ms. Tanner shouted. "Ladies, gentlemen, please walk to the cafeteria. Do not run!"

Tiara glanced over her shoulder at Ms. Tanner as she joined everyone else in the classroom trying to get through the doorway at the same time. Ms. Tanner was obviously talking to a brick wall because not one of the students was hanging around long enough to hear what she had to say.

The girls made their way down the four flights of stairs to the basement level of the building. They weren't the first ones downstairs but they certainly were not the last ones either.

"And this would be the cafeteria," Amanda declared as they stepped through a set of double doors, Karen and Aaron joining their group.

"Or don't eat," Karen added. Amanda gave her a grin.

"C'mon, Karen. You have to admit, the food here isn't *that* bad," Amanda said.

"Oh, no. Of course not!" Karen laughed, rolling her eyes. "If you walk on four legs and your name is Lassie."

Tiara laughed openly at that one. Throughout the morning, she had learned to register Karen's sarcastic comments not as insulting, but as an assessment of what she thought of a situation. Karen loved stating her opinion and admittedly, Tiara truly enjoyed hearing it.

"And what about you?" Brooke asked Aaron. "What do you think of the food?"

"It's all right by me," Aaron said with a shrug. "Then again, I'll eat anything."

As they approached the serving line, Tiara caught sight of a calendar menu. Today was pasta. She figured it was pretty hard to mess up pasta. She grabbed a tray and some food and followed the others to a table.

"All I'm saying is I can't wait until October when we can go out and eat," Karen said, spreading the sauce around on her pasta. "I don't even understand the whole 'freshmen can't go off campus for the first month of school' thing. What's the difference between a freshman and anyone else once they're off campus?" she asked the table in general.

"Could it be that maybe everybody else knows how to find their way back to campus?" Amanda suggested.

"Amanda, it's the same campus as the middle school," Karen pointed out. "We were here last year . . . and the last four years before that."

The middle school students shared the cafeteria, the

field, and pretty much everything else on campus with the high school students.

"Yes, but new kids didn't go to middle school," Amanda pointed out.

Tiara hoped they wouldn't bring her into the argument. Even though Amanda was Tiara's buddy and thus supposed to be her first friend in school, Tiara was pretty sure she liked Karen equally if not more than Amanda. She would feel torn if she had to choose between the two of them. Luckily they didn't ask her.

"Plus, as freshmen we have to learn first things first. Going out to lunch is a privilege we receive once we learn the more basic and crucial components of the high school," Amanda continued on with her explanation. Tiara could see why she had been chosen to act as a buddy. She was an authority on everything and everyone.

"Thank you, Steve Urkel," Karen said, opening her carton of iced tea. "But I'm still planning on going out to lunch as soon as October hits."

"You're going to go out for lunch every day?" Brooke asked. "Isn't that going to get a little expensive?"

Brooke had really outdone herself this time. She was now asking kids in what was practically the most costly school this side of Harvard if they found going out to lunch expensive.

"No way," Karen responded, much to Tiara's surprise. "I'd be begging hobos on the street for money if I did that. No, I'm just going to go out for lunch every once in a while."

"With Karen, it's not so much 'doing' something as it is having the ability to do it," Aaron explained. "Like in middle school, she always tried out for things . . . different activities, parts in the school play, and things like that. Then she would quit as soon as she got the position or the part."

"What kind of dunce cap teachers did you guys have in middle school anyway?" Brooke wanted to know. "I mean, how could they fall for that trick over and over again?"

"Hopeful teachers," Amanda said. "We had hopeful teachers . . . not dunce caps. You see, Karen is great at a lot of things. She was the best actor we had in middle school. She also has a great voice. They would always cast her as the lead in any of the plays or major activities we had in hopes that maybe she would take the part."

"I really just didn't have time for their productions," Karen explained, putting on an affected British accent. "But maybe I'll give one of the high school shows a chance."

"Of course, there's a lot more competition here at the high school level," Brooke said. "There's no guarantee that they'll want you in their shows."

Tiara looked around the table and saw eyebrows raise at Brooke's comment.

"That's true because they don't know me," Karen admitted just as Tiara was about to say something to Brooke. "It's kind of a double-edged sword, whether they know me or not. Know what I mean?"

"Yeah," Brooke said with a nod. "Like if the middle school teachers informed the high school teachers that you were a good actor but that you always quit the productions, they might not want to waste their time accepting you. But if the middle school teachers didn't tell them anything about you, then there's no guarantee that they'd even want you."

"Thanks for spelling it out for me," Karen said with a chuckle.

"And speaking of extracurricular activities," Amanda said, turning toward Tiara, "are you going to be doing any?"

"Well, I don't know." She was pretty good at acting and had a decent voice, but she didn't want to suggest that she was competition for Karen. Plus, she wasn't sure whether she was interested in doing any performances just yet. "I think I might try out for the tennis team."

"Really!" Amanda exclaimed. "I'm trying out too."

"Me too," Brooke said, not quite as enthusiastically as Amanda.

"This is really great! We'll be seeing each other all the time since we'll be together in all our classes and at tennis after school."

"Awesome," Tiara replied. She could only see one thing that was truly "awesome" about all of this . . . she would never have to endure one of those "new kid standing all alone" awkward moments.

Chapter 6

The afternoon session at Skidmore Prep flew by just as quickly as the morning session. Tiara hated to admit it, but surprisingly, she'd enjoyed every minute of it. Her three afternoon classes were definitely going to be fun. Science had been her first class after lunch. Her teacher, Mr. Sinclair, was to die for. Every one of his female students felt the same way. With his shoulder-length blond hair, blue eyes, and six feet of height, Mr. Sinclair was an older version of Justin Bieber, the teenage heartthrob.

"Call me Stephen," Mr. Sinclair had invited the class. "We're very low-key around here. I want you to feel free to come and see me anytime about any questions you may have about the subject matter."

"Wow. You can definitely count on that," Karen had replied under her breath but still loud enough for the class to hear, causing everyone to fall out with laughter.

If Mr. Sinclair heard what she'd said, he did a great job of concealing it, turning instead to Maxwell Blackstone and asking him to start passing out the brand-new science textbooks that were piled up on the floor next to his desk.

Just like all the other teachers from her morning classes, Mr. Sinclair wasted no time jumping into the science curriculum. He'd even assigned homework, which he expected them to complete by the following day.

"He may be cute," Tiara said to Karen, Brooke, and Amanda as they all left the classroom together, "but he's still expecting a lot of work out of us."

"Yeah, but at least we'll have something good to look at while we're doing it," Karen replied with a cheeky grin.

History had been everything she'd expected—old. Latin, however, had been a complete surprise. Amanda, Brooke, and Karen had all followed her into the Latin classroom. This really surprised Tiara. Who really took Latin in school these days? Anyone who had a parent who was a doctor, lawyer, or college English professor, apparently. Each one of her newfound friends, she soon discovered, had a parent or two who claimed one of those professions.

Tiara had discovered that Brooke's mom was an English professor at Georgetown University and her dad was a surgeon at the Washington Hospital Center. Amanda's dad was a partner at Brown, Cater, and Tyndale, another prestigious law firm in the district. Amanda's mother was a stay-at-home mom. Both of Karen's parents were also attorneys; her mom worked as a tax attorney for the federal government and her dad was a tax specialist at the law firm of Snelling and Barnes.

With all these type-A parents, each of the girls had pretty much been instructed to take Latin I. They'd all received the same speech about how this course would help them with the SAT exam when they finally made it to the eleventh grade.

Ms. Lopez, the Latin teacher, had really been on the defensive at the start of her class. Tiara assumed this was because of the subject matter. How did anyone make Latin interesting to a bunch of freshmen? With this in mind, Ms. Lopez had come to class armed with a syllabus filled with enough videos and teaching aids to make the most hardened freshman sit up and pay attention.

Sit up and pay attention, they did. By the time the last bell had rung, everyone in Latin I had been pleasantly surprised at how quickly the time had flown by.

"Mission accomplished!" Tiara heard Ms. Lopez mutter as the students filed out the door with smiles on their faces.

Tiara, Brooke, Karen, and Amanda were now seated in Skidmore's huge athletic locker room. As large as it was, the fifty students who had shown up for the tennis tryouts were still falling over each other. Tiara sat down on the bench directly in front of the locker she'd been told she could use, but only for today. Special lockers would later be assigned to the "chosen ones," those who were finally selected for the elite tennis team. For today, the tryout participants could use any of the empty assigned lockers that didn't already have a lock.

Tiara bent over and began lacing up her white Nike tennis shoes. Amanda, Karen, and Brooke sat beside her. They'd finished dressing and were now gazing around at the other Skidmore girls. Varsity tennis at Skidmore Prep was a big deal. It was no secret that most of the Ivy League colleges sent their recruiters to watch the Skidmore tennis matches in hopes of discovering the next Roger Federer or Serena Williams.

For the most part, though, athletic scholarships to the Ivy League was not the main draw for the typical Skidmore tennis player. Skidmore students on the whole could afford to pay the Ivy League tuition. No, the big draw for the Skidmore Prep student was the actual admission itself into the name-brand Ivy League school. The colleges had resorted to recruiting students from overseas. They were now going abroad in search of students who were great tennis players and wanted to come to the United States and play tennis in exchange for a scholarship.

For the last three years, seniors at Skidmore had been hearing about how difficult it was to get into the colleges of their choice. Everyone knew that it was a terrible time to be applying to these schools. By now, even the freshmen had heard this dismal tale. There were just too few slots available. The Ivy Leagues, however, always held a few positions open for their chosen incoming star athletes. So, the pressure was on, and although no one in the room would admit it, everyone knew that they had a lot riding on these tryouts. It was about more than just being on Skidmore's tennis team. It was also about a potential "in" to the college of their dreams. As a result, the room was overloaded with more students than was necessary to fill the sixteen available slots on the team. Students whose parents had undoubtedly urged, counseled, even threatened them in order to get them to try out for the team were here and every one of them was wired up and on edge.

There were one hundred and twenty students in the freshman class—sixty boys and sixty girls. Excluding herself, Karen, Brooke, and Amanda, Tiara had counted twenty-six other freshmen girls trying out for the team. The remaining twenty girls in the room were a combination of sophomores, juniors, and seniors.

"There's Sierra Morgan. Lindsey Battle is standing next to her," Amanda said in a loud whisper, gesturing to two girls in the corner.

"Who are they?" Brooke asked.

"Sierra Morgan is our star tennis player. She was the number-one player on Skidmore's team last year and the number-one player in the entire prep school league. All the colleges—I mean *all of them*—are trying to get her to come to their school after she graduates this year. She can write her own ticket and go wherever she wants."

"Whoa!" Tiara replied. "That's fantastic!"

"Yes, it is. The girl standing next to her is Lindsey Battle. Lindsey is also a senior. She's ranked number two in the prep school league."

"Are you saying that Skidmore has both the number-one and the number-two players in the whole prep school league?"

"Yes," Amanda replied. "But it doesn't matter if you played on Skidmore's team last year or if you're ranked number one or two. Everyone is treated the same. Everyone has to try out for this year's team just as if they'd never played for Skidmore before. That's why it's so crowded in here and that's also why it's so competitive. There are a lot of sophomores and juniors who didn't make the team last year. They're back again to give it another shot . . . and they're desperate."

"This whole tryout business sounds real serious," Karen said as she looked around at the crowd. "These girls even came dressed for the occasion. They're dressed to kill," she added, looking down first at her own outfit and then over at Tiara's, Brooke's, and Amanda's. The four girls had on the basic Skidmore athletic attire: gray shirt, navy shorts, both with Skidmore's name somewhere on the front.

"Look at that outfit!" Karen whispered loudly, shooting her eyes at a girl wearing a hot pink getup like what Serena or Venus Williams would wear.

"That's Joy Goldman. She's Skidmore's fashion diva."

The four girls looked down at their boring Skidmore attire. They knew without saying it that Joy was in a league by herself.

"Is she any good?" Brooke asked.

"I've seen her play," Amanda said. "And yes, she's good! We definitely are in for some stiff competition. That's why I'm *so* nervous about these tryouts," she continued as they exited the locker room. "I really want to make varsity, but I know that's never going to happen."

"Why not?" Tiara asked, and then in fear of sounding like Brooke added, "I mean, I'm sure there's nothing to worry about."

"I agree with Tiara," Brooke said with a nod. "Even if you *say* you *know* it will never happen, you obviously think that it might, otherwise you wouldn't have mentioned it at all. Unless of course, you just wanted us to tell you that you will make it, even if you know you won't. I don't see why that would be comforting, though, seeing as we've never seen you play, have nothing to base our assurances on, and would, therefore, obviously be lying."

Tiara, Karen, and Amanda all stopped walking and stared, open-mouthed, at Brooke.

"What?" Brooke asked. "I'm just *saying*."

"No, I totally get what you're saying," Amanda said. "I guess I just want to know now whether I'm going to be on the varsity team or not. Like, if I'm not going to make it, then I don't even want to try out . . . you know?"

"Yeah," Tiara agreed as they walked toward Skidmore's fenced-in tennis courts.

"Whatever," Brooke said with a shrug. "Are those the courts?" she asked, pointing to the set of tennis courts ahead of them.

"No," Tiara said sarcastically. She had been putting up with Brooke's stupidity and snide remarks all day. Now she was just sick and tired of it. Tiara hadn't actually meant to speak that sarcasm, but it was out now and there wasn't much she could do about it.

"Sarcasm from Miss Johnson?" Brooke asked, turning to Amanda and Karen with a patronizing look of astonishment on her face. "More than a smile and a nod from Miss Johnson? More than a simple 'yeah'?"

"Wow, this is unexpected," Amanda agreed with a frown.

This bothered Tiara. She didn't care much what Brooke thought about her. Brooke was too obnoxious for her opinion to really matter. Amanda, on the other hand, was Tiara's buddy. She had done nothing but help Tiara out all day. Of course, that was her job. That's what she was supposed to do, but still, she really hadn't been required to be nice about it. Tiara had seen plenty of buddies who had not been nearly as nice as Amanda had been.

"Sorry, guys," Tiara began before Brooke cut her off with a wave of her hand and an eye roll.

"No need to apologize," Brooke said. "I like you better this way."

"Much less awkward," Amanda agreed. "I don't really like it when people always agree with me."

"So basically, I've been annoying the crap out of you guys all day," Tiara concluded, going along with the sarcastic personality she had just created.

"Essentially yes," Brooke said as they approached the tennis courts. "But by this time next week, we will be laughing about that. Now, however, it's tennis time."

That was definitely true. They had finally arrived at Skidmore's tennis courts. There were three courts enclosed in one fence and three more located directly behind those. The latter were also fenced in. Tiara had also seen tennis courts on the other side of the locker room. In total, Skidmore had twelve full-size tennis courts.

Coach Bob Green was already positioned on center court surrounded by most of the girls who had been in the locker room a short while ago. Coach Bob was a tall, slender man around thirty-five years old. His sandy brown hair was thinning out in front and his eyebrows were so heavy it seemed like some of the hair should have been on top of his head. He had a long thin nose and thin lips that easily curved into a smile. He was smiling now as Tiara and her friends strolled over to join several other groups of girls who were already on the courts warming up. All six courts were in use.

Coach Bob signaled for the girls to gather near the net. He waited a few minutes as all fifty of them gathered close before he started giving his instructions. "We have fifty women here today who wish to try out for the Skidmore Prep varsity tennis team. I'm really sorry to have to tell you this, but only sixteen of you will be selected to represent Skidmore's tennis team—the best sixteen," he added. "Now I would like everyone to select a partner, find a space on the courts, and start to practice volleys over the net as a warm-up."

Amanda quickly turned toward Tiara. "I assume you're a good player . . . aren't you?" she asked almost hesitantly, not at all interested in having a lousy partner.

"I can hold my own," Tiara replied, staring back at Amanda. She knew she hadn't actually responded to Amanda's question, but in reality, she wasn't sure just how good any of the Skidmore girls really were. Tiara had been playing tennis since she was four years old. In fact, for the last four years, she'd trained seriously and had finally qualified to be on the Boston junior tennis team. The question for her wasn't how good a game she could play, but rather, what caliber of game these girls had.

Something in her demeanor must have satisfied Amanda because she nodded at Tiara and signaled for her to join her on center court. Out of the corner of her eye, Tiara noticed that Brooke had partnered up with Karen, and Alicia Blackstone and Molly "Olive Oyl" had joined forces. Of course, the two other members of Alicia's tag team, Megan and Brittany, did the expected and partnered up. Tiara didn't know the names of most of the other girls since they were from some of the other freshman sections, but everyone quickly found someone to partner with and ran to find a good space to hit.

Chapter 7

For the next ten minutes, fifty girls volleyed balls back and forth across the net until Coach Bob finally called them over to join him. "Okay, ladies. We're going to go through this selection by a process of elimination."

"Process of elimination?" Brooke whispered loudly to her three associates. "What does that mean?"

"I would think—"Amanda started to explain but immediately stopped when she heard Coach Bob's next statement.

"For those of you who have no clue what an elimination process is, let me explain," he announced, his wide grin directed at Brooke.

"So, you think he heard me?" Brooke asked in an undertone.

"Why would you ask that?" Tiara replied straight-faced, causing Karen to fall out laughing.

"Ladies! Ladies!" Coach Bob called out once again, trying his best to get everyone's attention. "As I said, fifty of you have shown up today to try out. You've partnered up, so now we have twenty-five teams of two players each.

Because we have an uneven number of groups, I'm going to select two members from last year's team to step aside so that we have an even split of forty-eight girls. Sierra Morgan. Lindsey Battle. Will you two step out?" Coach Bob asked, turning to last year's two superstars.

Tiara watched as the two seniors strutted over to stand next to Coach Bob at the net. Their walk said it all. It basically screamed out to the rest of the lowly competitors that as far as they were concerned, their positions as number one and two were set in stone.

"Now, I want the rest of you to find a court, two players on each side," Coach Bob explained. "I have a box with twenty-four long and twenty-four short straws in it. Each group will select one straw. Short straws will play the first round; long straws will play the second."

"Do we get to choose our opposing team?" a freshman from another section asked.

"No," Coach Bob replied. "I'll randomly assign you to your opponents. Now, are there any other questions?" he asked, scanning the faces of the young ladies who stood before him.

No one had anything else to say.

"Okay then. Sierra . . . Lindsey," he called to the two seniors standing by the net. "Those two boxes over there have the straws we'll be using. Would you allow one player from each of the partnered groups to select a straw? After that has been done, I want the ladies with the short straws to remain on the court. The ones holding the long straws can take a seat in the bleachers."

The next few minutes were a mad scramble. Amanda

dashed out to pull their straw. She soon returned to Tiara's side, a huge smile on her face. "We have a long one," she said, holding out the lengthy straw for Tiara to see. "We're in the second group."

"Great!" Tiara replied. As the girls jogged toward the bleachers, Tiara noticed that Karen and Brooke were also headed in that direction. Unfortunately, so were Alicia, Molly, Megan, and Brittany.

The first elimination round was fast and lethal. Twenty-four girls started out on the courts. Fifteen minutes later, twelve were headed back to the locker room. They had been eliminated.

Coach Bob gave the signal, motioning the long-straw group onto the court. Amanda and Tiara stood facing two other freshmen from one of the other sections. Alicia and Molly were on the court next to them. They too had selected two unknown freshmen as their opponents.

"Do you know these guys?" Tiara whispered to Amanda. Amanda shook her head. Tiara figured they had as much to lose as the other pair.

"M or W?" one of the other girls called, approaching the net.

"Umm . . ." Tiara said, looking at Amanda.

"M, okay?" the girl said as she spun her racket. All four girls watched as the racket began to spin. To anyone who didn't know anything about tennis, this probably looked strange—four girls staring at a tennis racket spinning on a court until it fell over. But anyone who was familiar with the sport would recognize this as the ritual that decided who would serve first.

"W," the girl's teammate said. "We serve first."

"Okay," Tiara agreed, even though technically the spin had not been fair since neither she nor her teammate had actually said M.

"Which side do you want?" Amanda asked Tiara.

Being left-handed, Tiara chose the left side. As a lefty, Tiara was equally good on both sides of the court. Most left-handed individuals were forced to develop their right hand since pretty much everything they ever used was designed for right-handed people. As a result, they were usually equally strong in their right and left hands. The reason Tiara chose the left side of the court, which she would never admit to Amanda, was the fact that right-handed people were just naturally weaker at sports like tennis. Tiara knew a few lefties who were terrible at tennis, but that was their fault. They just didn't have the ability to play tennis, and they admitted it. The truth was, every left-handed person had the potential to be better than any right-handed person, just because the lefty had always been forced to work harder at everything.

"Love, love," the girl who had spun her racket said as she prepared to serve. This was another thing any non-tennis-savvy person would be confused by. The term *love* had nothing to do with adoration for one's opponent; it was used as another word for zero. Tiara didn't know why. It was one of those things she didn't bother to question, though she figured one day she should probably find out.

The ball flew over to Amanda... nice and easy. Amanda slammed it back to the other side, winning the point. Tiara was slightly surprised. She hadn't expected so much power from Amanda and apparently she wasn't the only one. Their opponents exchanged shocked glances as Tiara gave Amanda a thumbs-up. Amanda winked and they shifted positions, preparing for the next point. Tiara mimicked Amanda in slamming the ball back, this time at the girl standing close to the net. The girl blocked it, probably in self-defense, and managed to get it back over the net. Amanda lunged for the ball and angled the shot for the back corner of the court, behind the girl at the net. Naturally, her partner wasn't able to get to it, causing Tiara and Amanda to win the point.

By the end of the first couple of points, Amanda and Tiara knew that this was going to be a piece of cake. The girls on the other side of the net couldn't even manage to score one point. Tiara and Amanda were having a blast. Tiara was such a skilled player that she was able to determine exactly where she wanted to place the ball and put it right in that spot. She managed to angle the ball from one side of the court to the other, forcing their opponents to run from side to side. Tiara knew they were going to win the game. There was just no way they wouldn't.

Halfway through their match, Coach Bob came over and stood a few feet behind Amanda and Tiara at the base line. He watched as Tiara strategically placed her shots, a look of admiration on his face. Her partner wasn't too bad either. Together, they were making quick work of their opponents. As a matter of fact, they finished their game well before any of the other girls with a leading score of four–love. After running to the net to shake hands with their opponents, Tiara and Amanda returned to the bleachers to watch Alicia and Molly struggle through their game.

Alicia was good. Tiara had to admit that. All of her shots went back with perfect aim and precision. She was good at the net but she also had good ground strokes. Tiara acknowledged this and so did the others watching the game. But unfortunately for Alicia, so did her opponents. Molly wasn't a bad player; she just wasn't as precise as Alicia. Their opponents soon figured this out and started hitting the ball only to her. Alicia noticed this and began to run around the court, going for any ball she could get. Molly was also aware of her limitation but it didn't seem to bother her. There was no doubt that Alicia was a much better player than she was and if that's what they needed to do in order to win, then so be it.

Alicia and Molly struggled through their game. They finally won the match, but just barely. The final score was four–three, which Alicia proudly reported to Coach Bob.

"Obviously Alicia's not as strong a player as she would like us to believe," Amanda said as she and Tiara stole quick glances at the twelve other girls who had been eliminated and were now making their way back to the locker room.

"Okay, ladies," Coach Bob yelled to the twenty-six girls who were left. "As you were playing, I walked around and ranked each of the groups, both individually and as pairs. As I said, only sixteen of you will be invited to join Skidmore's team. As I call out your name and rank, please head over to the locker room and get suited up for your uniforms. Does anyone have any questions?"

No one responded.

"All right. Sierra Morgan, rank number one; Lindsey Battle, rank number two; Tiara Johnson, rank number three."

"She's a freshman!" The mutters were a lot louder than expected. "A freshman ranked number three? That's incredible!" the other girls whispered.

"Ladies, please! May I have your attention?" Coach Bob said. "Amanda Carter, rank number four; Candy Spellman, rank number five; Kimberly Hall, rank number six; Joy Goldman, rank number seven; Michelle Leigh, rank number eight; Alicia Blackstone, rank number nine; Molly McKnight, rank number ten; Brooke Duncan, rank number eleven; Karen Samuels, rank number twelve; Leah Diamond, rank number thirteen; Rachel Jackson, rank number fourteen; Morgan Burke, rank number fifteen; and Brittany James, rank number sixteen."

The other ten girls who had not been selected tried their best to hide their disappointment as they made their way back to the locker room. Mentally, they were trying to come up with excuses to give their hopeful parents who were eagerly awaiting the outcome of the tryouts.

Tiara and Amanda were trying hard to play it cool and hide their joy. Halfway across the courts, Sierra Morgan caught up with them. Reaching out her hand, Sierra grabbed hold of Tiara's hand and gave it a good shake. "Welcome to Skidmore Prep's varsity team," she announced. "Your game is awesome!"

"Thank you," Tiara humbly replied.

"Have you been playing for a long time?" Lindsey asked, joining the two winning players.

"Since I was four years old," Tiara answered.

"You have a wicked left hand," Sierra pointed out. "Are you a lefty?"

"Yes," Tiara replied with a smirk. She had discovered at an early age just how lethal her left hand really was. Most tennis players, like the majority of the human race, were right-handed. A right-handed person generally learned to play against other right-handed people. Seldom would "righties" get an opportunity to play against lefties. When they did, they were always at a disadvantage because, more than likely, that lefty had always played against a right-handed player. As a result, the lefty always knew just where that shot was going to be placed. The right-handed player unfortunately had no clue how or where the lefty was going to end up. Tiara had worked on her left hand and had mastered her left-handed shots. Her left hand was now her "lethal weapon" . . . and she knew it.

"You're going to enjoy playing for Skidmore Prep," Sierra continued, thrilled to death that the team was getting a player like Tiara. She'd looked like a pro on the court. She had taken those players out with minimum effort.

"I'm sure I will," Tiara agreed.

"You know we rank number two in the prep league. We're trying to get to first place this year," Lindsey explained.

"No, I didn't know that Skidmore was ranked that high."

"Well, you're going to love it here," Sierra repeated, her smile infectious, her green eyes sparkling and her short red hair bouncing.

Tiara wanted to believe what the seniors were saying. Unfortunately, she'd caught a quick glance of Alicia staring at her. The nasty looks that Alicia and Molly had thrown her way told her quite a different story altogether. If looks could kill, Tiara knew she would be six feet under. It went without saying that Alicia didn't like the fact that she was ranked number nine. Worst yet, she definitely hated the thought that Tiara, a nobody from nowhere, was ranked number three. Even without saying it, Tiara knew that between Alicia and herself, *the battle was definitely on*!

Chapter 8

Marilyn had prepared blueberry pancakes with thick Vermont blueberry syrup they'd been saving from their last trip up north. A large platter of turkey sausages and freshly squeezed orange juice complemented the breakfast in celebration of the second day of school. By the time Tiara took her place at the kitchen table, everyone else was almost finished eating.

"Good morning, princess," Blake greeted his favorite daughter. "Sleep well?"

"Fine," Tiara mumbled, taking a solitary pancake from the platter and placing it on her plate.

"Tiara, I hope you're going to eat more than that!" Marilyn said curtly, not mincing words. She'd been taking care of Tiara and Spencer Jr. way too long to hold back any of her thoughts.

"I'm not really hungry," Tiara replied, pouring a little of the rich syrup over her pancake.

Lisa glanced at Tiara but said nothing. After fifteen years of raising two children she knew that missing a meal or two was no big deal.

"How was school yesterday?" Blake asked. He'd worked late the night before and arrived home well after both of his children had gone to bed.

"All right," Tiara replied.

"Just all right?"

"Yup," Tiara answered around a mouthful of pancake.

"Did you meet anyone interesting?"

"Not really. They're just regular kids. No different from the ones back home . . . back in Boston," she automatically corrected herself.

"I see." Still not giving up, he asked, "How many students are in your class?"

"Fifteen."

"Tiara tried out for Skidmore's tennis team yesterday," Lisa finally interjected, tired of the one-liners her daughter was serving.

"That's great!" Blake replied. "How did you do?"

"I'm ranked number three on the team," Tiara replied without emotion.

"Number three!" Blake repeated in amazement. "Did any upperclassmen try out?"

"Yes," Tiara answered, unable to hide her smile. "Several of the other competitors were seniors."

"And you ranked higher than they did?"

"Yup."

"That's incredible!" Blake glanced at Lisa, his pride evident. "That's what I'm talking about! How are you going to work that in with playing at the Tennis Foundation?" Lisa had signed Tiara and Spencer Jr. up to play in the tennis league that was run by the Arthur Ashe Tennis

Foundation. Blake knew they would be required to spend several hours each week training there after school.

"We don't have to be at the Foundation until four o'clock," Tiara explained. "Practice at Skidmore is scheduled right after school at two o'clock, so there should be no conflict."

"Great!" Blake said. "That really works out well."

"Yes, it does," Lisa agreed, already halfway out of her seat. "Tiara, I have an early-morning appointment at the jail, so if you want a ride we better be leaving now."

"Same here, Spencer," Blake said.

"All right, Dad. Just have to get my backpack," Spencer Jr. replied, jumping out of his seat. As usual, he was halfway up the stairs before the words had completely fallen out of his mouth.

Tiara glanced at the clock on the wall in her English class. Ten minutes to go before the bell. Ms. Tanner had passed out copies of *Great Expectations* and had already assigned thirty pages to be read by tomorrow. Tiara didn't mind. She enjoyed reading the classics.

"Psst."

Tiara looked across at Amanda. "What's up?" she mouthed. Amanda reached over and slipped her a note: *Alicia is on the warpath!*

Tiara nodded in agreement. She didn't need Amanda to tell her that. She'd already been given a large dose of Alicia's anger first thing that morning. Tiara had been standing at her locker exchanging books from her bag for the ones she needed for her first two classes. She was rushing, hoping to get into her advisory before the bell went off. She was paying no attention to her surroundings, so she was completely unaware that someone had walked up behind her.

"Nice sneakers," a syrupy voice called out from right beside her, surprising Tiara and causing her to spin around. Alicia was standing inches away from her. Molly "Olive Oyl," Brittany, and Megan were flanking their hero on either side.

"My sneakers?" Tiara asked, caught off guard by the surprise attack. Tiara had to call it that because that's exactly what it felt like, an attack.

"Yeah, your sneakers. Are they from Payless?"

Only then did Tiara realize what Alicia was trying to do. She had wondered how long it would take for Alicia and her cheering committee to pounce. The looks Alicia and Megan had given her yesterday at the tryouts had spoken volumes. Tiara didn't expect to be shown love, not after beating out a number of seniors, juniors, and sophomores, but she hadn't expected to be attacked by so many haters either. The surprising part was that the haters were not the upperclassmen who had taken the beating. They were Alicia and her "attached at the hip" crowd. Alicia was angry. Tiara guessed the reason for that was Alicia's "great expectations." There was no doubt Alicia had hopes of becoming the star of Skidmore's tennis team. Tiara was sure Alicia could have tolerated it if anyone other than Tiara had outranked her.

Tiara let out a long sigh and spoke as if to a child. "No, Alicia. My shoes did not come from Payless. Is there something else I can do for you?"

Alicia hadn't been expecting that. She'd been so sure her insult would hit its mark. Tiara didn't give her a second opportunity to make a comeback. The advisory bell rang and she slammed her locker shut, skirted around the little hate group, and made her quick getaway.

During the morning advisory, Tiara didn't get a chance to tell Amanda, Brooke, or Karen about her little mishap with Alicia. Now, here she was in English class, and Amanda was describing Alicia's sentiments to a tee.

The bell went off, finally announcing the end of class and the start of the lunch hour. As expected, everyone jumped up and bolted from the room, each student attempting to be the first to make it downstairs to the cafeteria. Karen and Brooke had been quick about packing up and were already waiting outside the door by the time Amanda and Tiara came out.

The four girls didn't waste any time making conversation; they quickly joined the flow of traffic. Once in the cafeteria, they purchased the choice items of the day and found a table that seated six. Aaron Peters had joined their group, maneuvering his tray so that he was seated between Karen and Amanda. Tiara was certain he liked one of the girls in their group; she just wasn't sure which one.

They'd only been eating for a few minutes when Alicia and Molly approached their table. All five of the friends looked up in surprise, certain that Alicia and Molly had no intentions of sitting at their table, but not understanding why they were there. No one said a word as they waited for one of the newcomers to make the first move.

"If you eat that," Alicia began, gesturing to the large piece of lasagna on Tiara's plate, "you definitely won't be able to play tennis today, not that I'm complaining."

"And if *you* eat *that*," Brooke interjected, pointing obnoxiously to the salad on Alicia's plate, "you'll turn even greener than you already are."

Alicia's mouth dropped open, like a goldfish out of water. What is wrong with this girl? Tiara wondered. She threw out these petty insults but was shocked when they were thrown right back into her face. Who did she think she was dealing with, a bunch of second-graders?

"I don't think anyone was talking to you, *number eleven*," Molly quipped, referencing Brooke's tennis rank.

"No one was talking to you either, oily," Brooke shot back.

"All I'm saying," Alicia continued smoothly, "is that something is going to knock you out of seat three. If it's not that lasagna, then it'll be me." She turned and walked away with a disgruntled Olive Oyl following close behind.

"Can you believe that girl?" Amanda asked the group. "Talk about being full of yourself. I wonder if she's ever received a compliment in her life; I mean, from someone besides herself or one of her minions."

"She needs to lay off the teen drama literature," Karen said, cutting into her own lasagna. "This isn't Sweet Valley High."

Amanda sighed. "I just don't get what the big deal is.

Seat three or seat ten, who cares? We're all on the same team. I don't see what difference it makes."

"The difference is that the number-three slot is much better than the number-ten spot," Karen stated flatly. "Alicia just wants to be better than everyone else. With what little common sense she has, she knows that there is no chance of her beating either Sierra or Lindsey, so she's looking at the next best thing: seat three."

"She's right," Aaron agreed. "Alicia has always assumed she should be first at everything. She's been in all of our classes since pre-kindergarten and she hasn't changed one bit. She thinks the world revolves around her. I bet this is the first time in her life that someone has beaten her out of something she really wants . . . and she really wants that third seat."

"Well, she's not gonna get it," Brooke said. Realizing it wasn't really her call, she added, "Is she, Tiara?"

Tiara looked around the table at the four expectant faces staring back at her. She had no desire to get into a confrontation with Alicia, but at the same time, she had no intention of backing down.

"No," Tiara said after a moment. "You're absolutely right about that, Brooke. Seat number three belongs to me, and there is no way Alicia's going to get it. Not if I can help it."

Chapter 9

Lisa flipped the switch to activate her left blinker before making the turn onto Wisconsin Avenue into the steady flow of traffic. Taking a quick glance in her rearview mirror, she moved smoothly into the fast lane, passing the twenty-six-foot truck ahead of her.

She had just left Tiara at the front entrance of Skidmore Prep after making another deadpan, silent trip from home. Lisa was concerned about Tiara. Two weeks had passed since her first day at Skidmore Prep. Unfortunately, the old Tiara was still nowhere to be found. Tiara was obviously still very unhappy about the family's move from Boston to Washington, DC, but worse yet, Lisa realized that there was something else bothering her oldest child. What it was remained a mystery. Lisa had tried several times to get Tiara to open up and talk, but the stubborn child wouldn't budge. She was shut as tight as a clam.

"Nothing's wrong, Mom!" she'd replied to Lisa's questions. "I'm having a great time. School's a blast!" she'd mumbled. "What did you expect? I'm the new kid in town, so of course it's a blast."

Lisa knew something was going on. It was something more than missing her old friends and her old school. There was something going on at Skidmore Prep, but as long as Tiara refused to communicate, there was very little Lisa could do to help.

Parking the BMW in the firm's underground parking lot, she climbed out of the driver's seat, reaching back in for her laptop and black leather Louis Vuitton briefcase. She was still deep in thought as she rode the elevator to the fifth floor. As the door slid open and she stepped into the hallway, Lisa made a mental note to give it one more week before taking matters into her own hands. She had no idea what actions she would take. She simply knew that something had to be done.

Walking through the solid mahogany doors, Lisa glanced around the reception area as she headed to her office. McKenzie, Kennedy, and McKenzie reeked of money—old money. Anyone stepping through those solid doors for the first time would naturally assume that the firm's clientele came from the bastions of the very wealthy. That assumption was actually far from the reality. Although the majority of the firm's clients were indeed very wealthy, McKenzie, Kennedy, and McKenzie maintained a very rigid policy of providing pro bono assistance to a large number of people in need. Low-income individuals were able to request free representation. A committee reviewed each petition and decided if they could handle the matter. If they could, then that person would get free legal services.

The one thing that Lisa had hated about giving up her job at the public defender's office in Roxbury was that she wouldn't be dealing with folks from the community. She'd gotten a lot of satisfaction from helping people in the community who could not afford to go to the major law firms, people who had never expected to receive good legal assistance. But now that Tiara and Spencer Jr. were a little more independent, Lisa wanted to take a shot at making partner at a major firm. She was hoping that McKenzie, Kennedy, and McKenzie would be the place where this would happen. Although she expected the next few months to be grueling, Lisa was willing to make the commitment in order to prove herself. She was determined to become the firm's first black female partner. It didn't hurt that her cousin Justin had recently been designated head of the firm's entertainment division and had become their first black male partner, but she also realized that her family connections would take her just so far.

"Good morning, Ellen. How was your weekend?" Lisa asked, giving the head receptionist a warm smile as she approached her desk.

"Just great," Ellen replied. "A few of us went to the jazz festival on the Mall. There were tons of people and vendors selling all sorts of things. Every type of food you could imagine was available and all kinds of souvenirs were on display. My parents are visiting from Charleston, South Carolina, so I took them there."

"Sounds like it was fun."

"It was. By the way, Ms. Singleton came in a few minutes ago. She asked me to tell you to give her a buzz when you arrived."

"Oh, okay. Thanks for the message," Lisa replied before

making her way down the corridor to her office. Unlocking the door, she entered the spacious room, taking a moment to admire its new decor. She'd added a few personal items from home last week: pictures of the children and Blake, her college and law school diplomas, and several awards she had acquired over the years. The office was now beginning to feel like it belonged to her, like it was really her space.

Taking a seat in the massive chair behind her mahogany desk, Lisa placed her laptop down next to her inbox. She had accomplished a lot over the weekend on one of the briefs she intended to file this week in district court. Glancing at her calendar, Lisa was reminded of her appointment with Senator and Mrs. Davis, the parents of Karen Davis, for nine o'clock, less than an hour away.

Lisa's interviews with Karen were definitely getting better. Karen had started opening up and the real facts about her case were now coming to light. In fact, Lisa had another appointment to meet with her over at the DC Jail later this afternoon.

The buzzer on her intercom went off just as Lisa pulled the last of the files she'd taken home over the weekend from her briefcase.

"Lisa Johnson," she answered, pressing down on the talk button.

"Lisa, it's Paige. Do you have a minute? I wanted to tap your brain."

"Sure," Lisa replied. "My office or yours?"

"Yours. I'll be there in a second."

Lisa and Paige had only recently met, but Lisa had

quickly grown to like her. They were currently the only two senior female attorneys at the firm. As coincidence would have it, they were also the only two black females in the entire firm.

Paige Singleton had joined McKenzie, Kennedy, and McKenzie within the last six months. She was twenty-eight years old, but already she was recognized as a brilliant criminal defense attorney who was highly sought after by a number of very prestigious law firms on both the east and west coasts. McKenzie, Kennedy, and McKenzie had snapped her up by default.

Up until six months ago, Paige had been climbing the ladder to success and a partnership at the elite Los Angeles law firm of Morris and Tate. She had been one of their best attorneys, well recognized in the legal circle. The idea of leaving Morris and Tate had never entered her mind.

Paige had returned to her hometown of Washington, DC, last March to attend a criminal law conference as a keynote speaker. She had been scheduled to give her presentation that week on Wednesday and Thursday. A change in the agenda had shifted her presentation to Monday and Tuesday, leaving her with the rest of the week free.

She had left the conference Tuesday evening and had spent Wednesday and Thursday visiting with her parents at their sprawling home in the Spring Valley section of Washington, DC. On Thursday, she'd accepted an invitation from her old friend, Justin Kramer III, to visit with him at McKenzie, Kennedy, and McKenzie, the law firm where Justin had recently become partner and head of their entertainment division. Only after arriving at the firm had she discovered that she had really been invited there for a job interview. McKenzie, Kennedy, and McKenzie was conducting a search for several experienced criminal attorneys. Justin Kramer had spoken very highly of Paige to several of the partners and had told Alex McKenzie to attend the criminal law conference and check her out.

Alex had done so. He had attended the seminar and had listened to Paige as she gave her presentation. He had been totally impressed with what he'd seen and heard. Immediately, Alex McKenzie had decided that he wanted to hire Paige and asked Justin to invite her over.

Paige had really enjoyed her visit at the firm. Unfortunately, she had disappointed the partners when she'd declined their immediate offer for a position, even with the exorbitant salary they had wanted to give her. Paige had explained that she intended to get married within the next few weeks and that her fiancé was in a hit television series in Los Angeles and couldn't relocate. Paige had been very disappointed that she couldn't accept the offer because although she enjoyed her work at Morris and Tate, she would have preferred to work and live in DC, near her family.

Two weeks after the law conference, Paige had made a complete reversal, accepting the job offer from McKenzie, Kennedy, and McKenzie. No one knew why she had suddenly changed her mind. They were just glad that she had.

Paige had already confided in Lisa and told her that the move had been a blessing in disguise. Within a week of returning to her hometown, Paige had met and become engaged to her future husband, Damian St. Jean, one of the most prominent promoters not only in the United States, but in the world.

Lisa had met Damian the week before at the firm's get-together. Damien was very good-looking, no doubt about it, and now he and Paige were planning to be married in a huge international wedding in June. Lisa wondered why Paige needed to see her; what could possibly be on the young woman's mind?

Chapter 10

Lisa looked up expectantly as Paige entered her office. "Hi, Paige. What's going on?"

"Oh, it's nothing critical," Paige quickly replied, trying to alleviate the concern she saw on Lisa's face. "I wanted to talk to you about something personal." Paige turned and closed the door before taking a seat in one of the large wingback chars stationed in front of Lisa's desk.

"Something personal?"

In the last few weeks, Lisa and Paige had met several times at the office to discuss cases. As the only two black female attorneys in the firm, there had been an instant bonding between the two women. They'd also met for lunch a few times in the firm's cafeteria, but for the most part, their conversations had been limited to legal issues. So Lisa was really curious now about what Paige wanted to discuss.

"I've been watching you with your children. I've seen them here at the office with you."

"Oh, really?" Lisa asked, curious now about what Paige could possibly want to discuss. It was a complete surprise to know that not only was she being observed, but that her children were being watched as well.

"They are such beautiful, well-behaved children."

"Oh, thank you." Lisa hadn't expected the compliment.

You really never knew when someone was watching you from afar. And Lisa was someone worth studying. Her caramel-colored skin had the same tone and glow as her young daughter's. Her shoulder-length hair had been pulled back into a French twist. Her large light brown eyes were probably one of her best features. The charcoal-gray suit she was wearing today, a classic Ralph Lauren purchased three years ago, looked great on her. She was a stunning woman, all five feet eight inches of her, but she was unaware, or at least she appeared to be unaware, of just how striking she really was.

Paige assumed that Lisa was around thirty-seven, thirty-eight years old, not because she looked that age but based on the time she had spent getting her legal education and the age of her two children.

"They are good kids, if I say so myself," Lisa agreed.

"Well, what I want to ask you is how you manage to raise them and work full-time in such a high-profile career like ours?"

"You want to know how I handle having a career and raising my children?" Lisa asked in surprise. She'd never have guessed that was the question Paige had on her mind.

"Yes," Paige responded. "How do you do it? As you know, Damian and I intend to get married in June. We both want to start a family, but realistically, Lisa, I spend hours here at the firm. I'm not sure I can handle children and a family. How do you do it? You make it look so easy."

Lisa chuckled. "I'm glad someone thinks I have it together." She thought about the drama she was currently going through with Tiara. "To the extent that I do, it's probably because I have help... lots of help. Finding good child care is probably going to be the most important factor in balancing your home and office life. As a parent, if you have to worry about your children while you're at work, you're definitely not going to be productive here at the firm. But if you get your child-care arrangements all worked out where you, Damian, and your children are all properly cared for, then you'll definitely be free to be the best you can be."

"How did you learn all this?"

"Trust me, it wasn't easy. My child-care education came through trial and error. The same way children come in all shapes, sizes, and colors, there's also all kinds of child-care arrangements. Now, if I was talking to your average career woman, I would probably tell her to look around the neighborhood and see what kind of child care is available, what's going to fit her budget. But let's face it," Lisa continued with a wide grin that filled the beauty of her face, "there is no way you're going to be the average housewife, certainly not with the salary you make here and definitely *not* with Damian for a husband."

Paige gave Lisa a brief smile. There was no secret between the two of them that McKenzie, Kennedy, and McKenzie was paying both women a good six-figure salary. Added to that, everyone in the firm was fully aware of

Damian St. Jean's net worth. Even if he hadn't been a client of McKenzie, Kennedy, and McKenzie, Damian was always in the tabloids. As one of the top international promoters, it was no secret that Paige was marrying a billionaire.

"You're right," Paige confirmed. "Money is not going to be a problem."

"Well, you're lucky. You won't have to consider all the options the typical American parent considers, like day care centers or taking your baby to a sitter. When Blake and I first got married, I had just completed my undergraduate degree. Blake had finished medical school, but he was still working on his residency. We didn't have any money to speak of. When Tiara was born two years later, I had just completed my second year at Harvard Law School. We couldn't afford to pay for help because we were paying my law school tuition and Blake's medical school loans. By himself, Blake has amassed several hundred thousand dollars' worth of college and medical school student loans. We certainly didn't have any extra money to pay for child care."

"So what did you do? Who took care of Tiara?"

"Blake did. He'd just completed his residency in July, exactly one month after Tiara was born. He found a position at Peter Brigham Hospital in Boston, in the anesthesiology department, but he told them that he would accept the position on condition that he would be allowed to work the night shift. They needed him badly, so they agreed to give him the shift he wanted. While he worked nights, I took care of Tiara. During the day, when I went to school, Blake took care of her. It worked out well for us. Actually, it worked out so well that I thought I could handle a job at one of the major law firms. Tiara was a year old when I graduated from law school and accepted a position at Bennett and O'Brian."

"Wow!" said Paige, obviously impressed at the prestigious law firm Lisa had just named. "You worked there?"

"Yes, but only for three years. Until a year after Spencer Jr. was born. I was on the partnership track, but it became too much for me to handle. I couldn't take it. I was working all the time. On several occasions, Blake had to call in sick or go into work late when I simply couldn't make it home on time. It was a mess! Our marriage started to suffer."

Paige looked on with concern in her eyes. That was exactly what she feared would happen in her marriage.

"Finally," Lisa continued, "I had to make a choice . . . partnership or my family. I chose family. I accepted a part-time job at the public defender's office in Roxbury. Part-time still turned out to average about seven hours a day. That's pretty much the amount of time most people work at any full-time position. The job change worked for me, though. It actually allowed me to get home at a decent hour so I could pick up the kids from nursery school. Blake also started working days, so we all had more time to spend together."

"Wow," Paige said. "I really admire you!"

"Thanks, but like I said, that's not going to be the problem for you. Money for you will not be an issue."

"I know, but I'm not sure I'll be able to leave my kids at home with just anyone," Paige replied.

"I know what you mean. I even had a hard time leaving

them with Blake, and he's their father . . . and a doctor at that. There was no doubt in my mind that he would be able to handle anything if they became sick or something, but it didn't matter. It was still hard for me to leave them. By the way, have you talked to Damian about all of this? He may want to do some of his work from home and spend time with the kids."

"Damian?" Paige looked at Lisa in shock. "I couldn't see him holding a baby let alone keeping one all day long . . . not even his own."

"Don't shortchange him, Paige. I didn't think Blake could do it either, but I have to say, he rose to the occasion. He turned out to be great with the kids. He really bonded with them and now that they're older, Tiara and Spencer Jr. are really close to him."

Paige still looked uncertain. For the life of her, she just couldn't see her suave, sophisticated husband changing diapers and doing the baby thing. Lisa saw the doubt on Paige's face and shook her head.

"Let's be real, Paige. If you're going to continue working here and shooting for partnership, then you're going to have to hire your own Mary Poppins. You know, some serene older woman; perhaps someone who retired from many years of teaching school and is searching for that one child that she can take care of and bake chocolate chip cookies for. Someone who will live in and make everything run smoothly."

"That only happens in the movies, not in real life."

"Oh, sometimes in real life too. We probably have the best housekeeper in the world," Lisa said. "We hired

Marilyn Goodly when Tiara was five and Spencer Jr. was two years old. She was an absolute godsend. She lives in and is just like one of the family. She does all the cleaning, laundry, and cooking. She keeps that house spotless and takes wonderful care of Spencer Jr. and Tiara, getting them to their appointments and other activities when I'm unable to make it. Marilyn has been wonderful. She makes me look good," Lisa said, not holding back but giving her housekeeper her props.

"Damn, that's a wealth of information," Paige stated appreciatively.

"Yes, it is," Lisa agreed. "And I suggest the minute you start thinking about having kids, start looking for a great housekeeper. Oh, and by the way, start training Damian as well."

Both women fell into hysterical laughter.

Chapter 11

Tiara had come to look forward to the daily tennis team practice after school. They were long—two hours—but fun. Sierra Morgan, Lindsey Battle, Candy Spellman, Kimberly Hall, Tiara, and Amanda were the six singles players on the team. When they competed against other schools, they played one-on-one against a member from the other team. The ten remaining girls on Skidmore's team were the doubles players. They were paired according to rank and played two-on-two against members from the other team.

To Tiara, the only flaw on Skidmore's team was Alicia Blackstone. It wasn't that Alicia was bad. Actually, as Tiara had discovered on the first day of tryouts, Alicia was a decent tennis player. No, Alicia's flaw was not her game. It was her attitude. Alicia no longer even tried to hide the fact that she hated Tiara. Not only that, but it had become apparent that she had managed to get a few other people on her side and turned them against Tiara.

Exactly one month had passed since Skidmore's tennis tryouts. Since then, Tiara had been trying to keep her distance from Alicia and her crowd. It hadn't been easy, nor was it working very well. No matter where she went, Alicia or one of her cronies always seemed to show up, subtly managing to get one of their snide remarks in. Alicia's behavior had not gone unnoticed either.

Tiara had become close to several of the girls on Skidmore's tennis team. They were totally impressed with her tennis ability. Added to that, they really liked the fact that Tiara was so humble about how good a player she was. Tiara never bragged or acted like she was better than everyone else. Her attitude had already won her a lot of friends.

Sierra was the first one to bring up Alicia's very obvious nasty behavior. "Do you know why she's acting the way she is?" It was after Friday's practice and Sierra and Tiara were sitting on the bench in the locker room. They were the last ones there, all the other girls on the team having already left to catch their rides home. Lisa had called Tiara on her cell a short while earlier to let her know that she was stuck in traffic and would probably arrive at Skidmore's front gate in about twenty minutes.

"I'm not really sure why she hates me," Tiara responded diplomatically. "Really, it's not her hate that bothers me the most."

"It isn't?"

"No. What really bugs me is that she's turning so many of the Skidmore students against me."

There was a definite, undeniable split between the students in room 401. Alicia had managed to grab a few of their classmates and had pulled them over to her side, against Tiara. Alicia's little clique now included Molly, her chief henchman, Megan, and Brittany. Maxwell Blackstone had no choice in the matter, being a relative. And of course, wherever Maxwell went, so did Jonathan Myers.

Amanda, Brooke, Karen, and Aaron Peters had joined forces with Tiara, but the other four members of the class—Patrick Simpson, Michael Richards, Sean Blaine, and Jessica Harden—were trying hard to remain neutral.

Alicia had also taken her hate campaign to the tennis team. She'd managed to win over several supporters there as well. Joy Goldman and Michelle Leigh had jumped on the bandwagon and had also joined her camp. Tiara couldn't understand the reason for Joy and Michelle joining the "haters" league since she hadn't done anything to either of them. The whole situation was really a mystery.

"I wonder why they would do that," Tiara mused to Sierra as the two girls left the locker room and walked around the school to the entrance gate of Skidmore Prep.

"Don't worry about it," Sierra said encouragingly. "Joy and Michelle probably don't even like Alicia, since few people at Skidmore actually do. They're probably just annoyed because two freshmen are ranked above them on the team."

This did seem to be the biggest concern for those who had teamed up with Alicia. So big, in fact, that Tiara knew that both of them had complained to Coach Bob. For some reason, both Alicia and Joy seemed to feel it was unfair that a pair of freshmen, though better than they were, should be ranked ahead of them on the team.

"I don't really know what they think complaining to

Coach will do," Amanda had said, obviously disgusted with the whole situation. "There's a team ladder. If they have a problem with their position, they can challenge the person above them and try to move their way up."

Tiara assumed that Coach Bob must have suggested the same thing to a few of the girls because several requests for ladder challenges had been made at that day's practice. Coach Bob scheduled Joy to play against Amanda and Tiara to play against Alicia at Monday's practice. Tiara was definitely looking forward to the challenge. She intended to put a stop to this nonsense once and for all.

When Sierra and Tiara arrived at the school entrance, Tiara's mother was there waiting for her. Tiara pulled the BMW's passenger door open. Climbing in, she waved good-bye to Sierra before closing the door.

"Hi, sweetie," Lisa greeted her. She turned the key in the ignition and drove out of the circular driveway.

"Hi." Tiara reached over to press the Play button on the CD changer. The smooth sound of Mozart's "Don Giovanni" filled the air. Tiara laid her head on the headrest and closed her eyes so she could enjoy the music.

"Traffic was awful!" Lisa explained. "I drove through downtown DC instead of going through Rock Creek Park. Was that ever a big mistake! I think everyone in town was trying to leave work early. I guess they all wanted to get a head start on the weekend."

"It's all right," Tiara calmly replied. "Sierra also had to wait for her mom to pick up her younger sister from the dentist, so I had company. We have orientation at the Tennis Foundation today. You didn't forget, did you?"

"No, I remembered," Lisa replied as she signaled a left turn into Spencer Jr.'s school.

Lisa drove straight up to the front entrance of St. Paul's and put the car in park. This was the advantage of arriving late for after-school pickup. Lisa would normally have had to queue up in a line of cars, inching her way until she finally arrived at the front door. Hopefully, Spencer Jr. would be waiting there. Spencer Jr. was generally pretty good about being where he was supposed to be, unlike a lot of the other boys who often forced their parents to send out search parties to find them. It was amazing how some of the boys would simply decide that they had better things to do than stand around in the entryway waiting for their ride home and simply wander off.

"There he is!" Tiara said, pointing to her brother. Spencer Jr. had exited the building from the side entrance instead of using the usual front door. His book bag was strung over his back. Lisa and Tiara could see that it was loaded down with homework for the weekend. Slung across his right shoulder was his Wilson tennis bag. Two tennis racket handles were sticking out from his bag.

Spencer Jr. was an easygoing guy. There was one thing he didn't play around with, though—that was his tennis. Spencer was deadly serious about his tennis game and even at the age of twelve, had already played on the Boston junior tennis team for two years.

Spencer Jr. pulled open the back passenger door, carefully placing his tennis bag on the seat before climbing in. He was also super particular about his tennis gear. Not just any racket would do for him. Spencer's rackets had to be

Wilson Pro Staff, the same racket his hero Roger Federer used. He always carried at least two of them around with him at all times. God forbid that anyone else should touch one of them.

"Hi, Mom. Hi, Tiara. Can we stop and get something to eat before we go to tennis?" he asked, getting straight to the point.

"Hello, Spencer," Lisa replied with a smile. "And how was your day?" she added, ignoring his request for food. Spencer knew better than to try and play tennis on a full stomach. He also knew his request was something Lisa would never entertain.

"Fine. We got our math homework back today—I got three check plusses. Three checks is the most anyone is able to get—I think I'm the only one in my class to ever get three check plusses." Spencer Jr.'s sentences ran together in his excitement to release all his information.

"That's great, Spencer! Three plusses is fantastic. Why do you think you did so well?" Lisa asked as she pulled up in front of the McDonald's on Connecticut Avenue and waited in line for the cars ahead to be served.

"Uh . . . because I studied?" Spencer Jr. replied, a big grin on his face.

"Try again," Lisa responded with a smile on her face. She knew Spencer didn't want to admit the real reason he was doing so much better than the other boys in his math class. Lisa had enrolled both kids in the Johns Hopkins gifted and talented program. During the summer vacation, both Tiara and Spencer Jr. had taken advanced math courses. Tiara had studied algebra II while Spencer had focused on prealgebra. Lisa had spent quite a few hours during the hot summer days trying to convince her son to finish his course. She'd finally given a loud sigh of relief the day Spencer Jr. had completed the last problem. Now that he was actually taking a prealgebra course at St. Paul's, Lisa could tell that he was loving it. Even though he refused to admit it, Spencer Jr. knew the real reason he was the only student in class receiving three check plusses was because of the extra work he'd completed in the Johns Hopkins program.

Lisa put the car in park after pulling up to the McDonald's express window. "Two milkshakes," she ordered. "One chocolate and one strawberry. And a diet Coke," she added, making her request to the high school student standing behind the glass window.

"A burger too," Spencer threw out, leaning over the front seat of the car.

"No, Spencer. That really would be too much food before dinner. We're not going to make a habit of this. A milkshake is enough." When the order came, Lisa passed the tray to Tiara to distribute the contents while she drove out of the fast-food chain.

Lisa's response had no negative impact on Spencer Jr. As Lisa merged into traffic once again, keeping her eyes on the road ahead, Spencer Jr. continued his conversation between slurps of chocolate milkshake. "I met with the voice teacher today," he informed his mother.

"How did that go?" Lisa asked, keeping her eyes on the road.

"Good. I had a very productive lesson."

"Wonderful," Lisa replied. Spencer had auditioned

for and been selected to join the renowned cathedral choir. St. Paul's had originally been founded as a choir school for boys. The school maintained its musical connection with the cathedral by selecting twenty of its lower school students to sing in the choir. Although it took up an enormous amount of time, Spencer Jr. was enjoying the experience a lot.

Lisa pulled into the Tennis Foundation's parking lot. She parked the car and watched as both of her children jumped out, each of them hoisting a Wilson tennis bag. Lisa remained behind the wheel of the car for a moment longer, marveling at how differently her two children were responding to the family's relocation. It was obvious that Spencer Jr. was making a conscious effort to adjust at his new school and fit in with his new friends. Actually, he was doing just fine. Tiara, on the other hand, was still resisting the change, looking backward instead of pushing ahead and developing new friendships. Lisa let out a loud sigh as she unhooked her seatbelt before climbing out of the car. No one ever said raising two kids would be easy. Sometimes it was just a little harder than others.

Tiara sat on the edge of her seat in the second row of the Tennis Foundation's large conference room. Sixty students ranging in age from ten to nineteen filled the metal folding chairs. Each one had tried out and successfully passed the stringent test that allowed them to play on the Arthur Ashe Tennis Foundation's elite tennis team.

The large group had just left the outside tennis courts where they'd been put through the paces. Tiara had really been surprised when she'd arrived on the outdoor tennis courts after changing into her shorts in the women's locker room. The small group of students who had come to try out for the team had gathered in front of the first tennis court on the Tennis Foundation's large athletic field. Two players were engaged in a quick warm-up match. Tiara had no idea who the player on the far side of the court was, but she could certainly identify the one closer to her. It was her next-door neighbor, Landon Andrews.

Although they lived next door to each other, Tiara hadn't seen her neighbor up close for weeks. It seemed that she and the Andrews kids were on a completely different schedule. She knew that both Kamilla and Landon attended Woodson, the local public high school. Students at Woodson High started their school day at eight-thirty in the morning, a whole half hour after Tiara was required to be in school, seated at her desk.

Tiara looked around, hoping to also catch a glimpse of Kamilla. She hadn't seen her anywhere in the crowd. Coach Wilson had walked over and joined the group, watching as the two teenagers played. Both guys were pretty good players, but Landon obviously had the better game. His form was tight; he was leaving very little room for error.

"Okay, ladies, gentlemen," Coach Wilson had said. "I'd like you to get into pairs. Spread out on the courts and spend the next ten minutes warming up. Coach Smith and I will be walking around to see who has what and what level each of you will be playing on."

Now, an hour later, after all sixty of the elite student players had been carefully scrutinized, everyone was sitting in the tennis center's conference room waiting for Coach Wilson to outline what he expected from each of them over the course of the school year. A large number of parents, Lisa included, had found seats at the back of the room. They too were eagerly awaiting Coach Wilson's presentation. The parents all knew that it was an honor for their children to have been selected to join the Foundation's elite tennis team. They also realized that being a part of this group was going to entail a lot of work, a good deal of it falling on their shoulders.

Tiara stole a quick glance at the back of the room. Her mom was seated in the first row in the section reserved for parents, an open notebook on her lap. Tiara knew her mom would take notes and memorize every piece of vital information by the end of the session. Tiara returned her eyes to the front of the room and glanced at Landon. He was seated on the first seat, one row ahead of her. She'd had no idea he was also a member of this elite tennis team. From where she was seated, she had a great view of his profile as he stared straight ahead. His features were prominent under the thick black hair that fell in waves over his forehead. His broad shoulders were outlined under the white polo tennis shirt he was wearing.

"Ladies and gentlemen," Coach Wilson called for the group's attention. "Welcome to the Arthur Ashe Tennis Foundation and our Academic Center for Excellence. Our purpose here at the Foundation is twofold. The Center for Excellence is a college preparatory program that provides

SAT prep courses four days a week for a select group of students enrolled between the third and twelfth grades. Each student in the program will be expected to participate in our intensive after-school, academic, and college preparatory series throughout the school year. Additionally, under the second phase of our program, our team of tennis coaches will be instructing each of you on how to compete and win at the elite level. We'll be going up against some other very high-caliber teams from all over the country. I want you to know that we are a very competitive team. We work hard and we play hard. If you think you will not be able to give the club everything you've got, I suggest you let me know right now."

Tiara took a quick glance around the room to see if any of the other students had anything to say. Of course, no one said a word or made a move to leave the room. For the next ten to fifteen minutes, Coach Wilson droned on instructing the students on what to expect. Tiara allowed her mind to wander back to her thoughts of Landon and whether or not he had a girlfriend at Woodson High.

Tiara was abruptly brought back to the present by the other students getting up from their seats. Spencer Jr. had already made his way to the back of the conference room and joined Lisa, who was huddled in a group with some of the other parents. They were standing in line gathered around to talk to Coach Wilson. Tiara made a move to join the group but was stopped by a hand on her shoulder before she reached halfway.

"Hi," Landon greeted Tiara.

"Hi," she replied, too surprised to say much more than that.

"I saw you earlier on the tennis courts. I didn't know you were on the team," Landon said, a wide smile spreading on his face.

"Yes, Spencer and I tried out earlier this summer. I didn't know you were on the team either. Is Kamilla a member also?"

"No. She tried out but missed it by a hair."

"That's too bad." Tiara continued inching her way toward the exit.

Landon kept pace with her. "Do you also play on your schools tennis team?"

"Yes. In fact, we just finished practicing before I arrived here at the Foundation," Tiara informed him just as she caught up with her mother and Spencer Jr. Lisa was still deep in conversation with Coach Wilson.

Landon wanted to keep talking to Tiara but quickly realized that Tiara might hang around for a while waiting for her mother to finish her conversation. "I'll see you at practice on Monday," he said before continuing out the door.

"Sure thing," Tiara replied, trying her best to act cool, as if a gorgeous high school junior spoke to her every day of the week. Out of the corner of her eye, Tiara noticed that a few of the other girls on the Foundation team were staring at her in wide-eyed amazement. Having Landon as a friend definitely wasn't bad for a girl's image, she thought.

Chapter 12

Tiara sat on the edge of her seat in the string section of the DC Youth Orchestra. As she waited, listening attentively to the music, she mentally counted out the beats to the concerto, anticipating when the violins should join in. She held her instrument on her shoulder, her fingers positioned to begin playing.

Tiara was seated on the "first chair," the most sought-after position in the orchestra. Eleven years of practice had allowed her to be selected for this coveted spot. An enchanting sound was now filling the auditorium. Tiara loved classical music. Playing in the orchestra was nothing new to her. She'd been playing the violin for years in the Boston Youth Orchestra. What was new and definitely interesting was the makeup of the kids in this orchestra. At least eighty percent of the students in the group were black—inner-city black—students who attended DC public schools. The remaining twenty percent were predominantly of Asian descent with one or two Caucasians sprinkled in the mix. Tiara had never been in an environment, whether at her former school in Boston or at her old church, where African Americans were in the majority. To be honest, Tiara had never really thought about it before. She'd simply taken it for granted that in any of the social settings she'd be placed in, the composition would pretty much be a mixed group or predominantly white. This was definitely not the case at the DC Youth Orchestra. The mix here was completely different. Tiara thought it was exciting.

"Whew! Wasn't that concerto difficult?" the dark-skinned girl sitting next to Tiara whispered softly, but still loud enough to be heard above the sound of the brass section.

"Yeah," Tiara agreed. She hadn't really thought the piece was all that difficult. In fact, the piece was one of her favorites—Mendelssohn's "Wedding March." Tiara had played it several times for some of her parents' friends at their own wedding ceremonies. There was nothing hard about the piece as far as Tiara was concerned, but there was no way she would ever say that out loud. To do so would make her sound like a snob.

"Have you been playing the violin a long time?" Tiara asked instead, trying hard to keep her voice down to a murmur as Mr. O'Connell, the orchestra director, continued working with the brass section.

"Four years," the girl replied. "How about yourself? How long have you been playing?"

Tiara really didn't want to respond to that question. She knew that no mater how she phrased it, there was no way she would come off sounding anything other than arrogant. Eleven years of private lessons in comparison to four years of group lessons was really no comparison at all.

Tiara was saved from having to respond as Mr. O'Connell raised his baton and proceeded to bring in the string instruments. The royal march filled the entire auditorium with its majestic sound. Rehearsal continued for another half hour before Mr. O'Connell allowed them to leave.

"I'm Kadesha Freeman," the girl said after practice.

"I'm Tiara Johnson."

"Nice to meet you."

"You too."

Kadesha watched as Tiara wrapped her violin in its velvet jacket and placed it inside her black leather violin case. "Is this your first year at the DC Youth Orchestra?" she asked. Her tight cornrows were evenly spaced on her head, and her dark eyes took in every one of Tiara's moves.

"Yes, this is my first year with the orchestra. I moved here from Boston, Massachusetts, about three months ago. I played in a youth orchestra in Boston, but it wasn't anything like this."

"What do you mean?"

"Our youth orchestra in Boston only had a few black kids in it. The majority of the students here are black. Why is that?"

Kadesha looked surprised, as if she'd never thought about it before. "Most of us attend public schools in the district. The public schools here don't have a music program. So we come here, to the DC Youth Orchestra, instead, and complete our music requirements."

"I didn't know music wasn't offered in the DC schools. That really explains a lot."

A tall, creamy chocolate boy approached the two girls. "Hi, Kadesha. Who's your friend?" he asked, staring intently at Tiara although his question had been directed to Kadesha.

"Tiara Johnson, Rashawn Lewis," Kadesha replied, introducing the two.

"Hi! Are you new?" There was definite interest in his eyes as he waited for her to respond.

Once again, Tiara repeated the monologue she'd just finished giving Kadesha. "How about yourself?" Tiara asked once she was through. "Have you been studying music at the DC Youth Orchestra for a long time?"

"I guess you could say that," Rashawn replied. "I started taking lessons here six years ago when I was ten years old."

"How do you like it?" Tiara asked as the trio made their way out of the large auditorium and down the stairwell leading to the front entrance.

"Well, it is a nice way to meet other kids from different schools in the district. Kadesha and I have been in the same section of the orchestra for the last three years. We actually go to different public schools, though. I'm at Roosevelt High. Kadesha comes here during the week, to Coolidge High."

"Really?" Tiara asked, glancing over at Kadesha with even more interest. Coolidge High was a straight-up urban high school. The kids who came here during the week were totally different from the ones who attended the music program on the weekends. Although the DC Youth

Orchestra housed its program in their building, very few of the Coolidge High students were actual members of the music program. It was obviously an image thing. Tiara realized that a lot of the urban kids from the hood just didn't think it was all that cool to be walking around town with a violin case in their hand. Somehow that image just didn't fit the picture most of them were trying to portray.

Tiara's glance at Kadesha must have spoken volumes because suddenly Kadesha looked embarrassed. "My mom was the one who wanted me to learn how to play the violin," she said sheepishly. "She thinks it'll help me get into college."

"Where do you go to school?" Rashawn cut in, once again directing his question to Tiara.

"Skidmore Prep."

"What!" he exclaimed, his amazement evident.

"I thought as much," Kadesha said in a derisive tone. "Once I heard you talk, I just knew you didn't go to a regular school."

They'd walked outside and were now standing on the loading dock at the back of the building where Lisa had instructed Tiara and Spencer Jr. to wait for her. A stream of other students who'd also finished their lessons walked by, heading for their parents' parked vehicles.

"What's it like going to Skidmore Prep?" Rashawn asked. "Every time I walk past that school, I wonder what it would be like to go there."

Before Tiara could respond, the trio were joined by two other students, a tall dark-skinned black boy and an Asian girl with long black hair. Tiara had seen them sitting in the string section of the orchestra.

"Yeah, I've always wondered about that myself," the tall boy who'd just joined the group agreed.

Tiara turned around to get a good look at him. His hair was dreadlocked, hanging halfway down his back. He looked like a young version of Bob Marley.

"I'm Jamal, by the way. You're new here aren't you?"

"Yes," Tiara replied. "The name's Tiara Johnson. I moved here over the summer, from Boston."

"So what's it like at that school?" Kadesha repeated the question that everyone wanted answered.

"It's all right. I guess it's like any other school."

"I bet it's not," the Asian girl replied with a whole lot of attitude. "Anyone can tell that it's not the same as our schools. Those kids over there are rich. I'm sure they drive up to the door in a Benz or a Lexus or a BMW, real top-of-the-line cars. They have to be different!"

Tiara hesitated, really caught off guard. It struck her that this group really had a bone to pick when it came to the kids at Skidmore. It dawned on Tiara that they were jealous, jealous because of what and who they perceived the Skidmore kids to be. Tiara knew that nothing she could say would make them change their minds. Nevertheless, she still had to say something. If she didn't, she knew she'd forever be classified as the girl from Skidmore... the outsider.

"Well, maybe you're right," Tiara finally agreed, "but I'll let you judge for yourself. The next time we have a function that's open to the public, I'll be sure to invite all of you. Then you can come and tell me what the differences are... if there are any."

"Wow! I'm all for that," the Asian girl replied excitedly. "By the way, my name's Michelle Kim. I'd love to see what's going on up in that school."

"Me too," Rashawn joined in.

"And me," Kadesha replied. "Well, see you next week. We gotta run or we'll miss the bus and the next one won't come for another hour. See ya!" Kadesha waved, then turned and broke into a sprint. The other kids followed suit.

"Bye!" Tiara called after them.

As she watched them dash off to catch the bus, their violin cases tucked under their arms to keep them from bumping against their legs, Tiara couldn't help thinking that they were an interesting bunch. No doubt about it, they were a little different from her classmates at Skidmore Prep, but very interesting. Tiara decided she would definitely invite them to Skidmore at the first available opportunity, just so they'd realize that there wasn't all that much of a difference between the Skidmore kids and themselves.

Tiara saw her mother pulling up in their sleek BMW. She was glad her new friends had already left. There was no need to have any of their opinions about the ritzy cars confirmed. Tiara started down the steps as her brother came bolting out of the building. Tiara guessed that he'd also been on the lookout for their car. Flying down the steps, he made a mad dash, trying to beat his sister to the vehicle. As usual, he did.

Tiara looked up from the algebra textbook in front of her. She had two more math problems before she could call it quits for the evening. Sunday had been quiet in the Johnson household. Tiara and her family had attended church at the cathedral that morning. Spencer Jr. had already taken his seat behind the altar with the other choirboys by the time Tiara and her parents got to their pew.

Tiara enjoyed the cathedral services. They gave her a sense of peace even though her mind often wandered throughout the sermon, like it had today. She had not been able to keep from thinking about the tennis challenge against Alicia the next day. Now, as she sat at her desk in her third-floor bedroom, her thoughts once again returned to the upcoming battle, the face-off she was expected to have with her arch-nemesis. Tiara had every intention of handling her business. She didn't normally act this way. She didn't often seek to put people in their place, but as far as she was concerned, Alicia Blackstone had started this foolishness. Tiara simply was about to end it.

Chapter 13

Monday morning. Tiara rushed downstairs and entered the kitchen, excited about the upcoming challenge against Alicia. She had dressed in her favorite blue flared-leg jeans and a navy-blue turtleneck sweater. Taking a seat at the kitchen table, Tiara tuned in and caught the tail end of the conversation between her dad and her brother.

"We're having a long rehearsal today," Spencer Jr. was explaining to his parents. "The combined choir is required to attend—that means the boys' choir, the girls' section, and the adult men's section."

"Why? What's going on?" Lisa asked.

"I'm not sure. I think someone special is coming to the cathedral soon, but we haven't been told who it is yet. Dad, are you going to pick me up on time?" Spencer switched the subject without a taking a breath, as he was prone to do.

"Yes, I'll try to be on time, Spencer," Blake replied sheepishly. Last week, Blake had kept Spencer Jr. waiting for almost two hours before he was finally able to call

Marilyn and ask her to pick him up. No one was allowing him to forget that incident. They'd been teasing him every day this week about forgetting he had a son.

"Dad, Marilyn can pick me up today if you're going to be too busy," Spencer Jr. suggested.

Both Tiara and Lisa tried to hide their smirks. Marilyn wasn't as polite. Peering into the refrigerator to grab another carton of milk, Marilyn laughed outright at Blake's tardiness. "I can pick him up if you'd like," she announced.

"That won't be necessary, Marilyn," Blake announced, stealing a quick glance at Lisa and Tiara. He knew they were silently laughing at him too. They'd nicknamed him the Absentminded Professor and had informed him that he would lose his head if it weren't attached to his neck. None of them wanted to believe him when he repeatedly told them that he had not forgotten Spencer Jr., that he had simply been tied up and couldn't get to his son's school. His excuse didn't matter to them. He knew he was going to be the butt of their jokes for some time to come.

"I'll be there to pick you up, Spencer," he repeated.

"Okay, Dad," Spencer Jr. responded with a smile. "And it doesn't matter if you're late. I'll wait."

"That's my boy. You know I'd never leave you at school . . . at least not overnight," he said with a smile. The reality was that Blake enjoyed the quality time he spent with Spencer, taking him back and forth to school. "How about you, Tiara? Do you have anything special planned for today?"

Tiara swallowed the last bit of yogurt and fruit salad

she had just spooned into her mouth before responding. "Nothing really. We have a quiz in algebra, but that shouldn't be any problem." She turned to her mother. "By the way, Mom, I'll be late today. We're going to have an extended tennis practice after school. Some of the girls want to challenge each other for different spots on the team, so practice is going to be a little longer than usual."

"Who's challenging who?" Blake wanted to know.

"They've challenged me and my partner, Amanda Carter."

"Who are the challengers?" Lisa asked.

"No one you know, Mom," Tiara answered abruptly. Her mom had known all her friends at her school in Boston, but since their move to DC, Lisa really had been too busy at the firm to get to know any of the Skidmore kids.

"That's not what I meant, Tiara," Lisa replied. "What I'm really asking is, whoever they are, are they any good?"

"Oh. Well, Joy Goldman is challenging Amanda. Joy's a good player, but I think Amanda's much better. Alicia Blackstone challenged me. Alicia actually is a pretty strong player, so it should be interesting."

"Well, I really wish I could be there to see it, but I'm up to my ears in work. I'll pick you up as close to four o'clock as possible." Lisa stood up and moved toward the front door. The charcoal-gray suit she had on was a designer classic. Tiara noticed that it gave her mom a really sleek corporate look.

"Right, Spencer. Let's hit the road too before we're late," Blake said. He and Spencer Jr. also stood up and left the kitchen, heading for the front door.

"I just have to run upstairs for my book bag," Spencer threw over his shoulder as he flew up the stairs.

"So what else is new?" Tiara asked sarcastically. "You're always running back upstairs for your book bag. See you later, Dad," she called, scooping up her own bag as she headed for her mother's car.

"How's Tiara doing?" Blake asked his wife as he helped her on with her coat. He couldn't help but admire how sophisticated Lisa looked in her suit. "She seems a lot better. Do you think she's finally adjusting to being here?"

"I'm not sure. She's definitely made some new friends, but I know she's still not the Tiara we knew in Boston."

"Give it some more time," Blake suggested, bending over and smoothly kissing his wife on the corner of her lips. "And we really need to stop meeting like this," he whispered in her ear.

"You're telling me. We haven't gone out by ourselves in ages! We definitely have to make plans to spend some time together."

"You're absolutely right. What about this—"

"Dad! I'm ready!" Spencer yelled as he came running up to the couple. "Let's go!"

"All right, all right, old man. I'm coming," Blake called after his son who was already halfway down the front steps.

Blake and Lisa closed the front door behind them and walked down the steps to their cars. Lisa eased into the BMW. "I'll see you tonight, honey," Blake said before pushing her car door shut.

"See you!" she replied with a soft smile through the

open car window. This was a perfect example of today's working couple—no time at all to spend with each other.

Tiara glanced at the clock on the wall in her homeroom class. It was one forty-five. Fifteen minutes to go before the last bell. The day had literally zipped by. No doubt about it. A tremendous amount of excitement had been permeating the air all day long, not only amongst the freshmen students, but the upperclassmen as well. A lot of the older students had heard about the upcoming tennis challenge. They were curious to see the match between Amanda and Joy but were especially interested in seeing Alicia and Tiara go up against each other. Word had already spread about how well Tiara could play. Everyone had also heard, namely from Alicia herself, what a great tennis player Alicia was. As a result, the tennis court was the place to be this afternoon.

Twenty minutes later, Tiara had changed into one of her new warm-up suits and her white Nikes. She left the locker room and headed to Skidmore's outside tennis courts, ready to do battle. The bleachers, which were usually stationed on the soccer field, had been moved to face the courts. They were packed with students who had come to watch the ladder challenges. Amanda against Joy Goldman, the winner playing Alicia, and finally the winner of the match playing Tiara. By now, everyone at Skidmore Prep knew there was an issue between Tiara and Alicia. Nobody was really saying much about it, not because it was a secret but rather because it was hard to be sure whose side a particular person was on. However, everyone knew the controversy existed.

Alicia was already on the courts, her entourage surrounding her. "I thought you'd stood me up." Her syrupy voice dripped with the artificial sweetness she was pouring out.

"No way!" Tiara replied, sidestepping her, just missing a head-on collision with Molly "Olive Oyl."

Tiara stalked toward the group in the stand and took a seat next to Brooke and Karen. Like many of the other students, neither Brooke nor Karen were particularly interested in tennis itself. Of course, they enjoyed playing the game and were definitely happy that they'd made the team, even if they had not landed in one of the highest spots. No, Karen and Brooke were really there just to support Amanda and Tiara. Other kids may have been there for this purpose as well, or maybe to support Alicia, or more likely than not, just to watch the game so they could be in the know the next day when everyone else would be talking about it.

Tiara was quiet as she sat next to Brooke and Karen. All around them, the other students were busy talking up a storm, but by now Tiara had tuned everything out. She was deep in thought. Amanda and Joy would be the first up to play, first to four. The winner of that match would then play Alicia.

Tiara wasn't quite sure who would win between Amanda and Joy; however, she was almost certain that no matter what, she would be the one playing against Alicia.

Tiara felt kind of bad in thinking this because Amanda was her friend. Still, facts were facts, and the fact was that Alicia was a better player than both Amanda and Joy.

"So," Brooke broke in to Tiara's thoughts. "We want your honest opinion: who do you think is going to win?"

"Between Amanda and Joy, it's hard to say," Tiara admitted. "Which is part of what makes watching the match so much fun."

"Tennis isn't even fun to play," Karen commented bleakly, "let alone watch. I'm just here to see Alicia get creamed."

"I second that," Brooke echoed. Tiara nodded, although she actually did enjoy playing tennis. The fact was, Tiara was just too preoccupied to debate the issue.

Amanda and Joy had just finished their warm-up and were about to start playing. They spun a racket to see who would serve first. Amanda won and retrieved the balls. Tiara was slightly amused by how seriously everyone was taking the whole thing. After all, it was just a challenge, and in the end, whether they were number one or number ten, it really didn't matter since they would still be on the team.

Tiara noticed with admiration that Amanda had a pretty good serve. For some reason, although Tiara had nothing to do with it, Amanda's serve made her proud. The first game of the match went by quickly. Amanda won it with two aces. The thing Tiara didn't like about challenge matches was that because they only played to four, every point was critical.

The next game began and was similar to the first one in that Joy's serves were as good as Amanda's had been. Joy won that game, but with only one ace. Their match lasted about twenty-five minutes, but when it was done both girls ran to the net breathing hard, as though they'd been playing for hours.

"Good job," Karen said when Amanda joined them on the bleachers. "Unless you lost, in which case, better luck next time."

"Karen, were you even watching?" Amanda asked, feigning hurt. Amanda knew that Karen wasn't particularly fond of tennis and was therefore more than likely to have zoned out.

"Well, did you win?" Karen asked.

Amanda rolled her eyes and nodded. "Which means I have to play Alicia in about fifteen minutes," she said, dread in her voice.

"You'll do fine," Tiara said. Of course, Tiara did not exactly believe her own words. It wasn't that Tiara wanted Amanda to lose; it just seemed pretty inevitable. "You'd better get back on the court. Alicia's already out there warming up."

"You're right." Amanda gave the girls a weak smile, then turned and jogged over to the court.

"Good luck," Tiara called after her.

"Yeah," Brooke said quietly. "Good luck. You're definitely going to need it."

Tiara hated to admit it, but Brooke was probably right. There was certainly a difference in the level of competition involved in the match between Amanda and Alicia. Amanda and Joy had been more or less fairly matched up; they played on the same level. That wasn't the case between Amanda and Alicia. There wasn't much competition between Amanda and Alicia, and as Tiara figured, Alicia won, slaughtering Amanda four–love.

"That'll be you in about fifteen minutes," Alicia said smartly to Tiara as she stepped off the court and headed for the water fountain.

"Not unless you can morph into Maria Sharapova," Tiara retorted before turning to Amanda and whispering, "Nice try."

"I'm actually glad I lost," Amanda said with a shrug. "If I had won, I would have had to play you."

"Yeah," Tiara said. "I hate it when I have to play my friends." This was true; Tiara hated having to beat people she liked. It was a good thing she wasn't friends with Alicia.

Their fifteen-minute break flew by. In no time at all, Coach Bob was calling both girls to the courts. Amanda had stayed by the net talking to Tiara and basically boosting her up. Her back was turned to the stands, so she failed to see Alicia's approach.

"Excuse me," Alicia snootily said to Amanda. "We're playing now. There's probably room on the bleachers for you."

Amanda turned and left the court wordlessly but gave Tiara the thumbs up behind Alicia's back. Tiara nodded and began her warm-up with Alicia. They volleyed back and forth for about five minutes before approaching the net for the racket spin, which Alicia won.

"Hmm, looks like I won," Alicia said, her voice oozing sugar. "I guess I serve first."

Tiara knew Alicia wanted to be the first out so that she

could avoid Tiara's wicked serve for as long as possible. The first round was a long one, which Tiara lost. It wasn't that Alicia did anything that made the game particularly hard, Tiara simply got bored with the endless volleys and would end up whacking them either way out or into the net, just to move the game along.

By the second round, Tiara had mastered Alicia's moves. Additionally, Alicia was no longer serving, which meant that Tiara was going to dominate the court anyway. Alicia's shots were hard, but it was apparent to everyone watching that Alicia just wasn't good enough. Tiara's first serve was wicked. There was no way Alicia could return it. That shot was followed by a deadly drop shot, a passing angle from the right side of the court over the net. Drop volley. It was incredible. After that, it was downhill all the way for Alicia. Tiara won four–love.

"Great match!" Coach Bob said, reaching the net before the girls could shake hands. "This just proves that we've got some wonderful talent on this team. Shake hands, girls."

Grudgingly, Alicia reached out for Tiara's hand, slapping it as a mask for a shake before turning to Coach Bob. "But this doesn't necessarily mean she's ahead of me on the ladder, does it?" Alicia inquired. "I mean, we only played to four. It wasn't a real game, so it shouldn't count for anything," she whined.

Coach Bob stared at Alicia, not comprehending. "Well, she is ahead of you," he finally said. "She beat you! It doesn't necessarily mean that she's better than you, but for now, she is ahead of you. Now, everyone on the courts," he ordered. "Let's get some practice going here!"

Chapter 14

Mondays were generally the busiest day of the week for Lisa and this one was no exception. She had arrived at the office extremely early since Tiara didn't have school today. The teachers were having one of their quarterly faculty meetings and the high school students were allowed to stay home and use it as a study day, so Lisa was able to avoid making her usual stop at Skidmore.

Lisa attacked the pile of work waiting in her inbox. By eight forty-five, she'd already reviewed three new cases and was trying to decide how to proceed with each one. She'd outlined some issues she intended to have Robert Brown, one of the young associates, research for her.

As she sat back in her oversized chair, Lisa listened to the sounds coming from beyond her office door. The firm was coming to life with the arrival of the other associates and some of the scheduled clients. Lisa found herself sitting quietly, staring into space, and mentally reviewing the list of things she had to accomplish today. Her daydream was interrupted by the buzzing of the intercom on her desk.

"Yes?"

"Ms. Johnson, your nine o'clock appointment has arrived—Senator and Mrs. Davis," Ellen stated in her crisp South Carolinian accent.

"Thanks a lot, Ellen. Would you show them in?"

"Of course."

Lisa had been expecting Kyra Davis's parents. She'd been talking to them continuously about their daughter and about her case in general, but last Friday, for some reason, Mrs. Davis had called, urgently requesting an appointment.

Glancing up at the knock on her door, Lisa stood up to greet the dignified middle-aged couple who entered the room ahead of Ellen.

"Ms. Johnson, Senator and Mrs. Davis," Ellen announced the couple.

"Good morning, Senator, Mrs. Davis," Lisa replied, walking around her desk to shake hands with the couple.

Senator Davis looked like your typical elected official. Almost six feet tall with salt-and-pepper hair, the senator was dressed in the standard conservative navy-blue suit and button-down white shirt. His wife stood by his side, also dressed in a navy-blue nautical dress with white piping at the hemline. Mary Davis wasn't a tall woman. About five feet, five inches, she looked almost childlike next to her husband, who towered over her. Her silver hair was freshly styled in an elegant short bob. Her blue eyes were somewhat puffy, as if she'd been crying.

"Please have a seat," Lisa said, encouraging the couple to take the two chairs facing her desk. "Can I have Ellen get you something to drink?"

"Nothing for me," Mary Davis replied, looking across at her husband.

"Nothing for me either," the senator replied.

Lisa nodded to Ellen, who quietly exited the room. Returning to sit behind her desk, Lisa pulled a legal pad from the middle drawer and picked up a pen from the desk.

"Well, Senator, Mrs. Davis. Something is definitely on your mind. Could you tell me what I can do for you today?"

Mary Davis glanced at her husband, waiting for him to take the lead. He finally did.

"Ms. Johnson. What will it take to get Kyra out of prison immediately? We want her out now!"

"Senator Davis, you know that's not a good idea. Threats have been made against your daughter. Since we have no definite idea who is making them, the safest place for her right now, until we go to trial, that is, is in protective custody in DC Jail," Lisa patiently explained to the couple.

Kyra had driven the car that the Heat gang members had been in when the drive-by shooting had taken place. Gang members from the Heat were seriously worried that Kyra Davis was going to cooperate with the prosecutors in exchange for a lesser sentence. They couldn't allow this to happen, but as long as Kyra remained in jail, they couldn't get to her either.

"Senator Davis, you retained my firm to represent your daughter. In doing so, you agreed to accept our advice," Lisa delicately pointed out. "Now you are pointedly telling me that you wish to ignore our recommendations and instead have us attempt to bond your daughter out of jail."

"Yes, Ms. Johnson," Senator Davis responded in a haggard tone. "That is what we want you to do."

Lisa stole a quick glance at Mary Davis, hoping to get some support from her. None was forthcoming. With a heavy sigh, Lisa returned her gaze to the senator. "All right, sir. I'll get in contact with the district attorney and see how soon we can schedule a bond hearing."

"Thank you, Ms. Johnson," Mary Davis replied, relief evident on her face.

"You're welcome. If you'll wait just a moment, I'll have one of the secretaries draw up a consent form indicating that this decision is being made against my legal advice."

"That will be fine."

Chapter 15

Lisa sat in front of the huge picture window and stared down at the busy traffic below. Senator Davis and his wife had left her office almost fifteen minutes earlier, but Lisa hadn't been able to move from her desk. She was still dumbfounded, trying hard to figure out why Kyra's parents were so insistent on getting her out of jail right away.

Lisa had been very serious when she'd informed the Davis couple that in her opinion, the best place for Kyra right now was in jail. The Heat gang members were no joke. They would definitely seek Kyra out if she was released from prison before the trial, and there was no telling what they would do to her when they found her.

Still, Lisa knew she didn't have a choice. She'd been retained by the Davis family to represent their daughter. She had no choice but to do what the family instructed her to do after fully advising them of the possible consequences of their decisions.

Turning from the scene outside her window, Lisa spun around in her chair and reached for the Rolodex on her desk. Riffling through, she came up with the phone number to the district attorney's office. Punching the numbers on the phone pad, Lisa waited quietly while the phone rang.

"District attorney's office, may I help you?" the voice on the other end replied.

"Yes, yes, you may. This is Lisa Johnson from the law firm of McKenzie, Kennedy, and McKenzie. I'm trying to reach Michael O'Leary."

"Just a minute, ma'am. I'll see if he's in."

After a short pause, Lisa heard the voice return to the line. "Just a minute, Ms. Johnson. Mr. O'Leary will be right with you."

"Thank you." A second later, she heard Mike's deep voice on the other end.

"Michael O'Leary speaking."

"Hi, Mike. It's Lisa Johnson."

"Oh, Lisa. How's everything going?" Mike warmly responded. "Are they treating you okay at McKenzie, Kennedy, and McKenzie?"

Lisa laughed. She knew Mike was teasing. There was no doubt in Mike's mind that Lisa was getting the royal treatment at the firm. Alex McKenzie, Mike, and Lisa had all attended Harvard Law School together. They had formed a study group and had spent almost every waking moment together for three years.

Lisa has been told the story time and time again about how Alex and Mike had met each other the first day of law school in the registration office. Having attended Harvard as an undergraduate, everything that first day had been pretty routine for Alex... but not for Mike. Michael O'Leary had completed his undergraduate degree at

Boston College and had been completely lost the first day of registration. In fact, Michael had been more than lost. None of his scholarship money had cleared the system, and so Mike was obviously not going to register that day . . . at least not without some kind of assistance.

"Do you need any help?" Alex had asked, walking up behind Michael in the registrar's line.

"Looks like my scholarship money hasn't hit my account yet," Michael responded. "They're not going to let me register."

"Until when?"

"The old bat over there says it could be a week or two. *No money, no classes.*" Mike changed his voice to mock the old woman's for the last bit.

"Where are you staying?"

"McKenzie Hall."

"Well, that's a coincidence. So am I. Let's go. I know I can at least get you moved into the dorm. Let me make a few phone calls and see if we can track down your scholarship money." Alex had taken Michael back to McKenzie Hall and maneuvered to get him a room in the student dorm.

"By the way, I'm Michael O'Leary," Michael said as he'd walked alongside Alex.

"And I'm Alex McKenzie, and yes, like in McKenzie Hall. My great-grandfather, my grandfather, and my dad all attended Harvard."

"Must be nice."

"It's all right. It has its benefits, like now." As he spoke, Alex had flipped open his cell phone and placed a direct call to his dad, Adam Alexander McKenzie IV. Mike's newfound friend told his father about him and asked his dad not only to track down Mike's scholarship award, but to front some money into his new friend's account to get him through this rough time.

The friendship between the two young men that had started sixteen years earlier had widened from that first day of class to include Lisa Johnson. Lisa had first met the two law students in her contracts class. She'd been the only black female in the class, which of course had not been unusual for her. Walking into the huge amphitheater at Harvard Law School, she'd spied an empty seat at the end of the last row. She'd taken it and pulled her textbook from out of her bag when the young man next to her had greeted her.

"Hi. I'm Alex McKenzie and he's Mike O'Leary." He'd pointed to the other young man seated next to him.

"Lisa Johnson," she'd replied, taking a closer look at Mike. "You look familiar. Where did you do your undergraduate studies?"

"Boston College."

"Really? So did I. That's why you look familiar."

From that day on, the three new law students had become a team, forming their own study group and meeting every day after class in the library to study and discuss their cases together. They had remained close friends during law school. Although Lisa had stayed in Boston after graduation, the two men had left Beantown and moved down to Washington, DC, together.

Over the last sixteen years, Alex and Mike had become

closer than brothers. Alex had gone directly into his father's and grandfather's law firm in Washington, DC, while Mike had joined the DC Office of the District Attorney.

Lisa thought it was amusing that after almost sixteen years, the trio was now back together again in the same city. Alex had only recently gotten married and was now expecting his first child. Mike, on the other hand, had been married for over six years and had become the super family man. Although the same age as Alex and Lisa, at thirty-eight, Mike was now quite settled with three daughters all under the age of five and a wife who was now pregnant with their fourth child. Mike claimed that it was an Irish Catholic thing.

Returning to the present, Lisa quickly outlined to Mike the problem she was having with the Davis couple. "Against my advice, they want to go forward with a bond hearing. I need to know which one of your assistants is going to prosecute this case. I'd like to see if we can schedule a bond hearing while we're waiting to see if we'll actually have to go to trial if we can't reach some kind of plea agreement."

"Lincoln James is scheduled to handle this one," Mike replied. "I'll have him call you ASAP with a date for a bond hearing."

"Great, Mike. I knew I could count on you."

"No problem. I'll have Lincoln get back to you right away. By the way, Ashley wanted to know when we're all going to get together."

"Set a time, Mike. We'll be there," Lisa responded with a laugh.

"All right, Lisa. Talk to you soon."

FRESHMAN YEAR

Mike instantly made good on his word. A short while later, Lisa was on the line with Lincoln James. It was obvious to Lisa that Mike had already told Lincoln about Lisa's request. Lincoln came back with a November twenty-ninth date—the Monday after Thanksgiving. "It was the earliest date I could get," he said apologetically. "The court calendar is loaded with cases."

"That's all right," Lisa replied. "We'll take it. By the way, maybe you can leave some free time on your calendar next week. I'd like to meet with you and see where we're headed on this case."

"No problem. I'll give you a call early next week to set a time."

Three hours later, after eating a sandwich that had been delivered to her office, Lisa sat waiting in the attorney/client meeting room of DC Jail. It was already two o'clock in the afternoon. The marshals had escorted Lisa to the private meeting room before leaving to get Kyra from the protective custody unit.

Lisa glanced around the room, taking in the hardback chairs and the table positioned in the center of the small space. Lisa knew that three US marshals were stationed outside the door and would remain there until she finished her interview with Kyra. That was two more marshals than were usually present at these interviews. The increased security was due to the ongoing investigation into the events that had led to the escape of two inmates a week before.

141

The previous Saturday, shortly after ten o'clock in the morning, two prisoners from the DC Jail men's unit had broken into the warden's empty office. They'd smashed through a reinforced glass window and slid down a canopy to freedom. Although the men had since been caught, the DC Department of Corrections was very concerned and investigating how the two men who were codefendants had not been separated during their incarceration and how they'd been allowed to be anywhere near the warden's office in the first place. As a result, in the last week, security had been beefed up at the jail.

A sharp knock on the door alerted Lisa to the fact that the marshals had returned. Pulling the door open, two of them entered the room with Kyra walking between them. They motioned for her to sit down in one of the chairs at the table. As usual, Lisa noticed the shackles that were on Kyra's hands and legs. All prisoners in protective custody were forced to wear them anytime they were removed from their cells, even if they were only going to meet with their attorney.

One of the marshals spoke to Lisa, informing her that they would be right outside the door.

Wow, Lisa thought to herself. Five huge men assigned to guard one puny young woman! Was that really necessary?

Kyra Davis was an attractive young lady even in the ugly orange jumpsuit she was forced to wear at the DC Jail. Her light brown curly hair was cut in a short stylish hairdo. Her green eyes, which were the exact same shade as her father's, were probably her second best feature. Her first was her genuine smile.

Lisa had been drawn to Kyra Davis from the first day they'd met. Her instincts over the last sixteen years had become pretty finely tuned. She'd become a good judge of character, especially when it came to her clients. Lisa could immediately spot the ones who were lying to her. Kyra Davis was not one of those.

Lisa had been asking herself how or why a young girl like this, someone who had everything going for her, would give it all up to become the getaway driver for a group of thugs... for a street gang. It just didn't make any sense.

"Ms. Johnson," Kyra began in her pleasant, cultured voice, "this is a surprise. I wasn't expecting to see you today."

"I know, Kyra. This is kind of sudden, but I met with your parents this morning and I felt I had to come and see you right away."

"What did they want?"

"A hearing. A bond hearing. They want you out of here as soon as possible. I can't understand what their motive is. As you know, in my opinion, the safest place for you right now is right here at the DC Jail under protective custody. Why would they want you bonded out?"

"They think I'm going to talk."

"What!" Lisa said, not realizing how loud her voice had become. "Talk about what?"

"The Heats... they think I'm going to turn state's evidence, become a snitch. If I'm not out of here and fast, the Heats have threatened to hurt Desmond, my younger brother."

Chapter 16

A general buzz had been circulating throughout Skidmore Prep for the last two weeks. The only serious topic of conversation was the homecoming dance. Now, less than two days away, Tiara still had not been asked to the dance. Granted, she wasn't the only one, but to her that didn't matter, it didn't make her feel any better. Not having a date two days before the biggest event of the school year was simply humiliating.

Everyone else in her crowd, with the exception of Brooke, had already been asked and was now eagerly making plans. Amanda was asked by Luke Weston, an upperclassman no less. Luke was an eleventh-grade Skidmore student and had known Amanda since middle school; Luke had been in the eighth grade when Amanda had been in the sixth. He had always talked to Amanda in a general sort of way, but this was the first time he'd ever asked her out. Amanda was thrilled. Luke was a hunk, no doubt about it. Almost six feet tall, he had dark brown hair and blue eyes. He also happened to be one of Skidmore's star football players—an added plus.

Karen too had already received an invitation from Aaron. Of course, no one had been surprised to hear that. Alicia and Brittany had also received invitations. They were pleased to announce to anyone who cared to listen, and even to those who weren't particularly interested, that they would be attending the dance with two upperclassmen. Alicia seemed to have made it her quest in life to let everyone know about her minor achievement. For some reason, in her mind, getting an invitation from an upperclassman redeemed her from her miserable defeat by Tiara at the tennis challenge two weeks ago. Now that she had something to gloat about, Alicia was not missing her opportunity to brag about it to everyone.

It was Friday, the day before Halloween... the day before the big dance. Tiara was seated in Ms. Tanner's classroom. She had been the first to arrive; the rest of the students were still in the hallway discussing—what else?—the dance. Tiara had just taken her seat when Brooke entered the room.

"Hi." Brooke took the desk on Tiara's left. "Where's everyone else?" she asked, glancing around at the still-empty room.

"Guess!" Tiara replied facetiously. "I'm sure they're somewhere in the hallway discussing the dance."

"Yeah. You're still going, right?"

The two girls had decided on Monday that if they still didn't have a date by Friday, they would attend the dance anyway. There was certainly no point in not going and ending up not being in the know just because they didn't have someone, of the male persuasion that is, to go with them. They were sure some of the other students would also be attending solo. The only problem was that neither Tiara nor Brooke knew any of these students, whoever they were. Still, both girls found solace in the fact that at least they would know each other and could hang around together.

The bell rang, signaling the start of class. Students poured in through the open doorway, rushing to take their seats. Amanda quickly sat at her desk on Tiara's right. Karen took the seat behind Amanda.

"You're not getting anything new to wear to the dance, are you?" Karen whispered loudly to Amanda.

"No, I'm wearing my Versace jeans," Amanda managed to reply before Ms. Tanner motioned for the class to come to order.

Brooke glanced at Tiara and released a soft sigh. Without a word being spoken, Tiara knew exactly what Brooke was thinking. It really would have been great if their only concern was what they were going to wear tomorrow night.

Tiara's mind drifted as Ms. Tanner talked on and on about England in the Middle Ages. She couldn't help thinking about the dance and the fact that no one had yet asked her. Had she been back with her old friends in Boston, Tiara knew there would never have been any issue of her not getting an invitation. She had been one of the most popular girls in her class... actually, one of the most popular students in the entire school. She was sure that not only would she have been asked to attend the dance, but she would have received several invitations by now.

Tiara realized that, like Brooke, a big part of the problem was that she was new to Skidmore. But that was only one part of the story. There was also a second reason, which Tiara was very much aware of. Throughout the entire freshman class, Tiara had counted a grand total of five black students, aside from herself. There were three other black girls, two in homeroom 405 and one in homeroom 406. There were only two black boys. Again, one was in homeroom 405 and the other was in room 407. Because these students were in different sections, Tiara didn't know them as well as she knew the kids in room 401, her homeroom section. Occasionally, she did see all of them in the hallways and they always greeted each other with a smile or a wave, but so far, she hadn't become as close to any of them as she was with her friends in her own homeroom class. Even if she had gotten to know them, with only two black boys in the entire freshman class, Tiara knew the four girls had them outnumbered, two to one. No matter what, two of the black girls in the freshman class were always going to have to look elsewhere for a date. The remaining two would also have no choice but to take what was available.

Tiara snapped out of her reverie as she heard the bell signaling the end of the last class of the day. As usual, the students made a mad dash for the door. Karen and Amanda made it out with the first wave of students. They had already told Tiara and Brooke that Karen was going over to Amanda's to borrow a sweater to wear to the dance. Tiara and Brooke had made plans to leave school together.

As she turned around to wait for Brooke, Tiara was surprised to see her friend talking to Patrick Simpson. Easing her way over to the door, Tiara walked outside the classroom and stood up against the lockers in the hallway. She was sure that whatever Patrick had to talk to Brooke about certainly wouldn't take all that long.

Tiara glanced across the hallway to the entrance of the classroom. Maxwell Blackstone walked out. She hadn't realized that he was still in the classroom.

"Hi!"

"Hi." Tiara responded to his greeting a little uncertainly. Although they had most of their classes together, Tiara very seldom spoke to Maxwell. His connection to Alicia was just too much of a barrier to start a friendship. Because of the family relationship, being cousins and all, Tiara knew where Maxwell's allegiance lay, and she had no intention of trying to change them.

"Aren't you going to tennis practice today?" Maxwell asked.

Tiara was really surprised. This was a lot more conversation than Maxwell Blackstone had ever had with her. She guessed it was because Alicia and her entourage were nowhere around.

"Yes, I am going to practice, but I'm waiting for Brooke. She's still inside the classroom talking to Patrick."

"Yes, I know. I saw her in there."

Tiara remained silent. She didn't really know what else to say.

"Are you going to the dance tomorrow?" Maxwell continued.

"Um, yeah. I plan on going." Now Tiara was really caught off guard. Was Maxwell trying to get information for Alicia? Why was he asking all these questions?

"Oh. Are you going with anyone?"

Tiara didn't get a chance to respond, thank God. What would it look like having to tell Alicia's cousin that she didn't have a date to the dance? That piece of news would certainly spread like wildfire around the school.

At that moment, Brooke came flying out of the classroom. "Tiara! You waited for me. Great! I have something to tell you." Brooke was hardly able to contain her excitement as she pulled Tiara along beside her.

"I'll see you tomorrow, all right, Tiara?" Maxwell called out to the two girls as they walked away.

"Oh, sure," Tiara replied absently as Brooke pulled her through the double doors leading downstairs.

"You won't believe this!" Brooke squealed once they were alone. "Patrick Simpson just asked me to the dance. Isn't that great?"

Tiara stood still for a moment, stunned. "Yes," she finally replied in a deadpan voice. "Just great."

Chapter 17

Tiara slowly made her way down the staircase leading from her second-floor bedroom. Although she should have been excited about going to the dance, she really wasn't. In fact, she was feeling just the opposite. Tiara was depressed and, in reality, would have preferred not to show up at the dance at all. Everyone there was going to have a date . . . everyone except her. Even Brooke had managed to snag an eleventh-hour date. This left Tiara by herself . . . flying solo.

As she approached the kitchen, Tiara could hear voices coming from inside. All conversation ceased when she entered.

"Wow! You look nice," Blake said, getting up from his chair at the kitchen table. Walking over to Tiara, he gave her a kiss on the forehead. "You're going to knock 'em dead."

"You do look very nice," Lisa pointed out to her daughter after realizing that Tiara wasn't going to respond to her dad's statement. Tiara had wanted to wear her blue jeans, but Lisa had convinced her to wear her black satin pants and tuxedo jacket with her white satin blouse underneath. Tiara did look very nice.

"I'm driving you to Skidmore. Your dad will pick you up at twelve midnight. The dance *will* be over at midnight, won't it?" Lisa asked.

"Yes, it will," Tiara replied. "I'll meet you at the front entrance," she said, turning to address her dad. "Mom, are you ready to go?"

"Yes, go ahead to the car. I'll be right out," Lisa replied as she turned to go upstairs to find her purse.

Wisconsin Avenue was lined with rows and rows of cars. Glancing out the passenger-side window, Tiara concluded that every student at Skidmore Prep had decided to attend the dance tonight. Tiara had been extremely quiet on the ride over. Lisa had taken note of that fact but decided not to say anything about it for the moment. Now that they'd pulled up in front of the school, Lisa felt this was the time to address what was on her daughter's mind.

Tiara reached for the door handle, getting ready to leave the car.

"Tiara! Wait a minute. I want to ask you something."

"What, Mom?" Tiara asked, a puzzled look on her face.

"Is something wrong?"

"Wrong? No, Mom, nothing's wrong."

"Are you sure?"

"Yes . . . nothing's wrong."

"Tiara, things have been pretty hectic at work the last

couple of weeks, but if there's anything you need to discuss, just let me know. You know I'll always find the time."

"Everything is fine, Mom. There's nothing going on."

Lisa hesitated but decided to leave it alone. "Okay. If you say so. Your dad will be here at twelve to pick you up."

"Twelve tonight or twelve tomorrow night?" Tiara asked teasingly, knowing her dad's tendency to be late.

"Tonight," Lisa replied with a chuckle. "I'll make sure of that. Have a good time."

"I will, Mom," Tiara said, hoping to herself that her statement would turn out to be true.

Tiara got out of the car and waved good-bye as Lisa pulled off into traffic. When Tiara could no longer see their car, she turned toward the building, scanning the crowd in search of some of her friends. It seemed most people had arrived in large groups. Tiara watched as a group of eight or nine, presumably upperclassmen girls, made their way into the dance. She couldn't help wishing that Brooke hadn't gotten her last-minute date so that they could have walked in together. Tiara didn't need a crowd. Just one friend would have been nice.

"So, are you gonna go in... or spend all night out here?"

Tiara jumped at the sound of the voice directly behind her. She turned quickly. "Oh, hi, Max. I was just waiting for some other people to get here."

"You might as well go in," Max said, grabbing her hand. "A lot of people are already in there."

Before Tiara had a chance to decide, she was following

Max into the high school and downstairs to the cafeteria where the dance was being held. In the process of entering the building, Tiara bumped into Ms. Tanner. She was standing by the door. At that moment, Tiara remembered that teachers would be in attendance to make sure nobody came in drunk. Tiara straightened up and greeted Ms. Tanner.

"Hello, Tiara," Ms. Tanner greeted her. "You two look nice."

"Thanks. You look nice too." Ms. Tanner was wearing a tailored black pantsuit that sort of made her look like a bouncer. Tiara wondered if that was the effect she was shooting for. Instead of asking, though, she and Max waved good-bye and headed for the cafeteria.

Tiara slowly took in the decorations as they entered the cafeteria. Most of the tables had been removed and the few that remained had been pushed to the side. The chairs were stacked against the walls. Gold and white crepe paper streamed from all sides of the room. Gold and white balloons were floating everywhere. Tiara hadn't really been expecting the decorations to be elaborate because the dance wasn't actually a formal. It was semiformal, which was supposed to be drastically different from formal. Tiara thought the decorations suited the general feel of the dance, which was classy casual, as Amanda had told her homecoming always was. Most girls were wearing summery dresses or nice jeans and flowery tops. Tiara didn't feel out of place, though, because it was really too dark to see and appreciate anybody's outfit unless you were standing right in front of the person.

"So how long have you been here?" Tiara asked Max. Tiara had planned to arrive a little late so as to avoid any awkward moments. She was curious to see if Max, who had also come solo, had thought along the same lines.

"Oh, about ten minutes," Max replied with a shrug. Tiara found this pretty reasonable. The dance had started at 8:30. It was now 9:10. Tiara had planned to get there around this time and Max, dateless as well, had probably planned his arrival time to be late as well. The only question Tiara had was what had Max been doing waiting outside if he'd already been at the dance for ten minutes?

"So what were you doing outside?" Tiara asked. "I mean, what made you leave the dance after only ten minutes?"

"No one to dance with," Max said. "Good thing you got here."

Tiara smiled and was just about to say how comforting it was to know there was at least one guy who didn't have a date so that she wouldn't have to stand around awkwardly the entire time, but she was interrupted by a shout.

"Tiara!" Tiara heard Brooke call out to her. A moment later, Brooke came rushing toward her with Patrick in tow.

"Tiara, I'm so glad you're here. This dance is so much fun," Brooke gushed. "You need to get out there and dance. They've already played a lot of good songs, but I'm sure they'll be playing more."

"Want to take a deep breath there, Brooke?" Max asked playfully.

"Oh, hi, Max," Brooke said, glancing at him before turning back to Tiara. "Well, anyway, Patrick and I have been dancing for like twenty minutes straight. Right, Patrick?"

"Uh, yeah," Patrick managed to say before Brooke started talking again.

"I suggest you find a partner and get out there as soon as you can!" And with that she dashed away quickly, pulling Patrick behind her.

"Well, that was entertaining," Max said when they were gone.

"That's what Brooke is known for," Tiara said jokingly.

"But maybe we should take her advice. Wanna get out there?"

"Umm . . . " Tiara was shocked. Was Max Blackstone really asking her to dance? Should she accept? After all, he was related to Alicia. At the same time, though, it was unfair to hold someone's relations against them. It wasn't Max's fault Alicia was related to him. Tiara decided to say yes.

In a matter of moments, Tiara and Max joined a group of other students and were dancing up a storm. Tiara was actually quite surprised. Max wasn't someone she would have thought could handle himself on a dance floor, but honestly, Tiara had to admit that he wasn't too bad. They danced three songs in a row before she waved her arms to catch his attention.

"Whew! Those songs were really long ones. Let's sit the next one out."

"Oh sure," Max agreed and followed behind Tiara as she went to the row of chairs along the wall. Brooke and Patrick were already standing nearby; apparently, they too were taking a break to catch their breaths. Tiara was surprised that Max was still hanging around. She was sure that he would have disappeared after dancing a few songs with her, but apparently not.

"Would you like something to drink?" Max asked Tiara.

Not to be outdone, Patrick turned and asked Brooke the same question.

"Yes," Tiara replied. "I'd definitely love something to drink."

Before either of the two could make a move, Alicia approached the group. Naturally.

"Well, well, well, a congregation of the dateless," Alicia cooed. "Except for me, of course. I have a date."

"Hi, Alicia," Max groaned.

"Max, Max, Max," Alicia said, apparently just remembering that he was related to her. "What do you think you're doing?"

"Talking... like any normal human being. That is, before you interrupted us."

"Really?" Alicia asked, seeming shocked. "That's interesting. So, Tiara, are you trying to prove some sort of point by hanging out with *my* cousin, or do you just like irony? Although I guess *you* don't have that many options."

Tiara wondered what she meant by that. It seemed obvious that Alicia was referring to the lack of black boys in class for Tiara to choose from but that seemed too raw, even for Alicia.

"Not that it's any of your business, but I was the one who started talking to her," Max interjected.

"Oh," Alicia said, again seeming surprised. "Well, I always thought we might not be related." She dismissed him with an eye roll. "I guess I'll see you later, Tiara." Then she turned and walked away, presumably going back to her date.

Tiara wondered what she meant by that. Why would Alicia ever make an effort to see her later? Tiara didn't have much longer to think about it, though, because just then, Karen and Aaron joined the group.

"Hey," Tiara said, happy to see two of her favorite people. She stepped forward to give each of them a hug.

"Hey, Tiara," Aaron said, returning the hug. "We saw you standing over here and came over to say hello."

"Why are you standing over here by yourself anyway?" Karen asked.

"Oh, I'm not," Tiara turned, ready to gesture to Max. He wasn't there, however.

"Well, Max was standing here a few seconds ago."

"Before he started talking to Alicia?" Aaron asked skeptically. He pointed past Tiara to where Max was now standing, chatting it up with Alicia. Tiara began to wonder even more what the whole episode with Max had been about. Was he her friend or wasn't he?

"Yeah, I guess," Tiara said.

"Well, don't just be a wallflower all night," Karen said, changing the subject. "You better find someone to dance with or I'll find someone for you."

"Is that a threat?" Tiara asked jokingly.

"No," Karen replied with a smile. "It's a promise." And with that, she and Aaron disappeared into the dancing crowd, leaving Tiara standing alone.

Tiara stood by herself for a few minutes until she

decided she was starting to look sort of pathetic. She wasn't sure what to do with herself. Her other friends had returned to the dance floor and no one else had come over to ask her to dance. Tiara found a seat in a dark corner at the far end of the room. She was sure no one could see her there. She sat and watched as song after song came on. Tiara tried to pretend she was enjoying herself, but that was a farce. She watched as Karen and Aaron did a slow dance together. They looked really nice. Brooke and Patrick also stayed on the dance floor forever. They too were having a blast.

Tiara found herself glancing at her watch, wondering when she would be able to make a discreet getaway. She'd only been at the dance an hour and she was already bored out of her mind. Half an hour later, she wasn't any less bored, even though Amanda, Aaron, Brooke, and Karen had visited her at her little secluded spot. Things became interesting, however, when the last person she expected walked over to her again.

Alicia had returned, but she was not alone. She brought along her date, an upperclassman that Tiara didn't know. She wasn't even sure if she'd ever seen him before, which probably meant he wasn't all that popular, but that didn't matter to Alicia. She had obviously brought him along to show him off. This sort of amused Tiara . . . the idea that Alicia clearly cared about what she thought, enough to even bother.

"Oh . . . here you are," Alicia shouted over the loud music. "Max sent me over with this glass of punch for you. He said he'd promised to get you something to drink and told me to tell you that he'd be right back." Alicia sat down in the chair next to Tiara. "He's in the men's room."

"Oh..." Tiara looked at Alicia suspiciously, very surprised by her act of kindness. "Thank you." She took a long drink from the glass.

"I think my cousin likes you," Alicia continued, watching as Tiara nervously continued to drink the punch.

"Well, you know how it is when you don't have a date," Tiara said in faux self-pity.

"No," Alicia said, smiling snottily and grabbing her date's hand. "I actually don't."

"I'm going to the bathroom," the date said, loosening Alicia's grip.

"Fine," Alicia huffed. Her date just shrugged and walked away. Alicia turned back to Tiara. "Do you even know who he is?" she asked.

"Nope," Tiara replied. "I don't particularly care either."

"That's Ross Washington." She paused, waiting for Tiara's response. Instead of being amazed, Tiara just blinked at her. Alicia rolled her eyes. "Well, that was a waste. You don't even know enough about this school to be impressed. Pathetic!"

"Yes," Tiara said sarcastically. "That must be it."

"You know, Tiara, it's really all about who you invest your friendship in. The only reason I'm mean to you is because you associate yourself with the wrong crowd."

"Is that the only reason?" Tiara asked, doubtful.

"Of course. Why else?"

"I don't know," Tiara said. But of course she did know. There was the fact that Tiara was blatantly better at tennis, that more people on the team liked her even though she was the new student. And then, there was one more thing that lingered in the back of Tiara's mind as a possibility. She wouldn't go so far as to say that Alicia was racist, but at the same time, Tiara sort of assumed that her being black had something to do with Alicia not liking her.

"Yeah, well that's why. You need to select your friends a little better."

Without realizing it, Tiara had emptied the glass of punch.

"Hope you enjoyed that drink," Alicia said as she looked into Tiara's cup.

"What?" She didn't understand why Alicia was being so nice to her or watching her drink the punch so closely.

"Oh, nothing. I really hope it doesn't make you sick," she said in her syrupy voice as she stood up to leave. "And if it does make you sick . . . oh well." She had a wicked grin on her face as she walked away, presumably going back to her date.

Tiara didn't get a chance to reflect on what Alicia had said. As Max came over to join her, Tiara could feel the bile starting to rise from the pit of her stomach.

Walking up to Tiara, Max immediately started to apologize. "Sorry for taking so long . . . Coach Bob wanted help moving some chairs. I hope Alicia wasn't a bother."

"No, she wasn't bothering me. She just brought me the glass of punch you sent over." She felt her stomach turning over again.

"I didn't send you a drink."

"You didn't? Alicia said you'd sent it over . . . that you had to go to the men's room."

"Alicia can be weird sometimes. Anyway, let's go dance some more."

"No, thanks. I don't really want to dance anymore."

"Oh. Why not?"

"I think I'm going to be sick. I think there was something in the drink I just had," Tiara said weakly.

"Tiara, man, what's wrong with you?" Karen asked, running up to her friend.

Tiara wasn't sure she could answer that question.

"I don't know," she moaned. "My stomach hurts and I can't see straight."

"What happened to her?" someone else asked. Tiara couldn't tell exactly who the voice belonged to.

"How am I supposed to know?" Karen snapped. "I've been with Aaron all night. Where's Patrick?"

So it was Brooke who was speaking, Tiara thought to herself.

"He said he was going to the bathroom," Brooke said. "Tiara, are you okay?"

"Not really. I think I'm going to throw up."

"Well, let's get her to the bathroom before that happens," Karen said. "Get her other arm."

Tiara felt Brooke reach for her other arm and they started pulling her along.

"What's going on here?" an adult female voice asked.

"Oh, hi, Ms. Tanner," Brooke said cheerfully.

"Hello, Brooke. Again I ask, what is going on here?"

"Well, Tiara said she felt sick," Karen said. Unfortu-

161

nately, by that point it was too late. By that point the rising sickness in Tiara's stomach was no longer containable. She threw up all over Ms. Tanner's "bouncer" pantsuit.

"Oooh . . . gross!"

Tiara heard the remarks from the other students before she stumbled her way out of the room.

Chapter 18

Blake opened his eyes and took another glance at the clock on his car's dashboard: eleven thirty. It was the fifth time he'd looked in the last fifteen minutes. He'd been parked outside the entrance to Skidmore Prep for the last thirty minutes. Blake had been determined not to arrive late to pick Tiara up from the dance, so he'd left home with more than an hour to spare. He noticed that he wasn't the only parent waiting. Several others had also parked their cars on Wisconsin Avenue and, like him, were now dozing on their front seats while they waited for their offspring to come out.

Blake looked across the dark interior of the car onto the walkway leading up to Skidmore's front entrance. At this time of night, the area was lit by streetlamps that cast a glow over the entranceway to the school. The bright light allowed Blake to see the lone figure making its way toward the car. It was Tiara.

Opening the door on the driver's side, Blake jumped out and quickly walked around the front of the vehicle. Tiara barely made it to the passenger door of the family's dark green Volvo before her dad approached her, a worried look on his face. Blake had not expected to see Tiara before twelve midnight. In fact, he'd naturally assumed his daughter would hang around after the dance gossiping with some of her friends. He was definitely surprised to see her so early . . . and by herself.

Blake silently waited as his daughter quietly climbed into the car. He waited again as she reached for her seatbelt and buckled it before he closed the car door behind her. Once back inside the Volvo, Blake hesitated just a moment before turning the key in the ignition. He had seen how red Tiara's eyes were as she stood under the streetlights moments before she'd entered the car. Blake knew, even without asking, that his daughter had been crying. Turning in his seat, he gave Tiara his full attention. "How's my baby girl?" he asked hesitantly.

Tiara gave her dad a weak smile. "Fine, Dad. I'm fine."

Blake watched the expression on his daughter's face and knew her statement was far from the truth. "Are you sure?" he tried once again.

Tiara stared back at him, holding his gaze for a few moments. Unknowingly, her bottom lip started to quiver. The emotions from the last four months—leaving Boston and all her close friends, moving to Washington, DC, and fighting to secure a niche for herself, having Alicia and all her cronies take potshots at her, and finally, the events at the dance tonight—all of this had simply come to a head. Tiara's expression faltered and all the emotions she'd been trying to keep bottled up inside simply erupted and started flowing out.

Blake quickly turned the key in the ignition, cutting the engine off. Reaching across the seat, he pulled his daughter into his arms and watched as the tears trickled down her cheeks. He let her cry for a few minutes, her tears breaking his heart in two. He knew if he waited awhile, she would finally stop and tell him what was bothering her.

It took a few minutes, but finally Tiara's sobs quieted down. "What is it, Tiara? What's on your mind?" Blake asked.

"When I first started at Skidmore, I really didn't want to like it. I wanted to be back in Boston with my old friends," Tiara explained, "but now, it's different."

"What do you mean *different*? Are you saying you like it here now?"

"I like it, Dad ... for the most part, that is ... but because I'm the only black student in my homeroom class, I always feel like I'm either in the spotlight or hidden in a corner somewhere. I don't get treated like the other kids."

Blake winced on hearing Tiara's statement. What could he say, though? He knew exactly what she was feeling. As the head of the anesthesiology department in a huge metropolitan hospital, Blake was the only black doctor in his entire division. How did he tell Tiara that her current experience at Skidmore was probably going to be the norm for her from now on?

Tiara took a deep breath and continued speaking. "I know that I stand out ... that a lot of the other kids listen to me because I'm different and they want to know what I'm thinking, but a lot of times, I feel invisible because I feel like I'm the only one making all the effort. Like tonight ...

"I was the only one who didn't get invited to the dance. Everyone else had someone to go with . . . but I didn't have anyone," Tiara said, her simple statement tearing Blake apart. "I'm sure it was because I'm the only black girl in my class. I'm sure no one thought about inviting me mainly for that reason," Tiara said, ending her statement almost at a whisper.

Blake let out a loud sigh. He had to work hard to keep his simmering rage from erupting at her words, spoken so matter-of-factly. Blake chose his next statements carefully, not wanting to upset Tiara any further. This, however, was something that needed to be said. He knew this was a subject that all black parents in America who wanted the best for their children confronted on a daily basis. They were always faced with the question: Was it better to send their children to a predominantly black school where they would fit in and be comfortable or should they force their offspring to learn at an early age what to expect and how to deal in the real world. Blake knew there was never going to be a real-life situation where Tiara would be in the majority. Not as a black woman . . . and like her mother, Blake knew Tiara would have to learn now how to deal with that situation.

Blake guessed that Tiara's problems weren't coming from all the students at Skidmore Prep. As she'd previously explained, her problems were really coming from one girl . . . Alicia Blackstone and her little clique. Blake was sure that they were the ones causing Tiara grief. Tiara had explained how Alicia was such a plague to her existence. Alicia Blackstone had this air of superiority she walked around with, as if she were better than everyone else, as if everyone should realize that and treat her accordingly.

"Tiara... I'm going to tell you something and I hope you hear me and understand. Both your mother and I have faced the same things you are facing right now. We still do sometimes."

Tiara looked at her father in shock. There was no way either her mom or dad could have ever faced what she was currently experiencing.

Blake saw the look of disbelief on her face. "You're really going to have to trust me and believe what I'm saying, Tiara. You are going to have to try not to let any of this bother you. You can't be bothered with Alicia Blackstone and her attitude. Trust me when I say that you're going to run into people like her for the rest of your life. I still have to deal with people who have those same limitations. If I allowed them to, they would drive me crazy. I don't allow it, and I want you to try and do the same."

Tiara stared at her father, holding his eyes for a long moment. Finally she nodded, a determined smile spreading across her face. "Okay, Dad. I'm going to give it my best shot. I'll try and ignore Alicia and her gang."

"That's my baby girl! That's what I'm really talking about!"

Chapter 19

Tiara stood at the sink in the third-floor bathroom she shared with Spencer Jr. Running cold water over the toothbrush she'd just finished using, she returned it to the holder attached to the marble vanity before turning off the lights and heading back to her bedroom. Standing in front of the bookshelf closest to her bed, Tiara looked for and found one of her Chopin CDs. Sure, it probably wasn't the preferred genre of most of her peers, but the soothing sounds always seemed to help put her to sleep.

Tiara lowered the volume before turning off the lights and getting into bed. It was ten o'clock Sunday night. As she lay in the dark, the half-moon shining outside her window casting a glow across the room, Tiara mentally reviewed the events of the homecoming dance and everything else that had happened thereafter.

The weekend had simply flown by. Early this morning, Tiara had received dozens of phone calls . . . not only from Amanda, Brooke, and Karen, but from Aaron, Patrick, and, surprisingly, even from Max Blackstone. The girls on the tennis team had also called to check on her and find out, firsthand, what had really happened at the dance. Everyone, other than her close friends who had witnessed the entire debacle at homecoming, had wanted to know two things: 1) Had Alicia Blackstone really spiked her punch? and 2) Had Tiara really thrown up all over Ms. Tanner's bouncer suit? Surprisingly, everyone, even Max, shared the same opinion—that Alicia was a really mean person (and that was putting it lightly) and she shouldn't be allowed to get away with what she had done.

Tiara couldn't help smiling to herself as she lay in her dark bedroom. Without ever intending to, she'd once again become the talk of Skidmore Prep. This time, however, Tiara was determined not to let all this gossip get to her. Her father's words from the previous night kept returning to her: "You are going to have to try and not let any of this bother you. You can't be bothered with that girl, Alicia Blackstone, and her attitude. Trust me when I say that you're going to run into people like her for the rest of your life. I still have to deal with people who have these limitations. If I allowed it to, it would drive me crazy. I don't allow it, and I want you to try and do the same." His statements had now become her theme song.

Okay, Tiara thought to herself. I'm going to follow his advice. I've had enough of Alicia and her crap. There's no way she's going to live rent-free inside my head. Tiara was about to show Ms. Alicia Blackstone exactly who was running this show. Tiara was about to start kicking ass . . . namely, Alicia Blackstone's ass.

By eight-fifteen the next morning, Tiara was tensed with excitement. The rest of the students in homeroom 401 were buzzing with information. The other students, except Alicia and her crew, had arrived early and were now circulating around the classroom rehashing the events of the dance. Of course, the episode with Tiara and Alicia was the number-one topic. Everyone was in agreement that this time Alicia had really gone too far. Unlike with previous incidents Alicia had either instigated, or, like this one, blatantly caused, they were even outwardly siding with the object of Alicia's antics—in this case, Tiara. The moral support of her classmates was encouraging to Tiara.

The door to the classroom opened. Suddenly, everyone grew quiet as Alicia and her entourage made their grand entrance. Within three seconds of the door closing, the room was dead silent. Tiara could feel the tension bouncing off every one of the students in the room. She stood still where she was, surrounded by her friends and the other homeroom students.

"You know, guys," Alicia said, turning to the other members of her group, "if I didn't know better, I'd say we were just being talked about."

"If we didn't know better, we'd agree," Molly said.

Without giving anyone in particular a second glance, Alicia and her royal court shifted out of the doorway and moved to their seats. Everyone else in the room realized that the moment of confrontation had passed. No one, however, was expecting what came next.

"I guess you think you're pretty cool, don't you, Alicia?"

This jeer came from none other than Alicia's own cousin, Max.

Alicia appeared to be somewhat taken aback. She recovered quickly, though, and plastered a false smile on her face. "What difference does it make what I think?" she said. "It's a reality I've come to accept."

"Well, that's where you're wrong," Max said boldly. "You see, while you're working so hard to make it seem like you're this big somebody, in reality, you're really just not. It's pathetic and now, even more than ever, it's embarrassing."

"Please, Max," Alicia said with a smirk. "Are you actually trying to tell me that *you're* embarrassed by *me*?"

"No," Max replied. "Your actions have nothing to do with me. I'm not embarrassed *by* you; I'm embarrassed *for* you."

The room erupted into *ooohs* as Mrs. Donovan entered the classroom.

"Silence," Mrs. Donovan demanded, not in a mean way, but sternly. "This is a classroom, not a zoo. Take your seats." As everyone dispersed from where they had gathered around Tiara, Tiara caught sight of Alicia's glare. It was a glare aimed directly at her. It was a glare that said, "This is nowhere near over."

Tiara was on pins and needles all day long as she moved with her friends from class to class. Although the others had seemingly pushed all thoughts of Alicia and her crowd from their minds, Tiara had not. She couldn't. Not this time. Tiara had a feeling that a make-or-break moment was about to occur. Her father was right, Tiara thought. Alicia did have, how did he word it... "limitations." Plainly speaking, Alicia seemed to love drama, reveled in confrontation. She had to be stopped.

Tiara was sure Alicia was plotting something devious. Although she didn't know what it was or when it would occur, she was absolutely certain that something was going to take place.

How right she was!

Tiara stood in front of her open locker stacking her textbooks from her morning classes on the top shelf. Amanda stood by her side listening as Tiara told her about the private meeting she'd had with Mrs. Donovan.

"Tiara, why didn't you just tell her that Alicia spiked your punch?" Amanda asked in exasperation.

"I don't want any more problems. You saw the look she gave me this morning. That girl hates me!"

Staring at her friend in amazement, Amanda could see that Tiara was visibly stressed out. "Hey, why don't we skip lunch and go play a game of tennis?" Amanda suggested. "That should definitely take your mind off our resident psycho."

Tiara readily agreed. That would give her the rest of the afternoon Alicia-free, since she had two study periods right after lunch that Alicia wasn't in, and her last class of the day was Latin, a course that was deemed way too uncool and unnecessary for the likes of Alicia, although Molly "Olive Oyl" was in it. Tiara was certain that Molly's parents were pushing her into becoming some sort of doctor because Tiara knew for sure that Olive Oyl wasn't taking Latin by choice.

Their tennis match proved to be the right diversion for Tiara as she whipped Amanda three–love before rushing off to quickly shower and change before their next two study periods. The two girls slipped into their final class of the day just as Ms. Lopez, the Latin teacher, was pulling the door shut. As a result, they had no advance warning that Alicia had already begun her offense.

Tiara and Amanda took their seats. Tiara was bending down to take out her notebook and find a pencil when Amanda whispered, "Here." Amanda had two blow-pops in her hand. "I know it's not a sandwich or a Frappuccino, but it'll help get us through that," Amanda said, nodding in the direction of the board. Ms. Lopez had already begun one of her famous PowerPoint lessons. As much as Tiara wanted to do well in the subject, she found the PowerPoints completely boring. Although Ms. Lopez made an effort, it was tough not to let your mind wander in Latin class.

Tiara smiled at Amanda, gratefully accepting the blow-pop. Amanda truly is a great friend, Tiara thought. As she began to focus on the meaning of *carpe diem*, she unwrapped the lollipop. Five minutes into the class, Tiara began to notice that something was amiss. Turning to her right, she looked across at Amanda in search of an explanation. Several students in the room were snickering as

Tiara and Amanda gave each other looks that meant "What the heck?" Finding no answer in her friend, Tiara's eyes scanned the semidark classroom and zeroed in on Olive Oyl, who was looking directly back at Tiara and pretending her pencil was something other than a lollipop. Olive Oyl then turned to look at Jonathan Myers as they both giggled conspiratorially.

Tiara immediately pulled the blow-pop from her mouth as she felt the blood rushing to her cheeks, realizing that in her attempts to get to the chewy center of the lollipop, her movements had appeared to be rather suggestive. "Very funny," Tiara mouthed to Olive Oyl and the other students who had relieved their boredom at her expense. She glanced at Amanda sheepishly as she chided herself inwardly for being caught in that position. She noticed that Amanda had also taken her blow-pop out of her mouth.

"Oops!" Amanda whispered, grinning back at Tiara. "I guess that did look kind of bad."

"Only to sick perverted minds," Tiara retorted laughingly.

"Ladies, is there a problem?" Ms. Lopez boomed.

"Ah, no, ma'am," Amanda replied, using the Latin word for good measure.

After another thirty minutes of Ms. Lopez's Latin, Tiara completely forgot the incident, not knowing that Alicia would use it to validate rumors she had already begun spreading earlier that afternoon. Alicia had a plan for a few weeks of hell for her number-one target: Tiara.

Of course, when Alicia wanted something on the radar,

it had to *become* the radar. Because he had clearly switched camps and was now on Tiara's side, Max was no longer immune. Unbeknownst to Tiara, both she and Max were entwined as objects of Alicia's dirty games.

While eating lunch and glancing though one of the weekly tabloids, Alicia had seen a picture of Paris Hilton, a celebrity whom many of the students thought Alicia was desperately trying to emulate. Paris was in her latest attention-grabbing stunt. The picture was of Paris kneeling in front of one of her many ex-boyfriends in a seriously suggestive position. The picture had Alicia plotting.

"Look at this," Alicia had exclaimed as she shifted the magazine over to Brittany.

"Eew, gross!" Brittany had remarked, disgust written all over her face.

Alicia had played coy. "Well—" She'd leaned in closer to Brittany and Olive Oyl, who was seated across from them. "I heard Max enjoys them."

"What?" Olive Oyl's eyes were now large saucers. "Who is doing that to Max?" she asked, a tinge of uncertainty mixed with jealously creeping into her voice.

"Yeah, Alicia," Brittany countered. "I didn't know Max was serious with anyone. I mean, I know he's been sticking up for that pathetic loser, Tiara, lately, but besides that . . ."

Alicia smirked and looked pointedly at Olive Oyl. "You have got to be kidding me!" Brittany laughed.

"That's absurd," Olive Oyl retorted.

Alicia did what she did best and feigned agreement. The girl loved drama. She was a great actress when she needed to be . . . when she needed to create the effect she desired. "I know, but I'm telling you, I wouldn't have believed it myself unless I had seen it with my own eyes."

Brittany and Olive Oyl exchanged questioning looks before deciding that it must be true. Why not? Alicia had said so, hadn't she? "When?" the two girls asked in unison.

"At the homecoming dance," Alicia replied. "And who knows what else they did?" she added as the final dig.

"No way!" Brittany squealed.

"You don't have to believe me," Alicia had cooed to her adoring henchmen, "but it happened when I was trying to find Max. Remember, Molly? I came up to you in the punch line and asked you if you'd seen Max anywhere. You told me that you'd seen him dancing with Tiara."

Alicia gave Brittany a knowing look. "He was definitely with Tiara when I found him and believe me, he was doing something a whole lot more intimate than dancing."

The suggestion had been planted, and in a matter of hours, Alicia knew the rumor would become the hottest piece of gossip at Skidmore Prep. She also knew that only three people in the entire school would know that none of it was true—that nothing had really occurred between Max and Tiara—and that was herself, her blood relative, Max, and the victim, Tiara. Really, there was no question who everyone was going to believe. Alicia knew that this was in the bag.

Chapter 20

Thanks to word of mouth, texting, and instant messages, within three weeks, everyone—not only the entire student body at Skidmore Prep, but everyone at all the prep schools in the tri-state area of Maryland, DC, and Virginia, had heard the further exaggerated rumor that Max Blackstone and Tiara Johnson had "gotten it on" at the Skidmore homecoming dance.

"The score is two to one for Kalorama Prep School's Caroline Miller against Skidmore Prep's Tiara Johnson," came over the loudspeaker as Tiara picked up her towel and sat down on the sidelines after completing her singles match.

"Tiara, what's gotten into you?" Coach Bob asked as he handed Tiara her Gatorade bottle. "You're clearly the better player out there, yet that Kalorama student was in complete control over the last two games and for most of the first." Coach Bob stooped down so that his eyes were level with Tiara's before he continued. "Where is that focus you usually have? What are you thinking about today? You know, for the past couple of weeks, you haven't really been the player I know you have the potential to be—in fact, the one you were up until about three weeks ago."

"Sorry, Coach," Tiara said sincerely. "I've just had a lot on my mind lately."

God, that's an understatement, Tiara thought. For the last few days, she'd been retreating to the library during her lunch hour or, alternatively, going off somewhere by herself.

Coach Bob patted Tiara on her arm as he stood up. "Tiara, I want you to go out there and I want to see some of that magic when you play your doubles game, okay? Can you try for me? Please?" he asked, smiling down at her. "You and Amanda should be up in about a half hour."

"All right, Coach, I'll give it a shot."

"Good! That's what I like to hear."

Tiara took a long sip of Gatorade and leaned back against the wall of the bleacher stands. She felt overwhelmed and alone. Even her tennis game was being affected by Alicia's evilness, and Tiara knew Alicia was the culprit. She was sure everyone at school was noticing how her game was suffering. Coach Bob had noticed, so she knew her teammates must have noticed as well. This was bad . . . really bad . . . and no one believed a word she was saying, Tiara thought to herself, not even Max.

Max had made it very clear during their brief conversation at the start of her three weeks in hell that he thought Tiara had started the rumors herself. Where he had gotten that idea, Tiara had no clue. She assumed Alicia was probably responsible for that as well.

Tiara could have dealt with Max siding with Alicia.

Although she and Max had danced a couple of times at homecoming and had had a few conversations, Tiara knew that blood ran thicker than water. She really couldn't blame Max for believing Alicia's lies about her, the new girl. No, Max wasn't the source of Tiara's stress. It was the others... Karen, Brooke, Patrick, Aaron, and even Amanda. It seemed as if they too were starting to believe the rumors.

The major problem surrounding all of this was that no one had seen either Tiara or Max at the homecoming dance for at least a half hour before Tiara had thrown up on Ms. Tanner. In essence, neither Tiara nor Max had an alibi. Tiara had deliberately been sitting by herself where no one would be able to see her, and Max had been off helping Coach Bob find some chairs... or so he'd said. Tiara still wasn't sure what to believe about Max. She still wasn't sure that Max wasn't in cahoots with Alicia or, conversely, really did believe that Tiara was the rumor starter. The jury was still out on that one.

Then there was the now-infamous Latin-class "blow-pop incident." It was hopeless. Tiara knew she was in a no-win situation. In the end, as the new student at Skidmore, no one was going to believe her. Additionally, she just wasn't evil and ruthless enough to even think of anything on the level of what Alicia had managed to devise.

Tiara also had to admit that her own actions had helped to make it look as if she was "experienced" and could very well have been alone with Max. Tiara knew she'd have to turn this mess around—that she'd have to take baby steps. Rising from her seat in the bleachers, Tiara looked to her right. About ten feet away, her teammates, Amanda included, were gathered around talking as they waited for the next match. As Tiara walked over to join Amanda, her only thought was her tennis game.

"Hey, Tiara," Amanda greeted her with a small, albeit wary smile.

"Hey!" Tiara replied. "Do you want to head over to our court?"

"Yeah, sure," Amanda agreed, standing up and grabbing her racket, towel, and water bottle. The atmosphere was still pretty tense between the two girls. Tiara knew she had to do something to diffuse the situation if they were going to have any chance at beating the other team.

"So what are we up against?" Tiara asked, turning to face Amanda.

"Honestly? These girls are good. Seniors. The rumors are that one of them has already been offered a full-ride scholarship to three top colleges, including U. Penn."

"Rumors, huh?" Tiara repeated, picking up on Amanda's relevant choice of words. "Well, I for one don't automatically believe rumors. Have you *seen* them play together? Actually *witnessed* their game?" Tiara asked.

Realizing the real issue at stake, Amanda didn't immediately reply. "Well, no, not together," she finally admitted.

"Look, I know you don't believe me about Max, and I don't blame you either, but I'm just going to put it out there, okay? You and I make a great doubles team. I, for one, am not going to let the knowledge of how great a player one girl might be parlay into rumors of how good a doubles team she makes with someone and I suggest you don't either. Not today. Besides, I'm 'supposedly'—" Tiara made quotation marks with her free hand "—a great player, and look at the BS game I just played!"

"I'm sure Alicia being here didn't help," Amanda offered softly.

Tiara stared at her friend. Was Amanda coming to her senses?

"No, it didn't," Tiara finally replied, "but she's been taking up way too much space in my head lately and she's not going to anymore."

"Ms. Johnson . . . Ms. Carter," the referee called out as he approached the two girls.

"Yes, sir," Tiara replied.

"If you two are ready, let's begin."

Tiara and Amanda put their water bottles down along with their towels and set off to take their positions on the court. "Which one is our 'supposed' threat?" Tiara whispered slyly to Amanda. "You know, just so I have a heads-up?"

The opposing team had already taken their place. A tall, Maria Sharapova type and a smaller girl with a cute brown pixie cut. "The small one," Amanda whispered back. "And by the way," she added, "don't turn around, but just to give you another heads-up, Max and Jonathan just sat down in the bleachers . . . on our left."

Tiara nodded her head to let Amanda know she'd heard but continued walking to the front of the court to take her position. Max was not going to ruin this game for her, she vowed. He didn't. Neither did the small pixie-haired supposed U. Penn–bound hotshot from Kalorama

Prep. Amanda and Tiara prevailed three to one. The small brown-haired girl was good, but the chemistry between her and her partner was completely absent. Maria Sharapova she was not.

"Great job, girls!" Coach Bob congratulated them. "Tiara, I'm glad to see you took my advice to heart. I liked what I saw out there."

"Thanks, Coach Bob," Tiara said as she discreetly looked around to see if Max and Jonathan were still in sight. They were and Alicia had joined them. "Good thing I didn't pay attention to the fact they were watching," Tiara whispered to Amanda as she caught Max's eye. There was no mistaking he had been watching her, but whether it was because, like Alicia, he wanted to make Tiara miserable or something else entirely, Tiara wasn't sure. She knew she would soon find out, though.

A breaking point finally occurred the next day, courtesy of Ms. Lopez. Tiara had taken her usual place next to Amanda in Latin. Since their conversation and subsequent win at the tennis match, all the other girls had warmed back up to Tiara, albeit slightly. At least they had asked her to go with them to Starbucks after school for a Frappuccino. It was still a little awkward because obviously no one wanted to broach the "blow-pop incident," but as they'd walked to class, they'd gossiped about the previous night's *Scandals* episode and tennis. Those were safe subjects for everyone.

The obvious reacceptance of Tiara by her friends was not lost on Alicia and her crew. As Tiara and her group passed Alicia, Molly, Brittany, and Megan in the hallway, Alicia called out, "Hey, Tiara!"

Tiara had a sinking feeling as she halted her steps and turned around. Karen, Brooke, and Amanda also stopped walking, as did several of the other students. All of them stood quietly, openly eavesdropping on the confrontation. "What do you want?" Tiara asked, trying to keep the animosity out of her voice.

"I was just wondering if you wanted some more practice," Alicia stated sweetly as she took a blow-pop from her purse and began unwrapping it. "You know, with the long weekend coming up, maybe you and Max might be able to manage some quality time alone together and you can always try to improve on your technique." Alicia placed the blow-pop in her mouth. "Mmm," she moaned and took the lollipop back out of her mouth and pretended to study it intensely.

Tiara was speechless and mortified as Alicia continued speaking. "Tell me, Tiara, how many licks you think it takes to get the desired effect?"

"Enough," Ms. Lopez announced sternly. "Ms. Blackstone . . . Ms. Johnson. Come with me. Now!"

Chapter 21

Lisa frowned as she sat in her office staring at the pile of folders in her inbox. It was Monday morning, the week of Thanksgiving. The managing attorney at McKenzie, Kennedy, and McKenzie had already informed the staff that the firm would be closing early on Wednesday, the day before Thanksgiving, in order to get an early start on the holiday. What this really meant was that Lisa would have to double up the first three days of the week to make sure all her clients' work was completed before the close of business on Wednesday.

For the next two hours, Lisa worked hard, steadily making a big dent in the pile. A soft knock on her door made her look up.

"Hi. Can I come in?" Paige asked.

"Sure," Lisa replied with a smile. "I'd be grateful if you did. I could use a break right about now. Come in and have a seat."

"I see you're doing the same thing I was—trying to make a dent in some of the cases before the holiday."

"Yes," Lisa agreed. "I wonder where it all comes from."

"Well, you know we're still short of staff. It's so difficult to find good attorneys, especially in the criminal defense area," Paige explained. "Are you doing anything special for the holidays?"

"Not really. I think we're going to have some downtime together . . . nothing special. How about yourself?"

"Montreal . . . Damian and I are going to Montreal for the long weekend. We're going to spend some time with his parents . . . my future in-laws."

"Sounds like fun. Have you met them before?"

"Once. They came to Washington, DC, to meet my parents when we first got engaged. I guess they also wanted to meet the woman who had snagged their baby boy."

Lisa laughed. She'd met Damian St. Jean and he was anything but a baby. "I love Montreal," she said. "Blake and I traveled to Quebec a long time ago . . . BK."

"'BK'? What's that?"

"Before kids. Tiara and Spencer Jr. weren't born at the time. We had a fantastic vacation, now that I think about it."

"Really? Where did you stay?"

"Well, we flew into Quebec City and splurged big-time on our accommodations there. At the time, we didn't have any money to speak of. Just the same, we decided to stay at the Chateau Frontenac, this historic hotel that looks like a castle. It was beautiful beyond words . . . but really expensive. We only stayed there two days before we drove down to Montreal. That was equally nice. We got a chance to practice our French, especially while we were in Quebec City. That's all they speak there, you know."

"Yes, I know. I love Montreal myself."

"You speak French too, don't you?"

"*Oui, je parle le francais,*" Paige responded in the affirmative. "The only time I get a chance to practice, though, is with Damian."

"Montreal is so cosmopolitan. Have you ever driven up to the top of Mount Royale?"

"Yes. I love that you can look out over the entire city from the top of the mountain."

Mount Royale was a medium-size mountain located in the heart of Montreal. A lot of first-generation Canadians who had emigrated from some of the European countries had settled at the base of Mount Royale, mingling with the early French Canadians who were longtime residents. The area at the foot of the "Mountains," as the area was typically called, had become a real Bohemian hotspot. Little outdoor cafes dotted the surrounding area much to the delight of the large tourist population that was constantly visiting the sophisticated city.

"I know exactly where you're talking about. I'm glad you brought it up. I'll have to remind Damian to take a ride up to Mount Royale."

"Yes, you should definitely go and enjoy yourself while you're still in the BK mode."

Both women chuckled. It was interesting how a strong camaraderie had developed between them. Lisa knew the main reason was that both of them were black and the only two high-ranking female employees at the firm.

The sharp buzz of the intercom interrupted the little rap session. Ellen's cheery voice came through on the other end. "Ms. Johnson, there's a Mrs. Donovan on line two for you. She says she's your daughter's teacher at Skidmore Prep."

"Oh, thank you, Ellen. I'll take it."

"I'll go so that you can handle that." Paige got up and quietly left the room. Lisa wasted no time pressing the button for line two, wondering why Mrs. Donovan would be calling.

"Hello, this is Lisa Johnson."

"Ms. Johnson, this is Mrs. Donovan, Tiara's homeroom teacher. I'm so sorry to have to bother you, but we're having a few problems with Tiara. I wondered if I could schedule an appointment for you to meet with me?"

"Of course . . . yes. What is it?" Lisa asked, unable to think what could be happening.

"Please don't get upset, Ms. Johnson. I'm sure everything can be straightened out once we have a talk. Can we meet today . . . around three o'clock? That way, you need only make one trip back to the school today. I know you usually pick Tiara up after her tennis practice."

"Yes . . . of course. Three o'clock will be fine. I'll see you then, and thank you for calling."

"No problem," Mrs. Donovan replied before disconnecting.

Chapter 22

Carolyn Donovan glanced up from the stack of papers she'd been grading as she heard the door to her classroom ease open. With a smile on her face, she quickly stood up from behind her desk, walking halfway across the room to greet Tiara's mother. "Ms. Johnson. It's so good of you to come on such short notice."

Lisa returned the greeting while glancing around the room, trying to get her bearings. She had met Carolyn Donovan on parents' night and once again at Tiara's parent/teacher conference. Still, she didn't feel as if she knew her all that well. Mrs. Donovan seemed to be a good teacher. Tiara certainly spoke highly of her. Her light blond hair was now pulled back from her face in a French twist. She was tall, with enough height to have been a model. But as Lisa looked at her, she noticed that there was something about her facial expression that was a little off, something that prevented her face from gracing the cover of any haute couture magazine. What that something was, Lisa couldn't exactly say . . . there was just something.

Mrs. Donovan's face had broken into a bright smile the

minute she'd seen Tiara's mother. From just that one little action, Lisa immediately knew that Mrs. Donovan was the type of teacher every student would want to have—friendly and likeable. Lisa was still a little uncertain only because she had no idea what this meeting was all about.

"Ms. Johnson, please take a seat," Mrs. Donovan requested, pointing to the chair next to her desk.

Lisa sat down on the hardback chair, glancing around at the maps and posters that decorated the front of the room before returning her attention to Mrs. Donovan. "What's this all about?" she asked, getting to the point.

Mrs. Donovan didn't skirt the issue. "It's Tiara."

"What about her?"

"Tiara, as you certainly know, is one of the very few students at Skidmore who isn't a lifer... someone who has attended the school since pre-kindergarten."

"Well, yes... of course I know that."

"Well, as in any school, some... and I do mean just a few... of the students have been testing Tiara... putting her through the hoops, so to speak."

Lisa had sensed that Tiara was going through something. The events of the homecoming dance had confirmed all of that. Tiara hadn't said a word to Lisa about what had happened at the dance, but she didn't have to. Blake had entered their bedroom that night after picking Tiara up. He had been furious as he'd relayed the events of the evening. He'd explained how Tiara suspected Alicia Blackstone of having spiked her punch, causing her to throw up all over the place. Lisa also knew that the following Monday, Tiara had been questioned by the Skidmore administration about the incident. Tiara had not revealed any of the facts to the administration. She'd led the Skidmore staff to believe that a twenty-four-hour virus had been the cause of her upset stomach.

"Do you know which students have been giving her a hard time?"

"We sort of suspected who they were, but without Tiara confirming anything, initially, there wasn't much we could do. But simply put, we are quite certain that the main person in this little escapade is a student named Alicia Blackstone. We have been informed by several other students that Alicia started rumors that Tiara and Max Blackstone, who happens to be Alicia's cousin, were engaged in an intimate moment at the homecoming dance."

"What!"

"Please, Ms. Johnson, let's stay calm," Mrs. Donovan tried to soothe Tiara's mother. "I believe we have gotten to the bottom of this," she explained, glancing toward the classroom door as it was pushed open. "Come in, Ms. Lopez," Mrs. Donovan said as Tiara's Latin teacher made an entrance.

"Ms. Johnson, I'm sure you've already met Ms. Lopez. She's your daughter's Latin teacher. I invited her to sit in on our discussion since she has some firsthand information that may be of help to us."

Lisa nodded to Ms. Lopez as the Latin teacher took a seat beside her. "Hello, Ms. Johnson," Elena Lopez offered with a warm smile and her hand outstretched. The women shook hands.

Mrs. Donovan continued with her explanation, "Upon

further investigation, we discovered the severity of your daughter's difficulties in acclimating to the rest of her fellow students." Mrs. Donovan paused briefly as she saw Lisa's surprised look. "Now, Ms. Johnson, before you begin to defend your daughter, let's listen to Ms. Lopez. I think you will agree with our assessment that it is in no way Tiara's fault she has been targeted." Facing Lisa, Mrs. Donovan explained the gesture that Ms. Lopez had witnessed the day before between Tiara and Alicia.

"Ms. Lopez," Mrs. Donovan addressed the slight, dark-haired Latin teacher, "why don't you continue from here?"

Ms. Lopez nodded and recounted the hallway episode and comments that had been made to Tiara the day before after lunch. "Naturally, I called Tiara, Alicia, and Max into my office. Initially, your daughter didn't reveal anything, I'm guessing in fear that more problems would arise. Only after we questioned Alicia about the comments she'd made and the words 'Internet rumors' came out did we begin piecing together what was really going on. We've spent most of this morning trying to get to the bottom of all of this."

"As I was saying," Mrs. Donovan continued, "the only reason we can think as to why Alicia Blackstone started these rumors in the first place was to distract everyone from the fact that she was the one who spiked your daughter's punch at the homecoming dance and from the fallout that incident caused amongst her fellow classmates."

Lisa sat silent, dumbfounded for a brief moment. Finally she asked, "What is being done to rectify all of this?

I can't believe this has been happening to Tiara all this time!"

"Ms. Johnson, we are quietly trying to do all we can to rectify this issue. Ms. Blackstone's parents are scheduled to meet here with members of the administration at four o'clock. Putting vodka in your daughter's punch, coupled with these malicious rumors and the lengths to which they were spread, in our opinion deserves severe punishment. We have recommended to the school's advisory board that Ms. Blackstone be suspended for ten days without a chance to make up any classwork. This includes all school-related activities, which in Ms. Blackstone's case means the semifinals of the prep league tennis matches. Furthermore, we feel Alicia should be forced to write a public retraction of the rumors to be published in the *Skidmore Gazette*."

"I see." Lisa felt a little better knowing the actions that were being taken.

"Additionally," Mrs. Donovan continued, "Coach Bob, Max Blackstone's coach, has offered to write a public alibi detailing Max's whereabouts at the time in question during the homecoming dance, to put to rest any lingering doubts that the students might still have. We are so sorry this incident escalated to this level. We only wish that Tiara or another student would have brought it to a staff member sooner."

Lisa released a loud sigh. "I really wish Tiara had come to me or her father before it reached this point. I don't understand it. This move is obviously affecting Tiara a whole lot more than we ever thought it would. My husband and I have been so busy lately; we didn't realize just how much Tiara was going through. What do you think we should do about Tiara?" Lisa presented the question to Mrs. Donovan, searching for a solution.

"Have you and your husband thought about sitting down and talking to Tiara about your new jobs . . . about why you've been so busy lately?"

Once again, Lisa released a loud sigh. "Not really," she finally answered. "We've been too busy to even do that."

"Well, maybe you should take some time and sit down with her," Mrs. Donovan suggested.

"Maybe I should just quit my job," Lisa said. "That way, I'd have more time to spend with both of my children."

"No, Ms. Johnson . . . I don't think that's the solution. You do have a life of your own. I'm also sure you and your husband need to make a living in order to pay your bills."

"Well, that is true," Lisa agreed, "but I do need to make more time to listen to Tiara. I need to do something to help her get through this freshman year."

"Why don't you invite some of her old friends from Boston to DC for a visit? I believe Tiara will long for her old friends back in Boston until she's made to realize that it's not an either/or situation . . . it's not a choice between making friends here at Skidmore or keeping her old friends back in Boston."

Lisa thought about it for a moment. "That's an excellent idea. Maybe we can invite her two best friends from Boston to spend the Christmas holidays with us. Let me talk to my husband about it, but I'm sure he'll agree that it's the best thing we can do right now to help Tiara."

"That sounds like a plan!" Mrs. Donovan happily

replied. "All teenagers go through a tough spell... just like all adults. New school, new friends, a whole slew of new and different pressures can make things really tough on a teenager. Contrary to popular belief, freshman year is not a piece of cake. Healthy kids—and Tiara is absolutely a healthy child—they all make it through. With our help, Tiara is definitely going to make it through freshman year."

Chapter 23

Lisa was in much better spirits that evening after her conference with Mrs. Donovan. Blake had been on time to pick Spencer Jr. up from school and they had returned home shortly after Lisa and Tiara had walked through the front door. Blake had been eager to hear the outcome of Lisa's meeting with Mrs. Donovan and had started asking questions within minutes of greeting his wife. Lisa had held him off, not wanting Tiara or Spencer Jr. to hear the details of their conversation. Now, with the kids upstairs doing their homework, Lisa and Blake were seated in the TV room, the wide flat-screen television set on but turned down low.

"Finally!" Blake announced. "We're alone! So tell me, what did Mrs. Donovan have to say about Tiara?"

Blake sat quietly listening to Lisa's soft voice as she explained the situation between Tiara and Alicia Blackstone. Although he seemed angry, he forced himself to sit back and listen calmly.

"Mrs. Donovan thinks it would be a good idea if we invited some of Tiara's old friends from Boston to come to DC for a visit. What do you think?" Lisa asked her husband.

"You mean Mya and Ebony? That sounds like a good idea," Blake agreed. "When were you thinking of having them come?"

"We did promise Mya and Ebony that Tiara would invite them to Washington, DC, once we were settled in. I think now would be the perfect time to have them come down."

"It sounds good to me. When should we tell her?"

"As soon as possible, I guess. We can invite the girls to come and spend the Christmas holidays with us. I'll get Marilyn to make the airline reservations," Lisa said.

"I want to be around to see Tiara's face when she hears the news."

"Why don't we tell her right now?" Lisa suggested.

A few minutes later, Tiara hesitantly entered the TV room. Her father had used the intercom system to call her, telling her to hurry downstairs.

"Yes," Tiara said, walking over to take a seat between her parents on the couch. "What's up?"

"Your mom was at your school today. She met with your homeroom teacher, Mrs. Donovan."

"Oh. What did she have to say?"

"She told us what's been happening between you and Alicia Blackstone. Tiara, why didn't you discuss this with us?" Blake asked.

"I didn't want to bother you. You've both been so busy lately, I didn't want to dump anything else on you."

Blake and Lisa glanced at each other over Tiara's head. They both knew what she was saying was absolutely true. Blake had been going to work early and had consistently been returning home late at night as various emergencies arose at the hospital. Lisa's schedule had been even worse. She had been averaging about sixty hours a week at the firm. At the rate she was going, Lisa was sure she would accumulate at least thirty-two hundred billable hours by the end of the year. The fact of the matter was, those hours were not considered an exceptional amount. Most of the other associates at McKenzie, Kennedy, and McKenzie billed the same number of hours on a routine basis. Lisa's schedule, on the contrary, was pretty much the norm at the firm. Lisa knew a lot of the associates pulled all-nighters. Several times, she'd found one or two of them the next morning, still asleep underneath the conference room table where they had gone to block out the brightness because of the firm's policy of not turning off the office lights.

Lisa and Blake stared at Tiara. Neither one of them had a response for their daughter. They both knew what she was saying was certainly close to the mark.

"Tiara, it doesn't matter how busy we appear to be. You and Spencer Jr. are our first priority. You two will always be our first concern. We want you to be able to come to us anytime," Blake said.

Before Tiara could respond, Lisa joined in to lend her support. "Tiara, I know you won't believe me when I say that your dad and I have gone through, and are still going through, a lot of the same issues you're facing right now at Skidmore, but I'm going to tell you something—we are always going to run into people who want to cause us grief. The only thing I can tell you is that, like your dad and I, you are going to have to keep rising above all of that and moving on. Believe it or not, you will have to find it in your heart to forgive, to let go of what that person has done to you. And it appears you have, from what Mrs. Donovan has said. I know Alicia has hurt you, that you might want to retaliate, but you're a much better person than that. You are not only our child, but you're also a child of God. That means that you have within you the great powers of God, and he has promised you that he will never leave you alone or forget you. So when you start to believe this, you won't have to fight your battles by yourself. He will be right there at your side to help you. I promise you that! And please, baby," Lisa continued, "don't count your father and I out of the picture as not being able to help. True, we might not have had 'blow-pop incidents' and the like to deal with back in the day, but we have had equivalent life experiences and a lot more of them because we're much older than you. Maybe if some adult—your coach or one of your teachers—had been taken into your confidence in the first place, Coach Bob could have squelched the rumors all the sooner by showing that Max had an alibi."

"Oh, Mom," Tiara whispered as she turned to give her mom a hug. "I love you!" she said, tears streaming down her cheeks.

"Well, what about me!" Blake demanded indignantly. "Don't I get a hug too?"

Tiara laughed as she turned to give him a hug as well.

"That's my baby girl," Blake replied, returning her hug. "Your mom also has a surprise for you."

"What?" Tiara asked, turning around once again to face her mother.

"Guess who'll be visiting us for the Christmas vacation?"

"Who?" Tiara asked with excitement.

"Mya and Ebony!" Lisa instantly replied, refusing to keep her daughter in suspense a moment longer than necessary.

"No!" Tiara screamed, her happiness evident.

"Ouch! Watch out for my ears!" Blake said, not really annoyed. He was thrilled to know their surprise had made his daughter so happy.

"Yes," Lisa responded. "All the arrangements have been made. I spoke to Mya's and Ebony's moms. The girls will be spending ten days with us at Christmas."

Tiara had thrown her arms around her mom even before Lisa completed her sentence. "Mom, you're the greatest!"

"Again, I say... what about me?" Blake repeated. "What am I, chopped liver?"

Tiara turned around to include her dad in her embrace, turning it into a group hug. "I have the best parents in the whole world!" she announced.

Lisa's eyes met Blake's above Tiara's head. Their looks said the same thing: I wonder how long this new attitude will last?

Chapter 24

Tiara had set her internal clock to wake up late on Sunday morning, knowing that it would be her last opportunity before the Christmas holidays. Thanksgiving break had flown by. Last night, their next-door neighbors Alex McKenzie and his wife had thrown a huge party and invited all the senior personnel from the firm. The party had continued until early this morning . . . till two o'clock, to be exact. Lisa and Blake had attended the function and stayed to the very end. Before heading to the party, Tiara's parents had informed both Tiara and Spencer Jr. that they would be allowed to sleep in the next day; they wouldn't have to get up early for church. This really was a once-in-a-lifetime opportunity.

Tying the sash of her thick green terry bathrobe around her waist, Tiara made her way downstairs to the kitchen. Sitting down at the breakfast table, she poured herself a bowl of raisin bran and used the remote to flip through the channels on the television set in the built-in wall unit.

About an hour earlier, Tiara had heard her parents

moving around upstairs, the evidence of which was a half pot of coffee still brewing in the coffeepot on top of the counter. Tiara guessed that either her mom or dad had already been downstairs and had made a breakfast tray to take to their bedroom. Tiara's parents didn't get a chance to sleep in or have breakfast in bed too often, only occasionally on holidays. For that reason, there was an unwritten rule, understood by both Tiara and Spencer Jr., that their parents were not to be disturbed.

Tiara pointed the remote at the television set, scrolling through the cable channel menu to see what was on. Blake and Lisa chose that moment to walk into the kitchen. Tiara glanced up and acknowledged their presence. "You guys look like you had a late night," she said.

Lisa smiled. "I guess you could say that," she agreed.

"Was it a good party?" Spencer Jr. asked, walking in behind his parents.

"Actually, it was a great party," Lisa answered his question. "There was tons of good food, great music, and lots of people from the office whom I don't get to see too often, even though we all work at the same place."

"How do you guys feel about helping me clear away the rest of the dead leaves in the yard?" Blake posed the question to his two offspring while he poured himself a second cup of coffee.

"Oh, Dad! Do we have to?" Tiara and Spencer Jr. asked, almost simultaneously.

"Well, it would be nice to get a little help," Blake solemnly replied, pretending to be hurt by the fact that neither one of his children wanted to help him.

"All right. We get the message, Dad," Tiara said. "We'll be out to help in a minute."

It was a perfect day for raking. Clear skies and a cool breeze blew across their spacious backyard still littered with a carpet of scattered leaves. Blake, Tiara, and Spencer Jr. had started raking the front yard, collecting bags of leaves and setting them by the side of the road for Monday-morning pickup. The small group had then moved to the back of the house where they'd started duplicating their efforts. They'd almost finished dumping the leaves into the large black lawn bags when the screen door to the neighbor's house eased open. Kamilla Andrews stepped out onto her back porch and stood watching the trio hard at work.

"Hello," she called out. She stepped down from her back porch and walked over to stand at the dividing fence. "You guys really look busy," she called across the yard. "How was your Thanksgiving? We haven't seen any of you in ages."

Tiara had seen Kamilla only in passing over the last few weeks. "It was good. How was your Thanksgiving?" Tiara asked in return.

"Great! Too bad it's over and we have to go back to school tomorrow."

"I know what you mean," Spencer Jr. replied, voicing his dismay over the end of the Thanksgiving vacation.

As the three young people chatted back and forth across the fence, the Andrews' screen door opened once again; this time Landon Andrews stepped out, looking to see who his sister was talking to. Spencer Jr. was the first to see him.

"Hi, Landon," Spencer Jr. shouted across the yard.

Landon waved and joined his sister by the fence.

"Hi," he said to Spencer Jr. before turning his gaze on Tiara and her dad. "How are you, Mr. Johnson?"

"Just fine, Landon. Are you enjoying the weather?"

"Yes, sir. It's really been nice lately," Landon supplied, his gaze shifting to Tiara.

"Yes, we have been having some nice weather lately," Blake agreed, even though he realized that Landon wasn't listening to a word he was saying. He could tell that Landon's undivided attention was focused on his daughter. Smiling to himself, Blake pulled off his yard gloves and headed for the house. "Well, guys," he said, looking at his two kids, "I'm leaving the rest of this for you to handle. Just place the bags outside the fence when you've finished collecting the leaves."

"Sure, Dad," Spencer Jr. replied. Tiara barely noticed her father's departure.

"We haven't seen too much of you guys," Landon continued.

Tiara had been certain Landon would head back inside his own house and had simply returned to raking the leaves. She hadn't even bothered to look up. Only after hearing his voice did she stop piling the leaves into the bags and turn around to respond to his statement.

"No, we've been real busy with everything at our new schools," Tiara replied.

"Right, your new schools. How's that going, by the way?" Landon asked, looking directly at Tiara so that she would understand that he was talking to her.

"It's going," Tiara responded in a noncommittal voice. "How are you doing at your school?"

"Not bad. I just made the varsity basketball team, so that's taking up a lot of my time, in addition to my tennis, of course."

"The basketball team! That's awesome!" Spencer Jr. announced, butting into the conversation.

"What are you going to do after you finish with the leaves?" Landon asked, once again directing his question to Tiara.

"Why?" Spencer Jr. asked, butting in before Tiara could get a word in edgewise.

"We're going to see a movie later on, at the Mazza Gallery Mall," Landon replied. "I thought you might like to come along," he invited, looking directly at Tiara.

"That sounds like fun," Spencer Jr. replied, turning to Tiara. "I'll go ask Mom if we can go." He sprinted through the back door and into the house. Spencer Jr. completely missed the surprised look that appeared on Landon's face. Kamilla, on the other hand, saw it and burst out laughing.

"Tiara, your little brother is so cute! I wish I had a younger brother or sister. They do the weirdest things, don't they?" she laughed.

"I guess," Tiara agreed, not quite sure what else to say as Spencer Jr. came tearing back out of the door.

"Mom says that if it's all right with your parents, then we can go with you guys."

"Great!" Landon replied. No one could ever say he wasn't quick on his feet and didn't seize an opportunity when it presented itself. "We'll be leaving in an hour," he informed Tiara.

"Cool," she replied. "We'll be ready. Come on, Spencer. Let's get the rest of these leaves up so we can go!"

Chapter 25

Blake entered the family room and found Lisa stretched out on the couch. Walking over, he dropped down beside her, stretching out his long legs in front of him. "It sounds so strange," he commented.

"What does?" Lisa asked. "I don't hear anything."

"That's just it," Blake pointed out. "There isn't anything. No noise. No kids. Nothing! Just peace and quiet."

Lisa laughed. "It is unusual, isn't it? Do you think this is the way it's going to be when they go off to college?"

"Probably. And believe it or not, we'll probably miss the noise at that point."

"Yes," Lisa agreed. "We probably will."

Blake stood up and walked across the room to the concealed mini refrigerator hidden in the wall unit. Pulling out two diet sodas, he filled two glasses with ice before returning to sit beside his wife. He poured the sodas into the glasses. "Here you go," he said, offering her one of the glasses. "Does it seem like Tiara is a lot happier since you told her we've invited Mya and Ebony for the Christmas holidays?"

"Well, to tell the truth, she's still acting a little moody, but not quite as much as she was during the summer," Lisa replied with a sigh. "Blake . . . do you think we made the right decision moving to DC during her freshman year of high school?"

"She's making some new friends," Blake pointed out.

"I know, but none of them seem to be as close to her as her old buddies, Mya and Ebony."

"She'll adjust, Lisa. Look, she's already going out with the Andrews kids next door. She'll be fine. Stop worrying. Kids adjust faster than you think. Trust me!"

"Okay, Blake. I'm going to trust you on this one simply because I'm so swamped at work, I don't have the time to intervene right now."

Blake exhaled with a loud sigh. "You don't have to do this, Lisa! You don't have to work twenty-four hours a day. You don't have anything to prove to anyone. Remember, most of the other associates at the firm are either single or they have a stay-at-home wife who's handling everything in the household. You have two teenagers . . . and me!"

"And you're worse than the teenagers," Lisa jokingly replied. "I know I don't have to do any of this, Blake. I'm doing it because I want to . . . okay?"

Blake remained silent for a moment. Finally, he reached over and pulled Lisa into his arms. He placed a soft kiss on her lips, then smiled. "Everything will be fine. We're going to make it through this freshman year."

Landon stepped out of the minivan and allowed Tiara and Spencer Jr. to get in. Tiara's quick glance took in the entire spectacular view of her next-door neighbor before she climbed inside the van. Landon looked as if he could be one of the male characters from *Laguna Beach*, the MTV show. His faded blue jeans hugged his thighs like he'd been poured into them. His crisp button-down shirt was neatly tucked into his pants and covered by a short denim jacket, opened down in front.

"Hi, Mrs. Andrews, Judge Andrews," Tiara greeted the adults who were sitting in the front seat. "Thank you so much for inviting us along with you."

"It's our pleasure, Tiara," Laura Andrews replied, watching as Tiara dropped into the second row of seats beside Kamilla. Landon and Spencer Jr. sat behind them in the third row. Spencer Jr. was in seventh heaven. For some reason, Tiara's brother had appointed their next-door neighbor his hero. Spencer Jr. sat back and hung on every word Landon said.

"How's school going?" Laura Andrews asked, turning around to talk to Tiara. "Is it keeping you busy?"

"Very much," Tiara replied and proceeded to bring them up to speed on what was happening at both Spencer Jr.'s and her school.

The ride to the movie theatre took no time at all. About fifteen minutes later, Judge Andrews pulled into the underground parking lot of the Mazza Gallery Mall. As Tiara glanced at Kamilla's father, she noticed that Judge Andrews was an older version of his son. Almost six feet, one inch in height, he had the same caramel color as

Landon and Kamilla. He was also extremely soft-spoken. Tiara had liked him instantly.

Tiara sensed that Laura Andrews was definitely the one in charge in her neighbor's household. Although she was only about five feet, five inches tall, when she spoke, everyone listened.

"Which movie are you and Dad going to see, Mom?" Kamilla wanted to know.

"That new one with Denzel Washington," Laura Andrews replied. "It's playing in Theatre One. Landon, I'm leaving you in charge. We'll meet you at the front entrance at seven o'clock . . . all of you together," she said, silently conveying to her son that he was responsible for keeping an eye on twelve-year-old Spencer Jr.

"Will do, Mom," Landon replied. "Let's go, guys. Head for Theatre Six," he instructed them. Walking toward the concession stand, Landon asked each of them what they would like. Finally, laden down with popcorn and sodas, the small group entered the dark theatre and found four seats toward the back. Kamilla took the lead into the row, followed by Tiara. Spencer Jr. couldn't wait to be seated and cut right in behind his sister. Landon hesitated a moment before following behind Spencer Jr.

The credits were already scrolling down the screen as the group settled in. Sitting at the end of the row, with Spencer Jr. on his right, Landon had a hard time concealing his disappointment over the seating arrangement. He placed his soda in the armrest holder and reached into his pants pocket for his wallet. Pulling out a ten-dollar bill, he leaned over and whispered into Spencer Jr.'s ear.

"Hey, buddy. Why don't you run out and get us some jujubes?"

Spencer Jr. looked at the money. "With all this?" he asked, astonished at the amount.

"Yeah. Keep the change," Landon whispered, hoping his last statement would get Spencer moving.

"Sure thing!" Spencer Jr. replied, leaping up and inching his way out of the row and down the darkened aisle. No sooner had he walked through the swinging doors leading to the concession stands than Landon stood up and eased himself into the seat Spencer Jr. had just vacated. Exchanging the younger boy's soda for his own, Landon settled back and made himself comfortable next to Tiara.

Tiara took a quick glance to her left and noticed that the seat next to her was now occupied by Landon. A few minutes later, Spencer Jr. came ambling back down the aisle holding the candy out for Landon to take.

"You can keep it, buddy," Landon whispered to him.

"Really?" Spencer Jr. asked in surprise.

"Yes. By the way, I put your soda in that holder over there," Landon said, pointing to his old seat.

"Okay," Spencer Jr. happily replied, taking his seat before popping the box of candy open.

Tiara had only been halfway paying attention to what was taking place on the screen. She'd actually been listening to Landon and Spencer Jr.'s whispered conversation. *I wonder if this constitutes a date*, Tiara thought to herself, realizing that Landon's actions had been one hundred percent premeditated.

Chapter 26

Lisa sat in her parked BMW outside Skidmore Prep's front gate, the car engine still running. She watched until Tiara entered the main building and the front door closed behind her, then quickly pulled off. She was in a hurry this morning. It was hard to believe that two weeks had already flown by since the Thanksgiving holiday, but they had. It was Monday morning and Lisa was pushing hard to get to District Court before nine o'clock.

She had circled the block and was now back on Wisconsin Avenue, only this time, she was headed in the opposite direction, downtown and directly to the District Courthouse. Her client, Kyra Davis, who was still incarcerated at DC Jail, was scheduled to have her bond hearing at nine o'clock in courtroom B. Lisa was rushing to find a parking space and make her appearance before the scheduled time.

Twenty minutes later, she was flying up the steps of the courthouse. She was flustered. Initially, she'd driven into the courthouse's underground parking lot. Although it had only been eight-fifteen at the time, the lot had already been filled to capacity. Lisa was forced to circle around the garage, drive outside, and go more than three blocks away before she was able to find a parking space in an outside parking lot. Already tense, Lisa simply dropped a twenty-dollar bill into the young Ethiopian valet's hand, asking him to park her BMW before rushing off to cover the three blocks to the courthouse before her nine o'clock deadline.

Out of breath, Lisa now stepped off the elevator and quickly looked around, trying to locate the courtroom she was scheduled to be in. It was directly in front of her. Glancing at her watch, she noticed it was now eight fifty-five. Great, she thought. Five minutes to spare before court would be called to order.

Lisa glanced down the rows of seats in the courtroom and spotted Robert Brown, the junior associate from McKenzie, Kennedy, and McKenzie who had been assigned to assist her. He was sitting in the first row directly behind defense counsel's table. Walking down the aisle, she took the seat beside him. "Good morning," she whispered, glancing over at him. "Have you been here very long?"

"No. Only about ten minutes," Robert replied.

"I really had a tough time finding a parking space. The courthouse garage is full."

"Yes, I know. I had to park three blocks away."

Lisa gave him a smile. She could definitely relate to that. Robert had been proving to be a big help on this case. He'd been doing quite a bit of the research for her and was turning out to be a very organized individual. A product of Boston College, one of the elite Jesuit institutions in Massachusetts and Lisa's undergraduate college, Robert was also a very pleasant young man to be around.

Lisa pulled out her notes and reviewed them while they waited for Kyra's case to be called. Twenty minutes later, Lincoln James, the government's attorney, walked in, taking a few moments to stand at the back of the courtroom and gather his thoughts. It took him a minute or two before he was able to make eye contact with Lisa. She turned and returned his smile just as the court bailiff walked in and took his position by the side door.

"All rise... all rise!" the bailiff called out, waiting as everyone in the courtroom stood up. "Hear ye! Hear ye! This court is now in session. The Honorable Judge Wilson presiding," the bailiff announced in a loud booming voice.

Judge Wilson entered the room by the opposite side door. Seating himself in the huge black leather chair behind the podium, Judge Wilson nodded to the bailiff to continue.

"The court will now call the first case. United States versus Kyra Davis."

In a matter of seconds, the huge paneled door directly behind the bailiff opened. Two US marshals came forward escorting Kyra Davis, who was walking between them. Lisa's request that Kyra be allowed to wear her regular street clothes had been denied. She had been told that since this was only a bond hearing and no jury would be present to be influenced, it really didn't matter what her client wore. Lisa didn't agree. She thought that for her own self-esteem, Kyra should have been allowed to wear her street clothes. However, in the overall scheme of things, this wasn't the issue she was going to take on. She knew they had bigger fish to fry.

Lisa and Robert had already approached the defense counsel's desk and taken their seats. Kyra was quickly escorted to her table and took the seat between them. Lisa gave her a comforting smile as she glanced at the bright orange prison jumpsuit Kyra had on. She could see the fear in Kyra's eyes and wished there was something she could do to get rid of it. At the moment, she knew there wasn't anything she could do to solve that problem. Lincoln had also moved from the back of the courtroom and had come to join them, taking his seat at the prosecutor's desk.

"You may proceed," Judge Wilson finally instructed the two lead attorneys.

"Your honor," Lisa started her presentation, "my firm, the law office of McKenzie, Kennedy, and McKenzie, has filed a motion for a bond on behalf of my client, Ms. Kyra Davis. In support of this motion, I would like to bring to the court's attention the fact that Ms. Davis is the only daughter of Senator and Mrs. Davis, two very prominent and respected individuals in the Washington community. Without a doubt, my client's parents are definitely willing to vouch for their daughter and will guarantee her presence at all future hearings. Senator and Mrs. Davis are also willing to post any bond that this court decides to issue."

When Lisa had started speaking, the senator and his wife, who were seated on the first row, stood up. They now remained standing while Lisa finished her presentation and waited to hear what Lincoln had to say. He stood up. The tall, dark black man looked impressive in his navy-blue suit. "Your honor, the government does not have any objections to the issuance of a bond."

Lisa had already known Lincoln was not going to object to the bond. Lincoln and Lisa had met a couple of days before and had agreed on this issue.

"What is Ms. Davis charged with?" Judge Wilson asked.

"Second degree murder, your honor," Lincoln answered. "Ms. Davis was arrested for allegedly driving the car from which gang members opened fire on a rival gang. An uninvolved bystander was shot and killed in the process."

"I see," Judge Wilson replied. "And, Ms. Johnson, are you saying that Ms. Davis is the type of person I should release to the streets, that she isn't a menace to society?"

Lisa's heart sank. She had known from the very beginning that the possibility of winning this bond hearing was slim to none. That had been the main reason she'd tried to discourage the senator and his wife from pursuing one. A murder had been involved, and Lisa knew that no judge was going to allow the key suspect to simply walk out of the jurisdiction. Still, because of Kyra's parents, Lisa had felt that she needed to give it a shot. She continued with her presentation.

"Your honor, Ms. Davis comes from a very well-known family. Senator Davis is a member of congress. The family has maintained a home here in the district for the last eight years. Their youngest child has been attending school in the area the entire time they've lived in DC and is now a senior at Whitman High School. Ms. Davis has strong ties to the community and is certainly not a flight risk," Lisa concluded. "We are therefore requesting that Ms. Davis be granted a bond pending her trial."

Judge Wilson stared back at Lisa for a moment before shifting his gaze to Kyra. Lisa wondered what was going through his mind—probably the same thing that had gone through hers when she had first taken the case. Judge Wilson was probably trying to understand why a young woman from such a prominent family would get caught up in such a messy situation.

Judge Wilson finally returned his gaze to Lincoln, who had remained standing by the prosecutor's desk. "Ms. Johnson, do you have anything else you'd like to add?"

"No, your honor. I have nothing further."

"In that case, Ms. Johnson, I will render my decision. I am going to deny your request for bond. Ms. Davis will remain at DC Jail under protective custody until her trial, which I've set for April first. Ms. Davis has a very high-profile case and, unfortunately, I do consider her to be a flight risk. She will be much safer at the DC Jail instead of out and about in the community. Bailiff, would you call the next case?"

Within moments, the two US marshals stepped forward and once again positioned Kyra between them. They proceeded to escort her through the side doors and back downstairs to the government van that would return her to her holding cell at DC Jail. Lisa had taken a moment to whisper to Kyra just before she left, explaining that she would be over to see her at the jail later on that day.

As the bailiff cleared the courtroom in preparation for the next case, Lisa turned and walked over to Senator and Mrs. Davis. Lisa knew they were terribly disappointed with the judge's decision. She was too, for that matter, even though she completely agreed with his ruling.

"Senator Davis. You know how I felt about scheduling a bond hearing. I still think Kyra is better off staying at the jail until her trial is over. She'll be much safer there," Lisa tried to explain.

"Ms. Johnson, we actually agree with you. The problem is Desmond... our son. We've received several threats against him. The gang members think the longer Kyra is held in custody, the more likely she'll be convinced to turn against them and testify for the government as one of their witnesses."

Lisa stood still, shocked into silence. She'd been afraid something like that was behind the senator's request for a bond hearing. Now her fears had been confirmed.

Chapter 27

As excited as Tiara was for the arrival of her two friends, she was also somewhat nervous. After all, six months was a long time to not see someone. She worried that they might not have anything to talk about. The only thing worse than not seeing her friends for so long would be to not have anything to say to them once she finally did see them.

This fear instantly vanished as Tiara saw the pair exit the terminal and enter the lobby of the airport. Both girls looked exactly the same, and Tiara was sure that their personalities had not changed either.

"Mya," Tiara called eagerly across the lobby. "Ebony! Over here!"

"Tiara, stop yelling," Lisa hissed, although she herself couldn't help smiling. Since their move Lisa had felt bad for separating Tiara from everything she had ever known. She was fully aware that Tiara's entire life was Boston, but she had also known that moving to DC was the right choice. While she knew the move would hurt both of her children, it was obvious that Tiara would take it much harder than Spencer Jr., as she was leaving just when things would be getting good, right before high school. Seeing her with her friends made Lisa feel almost as good as Tiara clearly felt.

"Tiara!" the two girls cheered in unison. The three met in a group hug that went on and on.

"C'mon, girls," Lisa said lightheartedly. "You'll have plenty of time for catching up. Right now let's get your bags and get out of here."

The girls spent the ride home catching Tiara up on the various things that had been happening in Boston. They had also recently had their homecoming dance and of course both Mya and Ebony had been asked. Tiara couldn't help thinking that back in Boston, there was no way she would have gone to homecoming without a date. She, Mya, and Ebony would have gone in a group together with their handsome dates and been the center of attention. She certainly wouldn't have spent most of the night sitting in a lonely corner, nor would she have had to defend herself from a reputation-shattering rumor for weeks.

It seemed life back in Boston was in fact the peachiest it had ever been. It was no surprise that Mya had a steady boyfriend—that was usually the case—but even Ebony was branching out. Tiara was surprised to learn that the guy Ebony had gone to their homecoming dance with, a sophomore on the football team, was not just a random date but in fact Ebony's boyfriend. Shy, quiet Ebony had a boyfriend who was not only older but also a football player? Tiara couldn't help but feel she was missing something.

As soon as they reached Tiara's house, they went

straight to her room. "Wow, this is an amazing room, Tiara," Mya cooed, flopping down on Tiara's bed.

Ebony took a seat at Tiara's desk, nodding her head in approval. "Did you pick the furniture yourself or did your mom get everything for you?" she asked.

"We both worked on it," Tiara replied, glancing around her bedroom, seeing it for the first time through her friend's eyes. It was a nice room. Her four-poster bed with its white bedspread was the main item in the room, but the rest of the furniture was equally beautiful. Her mom had bought four bookcases, each six feet tall but with different interiors. The first one had a cabinet where Tiara stored her laptop computer. The other three bookcases had shelves, each spaced at different intervals. All of Tiara's books and tennis trophies were neatly stacked inside. Her dresser, desk, and night table were all made from the same deep cherry wood. Her cream-colored walls were adorned with framed pictures. A walk-in closet, where her clothes were neatly organized, took up one entire side of the room. Tiara knew the girls were right. She was extremely fortunate to have such a pretty room and everything else that had come compliments of her mom and dad's new jobs and, of course, the move to Washington, DC.

"Thanks, guys," Tiara responded graciously. "I must admit, I do like it more than my old room, but I still miss being in Boston."

"Why?" Ebony asked. "DC seems pretty cool . . ."

"Yeah," Mya agreed, then added with a laugh, "I mean you're down here with all these *southern boys*. I'm sure you already have a boyfriend here . . ."

"Well, first of all, DC is not the south," Tiara said with a smirk. "And secondly, to answer your question, no I do *not* have a boyfriend. I guess I'm not as cool as you two."

"That doesn't make you uncool, Tiara," Ebony said.

"I was joking," Tiara replied defensively. "Things just aren't as easy here for me as they were in Boston."

"What do you mean?" Mya asked, sitting up on the bed.

Tiara sat down next to her and sighed. "It's just different," she said. Then without expecting to, she launched into explaining everything that had happened at Skidmore since she had arrived. These were things that she had avoided telling Ebony and Mya over the phone because she didn't want them to worry or think things were worse than they really were. Now as Tiara was recalling the events, she realized that things might have been worse than she'd even thought. Not being asked to the homecoming dance sucked, but it was certainly not the biggest of her problems.

"There's a simple solution to your problem," Mya said conclusively when Tiara had finished.

"Which one?" Tiara laughed.

"Well, the boys one," Mya said as though it were obvious. Mya was the type of person who didn't really care too much about what other people thought about her as long as she had a steady boyfriend and friends that cared about her. Tiara was not surprised that Mya was unmoved by the Alicia situation. Ebony, who was more sensitive to other people's thoughts, might have some advice on that subject.

"Okay, what's your advice?"

"First, you need to forget about any of those dudes

at your school. Clearly there's too much potential drama there. And anyway, why limit your options?"

"That's true." Ebony nodded in agreement. Tiara glanced at Ebony. Since when had she become an authority on social issues?

"Right, so what you need to do is find someone from *outside* of school," Mya explained. "That way you can show everybody up at the next dance. Plus, whoever you find is sure to take your mind off Allison."

"Who's Allison?" Tiara asked. "You mean Alicia."

"Whatever," Mya said, sighing and rolling her eyes. "Do you get what I'm saying?"

"Sure," Tiara said, returning the eye roll. "You want me to find some imaginary guy that will make everyone at school jealous?"

"Not an *imaginary* guy." Mya frowned. "A real one. Who's gonna be jealous of an imaginary guy?"

"Okay, so where am I supposed to find this real guy?" Tiara asked. She wanted to see where this was going, even though she had little faith in it.

"Anywhere," Mya exclaimed, standing up. "The mall! Where's the closest mall?"

"There's a mall in Maryland that's close," Tiara said. "There aren't really any malls in DC . . ."

"Okay, cool," Mya cheered, clapping her hands. "So as soon as your break starts, we hit the mall to scout, okay?"

"Okay . . ." Tiara said, still unsure.

"Cool."

Just as Tiara was about to question exactly how the

scouting process was going to work, there was a knock at the door.

"Hey." Spencer's voice traveled from the other side of the bedroom door. "Can we come in?"

"Sure," Tiara called.

"Spencer!" Mya exclaimed. "Mr. Johnson! I haven't seen you guys in forever!" She ran over and gave them both hugs.

"Hey, Mya," Blake said in greeting. "Hey, Ebony."

"Welcome to our humble abode," Spencer said, laughing.

"It looks great!" Ebony said, getting up to give Spencer and Blake a hug.

"Well, make yourselves at home. Are you two going to school with Tiara tomorrow or are you just going to relax here?"

"Well, going to school would be cool . . ." Mya began, not sure whether the invitation was coming from Tiara or was just a suggestion of her father's.

"I didn't really think you guys would want to." Tiara shrugged. "You're more than welcome to if you want, though. All we're doing is having parties in, like, every class."

"It would be cool to meet your new friends," Ebony said.

"Yeah, that would be fun," Mya agreed.

"So it's settled," Tiara said with a laugh. "Tomorrow, you two will be the two newest students at Skidmore Prep."

It hadn't occurred to Tiara to be nervous about bringing Mya and Ebony to school until it was too late. The moment they stepped out of Lisa's car, Tiara wondered whether she had made a huge mistake. There was no particular reason why she felt that way at that moment, but as soon as her mother said "Have a nice day, ladies," Tiara knew something bad was going to happen; she didn't know what.

Tiara apprehensively led the way to her homeroom. They were early enough that there were only a few students in the room. The girls approached Mrs. Donovan's desk so Tiara could explain the two extra students for the day.

"That's wonderful, Tiara," Mrs. Donovan said when Tiara explained who her guests were. "I'm glad you ladies could visit. There's not going to be much actual school going on today, but I don't think that will be a problem."

"We don't even like doing schoolwork at our own school," Mya said, laughing. "Let alone while we're on vacation."

"Well, make yourselves comfortable," Mrs. Donovan offered with a smile.

Tiara pulled out two folding chairs from the back of the room, then led the way to her usual seat. She had just begun to give brief descriptions of the people in the homeroom when Amanda and Karen walked in. As soon as they noticed Tiara, they hustled over and introduced themselves.

"Amanda, Karen, meet Mya and Ebony," Tiara said, cheerfully introducing her friends.

"Welcome to Skidmore," Amanda said. "You guys are

lucky; you came on the best day of the year. Parties, parties, parties in every class!"

"So we've heard." Ebony smiled.

"You'll probably never want to see another brownie again." Karen laughed, flipping her black ponytail.

"Well, I don't know about that," Mya said doubtfully. "I love brownies." The quartet then began to discuss their favorite desserts. This conversation was going strong when an all-too-familiar shadow fell over the group.

"Well, what have we here?" asked the ever artificially sweet voice of Alicia. "Triplets?"

"What?" Mya asked, turning to face Alicia, a confused smile on her face. "No, we're friends from Boston." Ebony glanced at Tiara with a questioning look and Tiara nodded.

It wasn't that the three girls were offended by being called sisters; many of Tiara's old classmates considered them just that. They were mostly just confused by the abrupt approach of this person they didn't know.

"Oh, how cute!" Alicia jeered. "You could all be sisters, seriously. I'm sure you get that all the time . . ."

"Sometimes," Mya agreed, only then noticing the look of doubt Tiara had been trying to convey. Tiara wasn't sure where Alicia was going with this, but she was certain it could be nowhere good.

"Are you guys thinking of coming to Skidmore?" Alicia asked, as though she truly cared.

"No, they're just visiting," Tiara filled in with an edge in her voice, hinting that she wanted the conversation to end soon.

"That makes sense," Alicia said, beginning to turn. "After all, Skidmore has a quota to fill: no more, no less."

"Excuse me?" Mya asked, not sure if she had really heard correctly. Tiara knew, of course, exactly what Alicia had meant by "quota." To her it didn't need to be explained any further. Alicia, however, did not agree.

"Their quota," Alicia explained. "Skidmore only has a certain amount of black students and for good reason. We wouldn't want the credentials of the institution to go down." And with that final slap, she walked away.

Mya turned to Tiara, speechless. Tiara shrugged.

"Told you," Tiara said flatly.

"Oh *hell* no," Mya whispered, a scowl on her face. "There's no way she's getting away with that."

Tiara had no idea what Mya was planning on doing to get back at Alicia, but she was worried. She didn't think Mya would do anything to deliberately get her in trouble, but intentions had little to do with results. Tiara knew Mya could be fairly irrational, especially when it came to hurt feelings.

That's why she was surprised when the subject of Alicia was not brought up all through the morning. Tiara almost believed that Mya had forgotten about the incident altogether, until lunchtime.

There was no rush to the cafeteria, as everyone was stuffed with the cakes, cookies, and brownies that had been available every period. Instead, all of Skidmore Prep was crammed into the gym, watching the teachers versus seniors dodgeball game. Amanda, Karen, Tiara, Brooke, Mya, and Ebony had only been in the gym for a few minutes when the scheming began.

"Hey," Ebony mumbled. "There's our friend."

"Who?" Tiara asked and then noticed where Ebony was looking. There was Alicia on the other side of the gym, chatting it up with Molly and Brittany.

"Good old Alicia," Amanda said with an eye roll. "Always lurking around."

"I say we have some fun with that," Mya suggested, a smirk on her face. She turned quickly and ushered the other girls into a huddle. "We have to get her back for what she said this morning. That was too rude."

"I agree," Karen said. "She gets away with that stuff way too much."

"If I went to school here, she wouldn't get away with it at all," Mya scoffed. "Now what should we do to get her back?"

"I don't think we should do anything," Tiara said. "It's Alicia. There's no need to get into it with her, she'll never learn."

"I'm with Tiara," Ebony agreed. "We don't even go here, Mya. I understand why you're bothered, but it's not really a worthwhile battle."

"I know we don't go here," Mya said, rolling her eyes. "But Tiara does, and she shouldn't have to put up with that."

"We should have done something a long time ago," Brooke concurred. "But what are we going to do now—get into it with her? She'll never learn."

"Well, everyone in the school is in here, right?" Mya hinted. "So I think we should pay Alicia's locker a special visit . . ."

Tiara listened to Mya's plan, looking for traces of trouble. As it turned out, the plan was fairly foolproof, with no chance of the girls getting caught.

"Okay," she said, giving in. "Let's do it."

The girls had managed to get back into the building completely undetected. There was no way to know if their plan had worked until the end of the school day. They wouldn't know until then if they had gotten their revenge on Alicia.

They found her surrounded by her usual group at her locker. She was all smiles, waving around a piece of lined paper she had no idea Tiara and her crew were quite familiar with.

". . . I mean, I wasn't sure if Ross was really into me at homecoming," Alicia was saying, "but obviously he's in love with me."

"I could have told you that much!" Molly "Olive Oyl" sighed happily. Tiara couldn't help thinking how weird it was how much stock Molly had in Alicia's happiness.

"Hey, Alicia," Amanda said in greeting, leading Tiara's group up to Alicia's circle. "What's going on?"

"Oh, someone's nosy." Alicia laughed. Normally she would have told the entire group to go away, but of course normally they wouldn't have been interested.

"Basic curiosity is a more appropriate characterization," Brooke responded.

"Umm, whatever," Molly quipped, as though she had been spoken to. "Alicia, don't you think you should hurry and meet with Ross?"

"She's right," Brittany agreed. "He is a senior, with places to go and things to do . . ."

"You're right, you're right." Alicia nodded. "Adios, losers," she called over her shoulder as she hurried off.

Tiara watched Alicia walk away before turning to Olive Oyl and Brittany. "So what's that all about?" she asked innocently.

"We probably shouldn't tell you," Molly said slowly, waiting for the girls to beg.

"Oh. Please do," Karen asked, sounding as eager as Karen could, which was not very.

"Ross Washington left a note in Alicia's locker," Brittany eagerly piped up. Molly shot her a look of annoyance but Brittany only shrugged. "Hey, this is the best gossip of the week. I wanna be able to tell people before Alicia starts bragging and it becomes old news."

"That's pretty cool," Amanda said with a smile. "Where are they meeting? We should go see, then we would really have the best gossip."

"O-M-G, you're so right!" Brittany agreed. "They're at the senior center!"

"What are we waiting for, then?" Karen asked, and turned to lead the group to the restricted senior area.

The only special thing about the senior center was that if you were an underclassman, you could only be invited in by a senior. The room itself was not that remarkable: a few couches and a Ping-Pong table. At one point there had been a TV, but that had been taken out a few years ago because too many seniors had been missing class and it was hard enough to get them to school in the first place.

To enter the senior center without an invitation was a huge offense. The seniors would presumably punish any trespassers any way they saw fit. Alicia had no idea that she was about to be one of those trespassers. Tiara felt no guilt for what they were about to witness. In fact, she was pleased that she had agreed to the plan that Mya and Karen had essentially thought up. Unlike the tricks that Alicia had played on her, this one was untraceable and thus thoroughly rewarding.

"There she is!" Brittany cheered.

"Shh," Brooke directed. The pack of girls hid behind a row of trash cans and recycling bins, ready to watch the action.

Alicia knocked on the door of the restricted room. Technically the door was not supposed to be closed, but seniors essentially did whatever they wanted. A girl with dirty blond hair, clad completely in spandex, opened the door.

"What?" she asked flatly after looking Alicia up and down. Tiara couldn't help smiling at that. As big and bad as Alicia acted around freshmen, she was clearly quaking in the presence of this senior girl.

"Um, is Ross in there?" she asked almost inaudibly. "Ross Washington?"

"There's only one Ross," the girl responded slowly,

squinting at Alicia. "And yeah, he's in here. What do you want with him?"

"He left me a note . . . in my locker," Alicia responded, her confidence clearly depleting.

"Okay, right," the girl said, laughing. She closed the door and disappeared into the room.

Alicia stood there dumbly for a few moments, clearly not sure whether she should leave or stay.

"What's going on?" Molly wondered out loud, a frown stretched across her face. The part of Alicia that knew she would have to answer to Molly and Brittany made her stay long enough for the door to open again.

"The door's opening," Brittany pointed out. Ross Washington, who Tiara recognized from homecoming, stepped out cautiously. Tiara noticed a bunch of faces behind him and in the windows of the room. Clearly Alicia was about to be the day's entertainment.

"Hey!" Alicia exclaimed, throwing her arms around Ross's neck. "You wanted to see me?"

"Umm . . ." Ross frowned, obviously totally confused. He awkwardly patted Alicia on the back. "Umm . . . No . . ."

"What do you mean no?" Alicia laughed, still smiling in his face. She glanced at the people behind him. "Oh, did you want to go somewhere private?"

"I'm not sure what you're talking about," Ross said. "But I hadn't really planned on talking to you after homecoming . . . so . . ."

This got a laugh out of the growing crowd behind him.

"Then why'd you put that note in my locker?" Alicia asked, her smile fading by the second.

"What note?" Ross asked, a tension in his voice signaling that he was growing annoyed and probably even embarrassed by the conversation. "I don't even know where your locker is . . ."

"So then who put the note there?" Alicia asked, unquestionably angry.

"Not me," Ross responded harshly, stepping back into the senior center and closing the door behind him.

Chapter 28

Mya lay stretched out across Tiara's large four-poster bed, staring across the room. Ebony was at work brushing Tiara's shoulder-length hair into place. The girls had spent the last two hours getting ready to attend the evening service at the National Cathedral. The cathedral's Christmas Eve service was always special. It was televised each year and seen nationwide. Mya and Ebony were excited that they would be attending. They'd already expressed their hopes of having the television cameras turned on them so their friends in Boston would see them.

"I love Washington, DC!" Mya cried out unexpectedly. "I can't understand why you don't like it here."

"I don't hate it here... well, not as much as I did before," Tiara replied. "It's just that when we first arrived, all my friends were back in Boston. You guys are in Boston!"

"So what!" Ebony said. "We can always come and visit you here. We've had the best time this week with you and I can hardly wait to come back again."

"And you've made friends down here," Mya added. "You can't say that you haven't. You have Brooke, Amanda,

Karen, all the girls on Skidmore's tennis team, Kamilla, and yes . . . don't forget Kamilla's gorgeous brother, Landon."

"Right!" Ebony agreed. "Pleeeeeeease . . . don't forget the cute older brother!"

Tiara laughed. "Well, you two are right about a few things. I have met some nice people here, but I still miss all my old friends from Boston . . . all of you," Tiara whined.

"Well, if I were you," Mya said, "I'd get over it. You've moved to a great city, you're at a wonderful school, and your new home is to die for."

The girls had been chatting in Tiara's room, hating to admit that their time together would be coming to an end in just two more days.

"By the way, where do your neighbors go to school? They don't attend Skidmore, do they?" Mya asked.

"No, they go to Woodson High, the local high school. Their mom teaches there."

"Too bad. It would have been nice if Landon went to Skidmore Prep," Ebony piped in. "Then you'd be able to see him every day."

"Yeah!" Mya agreed. "He's such a hunk."

"He's okay," Tiara agreed nonchalantly.

"Oh, come off it, Tiara." Mya refused to be taken in. "You know he's cute."

Tiara was saved from having to respond by a knock on her bedroom door.

"Are you girls ready?" Lisa asked after easing the door open. "Spencer Jr. is singing in the cathedral choir so we have to be there no later than seven-thirty."

"We're ready now," Tiara said.

"Good. Your dad just went outside to warm up the car. Don't be long."

"Okay," Tiara replied.

"All right, Ms. Johnson," both girls echoed. "We'll be right down."

Chapter 29

Blake pulled up to the side entrance of the cathedral and double parked. There was no way he was going to be able to find a parking space this close to the cathedral, and from past experience, he knew better than to even try.

Lisa opened the passenger-side door of the family's green Volvo and stepped out. Spencer Jr. had already hopped out of the car. He had been sitting on the bumper seat, which had been flipped down to make room for Tiara's friends. He took off like a bullet, running up the steps of the cathedral. The choirboys were required to be in the small chapel in the lower part of the cathedral, dressed in their choir robes, at least fifteen minutes before the service was scheduled to start.

"Don't run!" Lisa shouted to Spencer Jr.'s departing back. Of course, her warning went unheeded.

Tiara, Mya, and Ebony joined Lisa as the group mounted the stairs to the cathedral's main entrance. Tiara was now used to the majestic building since the family attended church there every Sunday. She could tell that Ebony and Mya, however, were impressed by the magnificence of the huge structure.

Washington, DC, had a number of imposing religious buildings, but the largest church in the city was definitely the Episcopal Cathedral Church of St. Peter and St. Paul, generally referred to as the Washington Cathedral. Located in the heart of Washington, DC, the cathedral was first constructed in 1907 in the Gothic style, along the same lines as the old cathedrals in England. Its central tower was the highest point in Washington, DC. At one time or other, the facility had hosted almost every religious dignitary in the world. Their Christmas service was always televised and tonight was no exception.

Tiara, Mya, and Ebony trailed behind Lisa as she went through the front door of the main chapel. The girls' excitement became evident when they saw the television equipment and the camera crew already in position. An usher appeared to escort the group down the center aisle that led to the main altar. Halfway down the long aisle he stopped, directing them to a row of empty seats.

Tiara allowed Mya to enter the row first. She then followed behind so she'd be seated between her two friends. Lisa came behind Ebony and held a space for Blake. As she made a move to sit down, Lisa glanced ahead and caught sight of Alex McKenzie and his wife, Kathleen, seated a few rows ahead of them. She stood up and walked over to chat with the couple before the service started, leaving the girls alone in the pew.

"This place is incredible!" Mya leaned over and whispered to Tiara, speaking loudly enough that Ebony could also hear.

"You don't have to whisper," Tiara responded in her normal tone of voice. "It is pretty awesome, isn't it?" she said, taking some personal pride in the building.

"It's huge!" Ebony said.

"Don't worry about that. It'll be filled to the hilt within the next fifteen minutes. We had special tickets to get in, compliments of Spencer Jr.," Tiara informed them. "All the choirboys and their families received special passes. Everyone else has to line up to get their entrance tickets, first come, first serve. It's going to be packed."

"I didn't know your brother could sing," Ebony said.

"We didn't know it either. All the boys in the choir attend his school so he tried out and got in. Spencer Jr. has been playing two instruments for the last eight years and apparently has perfect pitch. He had no problem making the cut. All the boys in the choir get private voice lessons as well."

"Wow! That's great," Ebony said.

"Yeah, it is. The Cathedral Choir is one of the few all-male choirs in the country. It's really an honor to be invited to join."

"Don't look now, Tiara, but your neighbors just walked in," Mya whispered. "Landon, Kamilla, and their parents."

"Where are they?" Ebony whispered back, resisting the urge to turn around.

"They're coming this way," Mya said after taking another quick glance over her shoulder. "Oh my God . . . I think they're going to sit directly behind us."

"No way!" Tiara replied. "Ebony... take a quick look and see if they're behind us."

"Not directly behind us," Ebony whispered back. "They're two rows down. I think your mom is going back there to talk to them."

"Really?"

"Yes," Ebony replied after taking a second look. "She's talking to them now."

"We'll find out in one second what she said," Tiara whispered to her friends, continuing to face forward.

It was apparent that the service was about to begin. Lisa returned to her seat, Tiara's dad following right behind. Leaning toward her daughter just as the first hymn began, Lisa told the girls that she'd just invited both of their neighbors—Alex McKenzie and his wife and the Andrews family—to come over to the house after the service for some eggnog. The girls looked at each other and started to giggle.

"I love Washington, DC!" Mya said again.

"Me too," Ebony echoed. "I wish I lived here!"

Chapter 30

The service was almost over. The pastor had just announced the final hymn, the one Spencer Jr. was going to sing... solo. The position of lead altar boy was an honor all the choirboys had been vying for. As everyone picked up their hymnals and stood up to sing, Spencer Jr. walked over to the microphone.

"I wonder if he's nervous," Ebony whispered to Lisa. "Does he know this service is being televised all over the United States?"

"No," Lisa whispered back. "We didn't want him to go into shock or anything like that, so we didn't tell him that part."

Spencer opened his mouth and started singing. His voice blended in with the beautiful tone of the gigantic organ playing in the background. Spencer was singing the first verse of "Silent Night." His soulful, melodic soprano voice filled the entire cathedral. The acoustics in the Gothic building were spectacular, making Spencer Jr.'s voice sound like that of a celestial being. If Tiara hadn't known him as well as she did, she would have thought he actually was one.

"He sounds like an angel," Mya whispered loud enough for everyone to hear.

"He even looks like one in his white choir robe," Ebony whispered back.

"Who would have ever thought my brother could sound like that? Go figure!" Tiara agreed.

The full choir joined in on the second verse and Spencer Jr. ended the hymn by singing the last verse solo. As he sang the last few notes, the entire cathedral went silent, everyone simply staring at the little angel at the altar.

"Spencer Jr., you were awesome," Alex McKenzie's wife, Kathleen, repeated for at least the third time.

Spencer Jr. had heard that compliment, or one very similar to it, at least a hundred times since they'd left the cathedral. The group had returned to the Johnsons' house where an impromptu Christmas party was now in full swing. The Johnsons' living room was filled with people crowding around the huge Christmas tree. The energy level was high. The living room, the foyer, and the entryway of the Johnsons' house had been decorated with bright red garlands and sprigs of holly and ivy. Mistletoe was also suspended throughout the house in strategic places. The twelve-foot Christmas tree in the corner of the living room by the window was decorated in gauzy gold ribbon with gold and white artificial birds.

For such an impromptu event, Lisa had managed to produce a wide assortment of hors d'oeuvres, eggnog, hot chocolate, and rum punch. Blake had dimmed the overhead lights and loaded several CDs on the CD player. Nat King Cole's rendition of "Chestnuts Roasting on an Open Fire" was drifting across the room from the concealed speaker system, filling the entire house with music. Hundreds of sparkling white lights from the huge Christmas tree lit the room, giving it a magical glow.

It was after midnight by the time Alex and Kathleen made the first move to depart. Laura and Judge Andrews also stood up and made their way over to the front door, standing there for a moment to say their good-byes to Lisa and Blake. Spencer Jr. had long since fallen asleep while the girls and Landon had been having a wonderful time talking about the latest hip-hop artists and their most recent concert tours.

Kamilla saw her parents get up to leave. "I guess we better go too," she said, glancing at her brother. "We had a great time, Tiara. Merry Christmas . . . and it was wonderful seeing both of you again," she added, turning toward Mya and Ebony.

The two girls followed Kamilla, leaving Tiara to escort Landon to the front door. "This was really fun, Tiara. We should get together sometime."

"Ahhh . . . thank you," Tiara replied, somewhat surprised. She didn't know what else to say. Landon had really caught her off guard.

As they left the living room, Landon reached over and stopped Tiara. Turning to her, he quickly planted a kiss on her lips. "Merry Christmas," he said with a grin, pointing to the piece of mistletoe that hung from the arborway separating the living room from the foyer. Landon knew he had caught her completely off guard.

Tiara couldn't think quickly enough to come up with a creative response before Landon joined Kamilla and his parents. In fact, they had all walked out the front door before she could pull it together.

"Tiara!"

Spinning around, Tiara looked up at the staircase leading to the second-floor landing. Mya and Ebony were sitting on the steps hidden from sight behind the handrails. Tiara shot up the stairs to join them. She really didn't have to guess if they'd seen the kiss. Their expressions of envy, admiration, and complete awe said it all.

Chapter 31

Sunday afternoon came all too soon for Tiara, Mya, and Ebony. It had been a wonderful ten days, but Tiara's two best friends were heading back to Boston. Blake was behind the wheel of the family's Volvo on his way to National Airport. Tiara sat on the front seat with her dad but twisted halfway around so she could see her two friends on the backseat. Flurries of snowflakes had been falling all morning, adding to the pile of snow that had accumulated the day before.

Last night, the girls had chosen to sleep in sleeping bags on the floor in Tiara's bedroom instead of in the two guest rooms that had been prepared for them. They'd been too excited to sleep, so they stayed up, rehashing the events of the Christmas Eve party.

"No one in Boston is going to believe it when we tell them about your 'friend' Landon," Mya whispered in the darkened room. "Can you believe that kiss?" she'd asked, still unable to conceal her amazement hours after the event.

"He only kissed me because we were standing under that silly mistletoe," Tiara pointed out.

"No, that's not true!" Mya argued. "I stood under that same mistletoe—so did Ebony, for that matter—and neither one of us got anything that resembled a kiss. How do you explain that?"

Tiara had not been able to come up with a response, especially since Ebony had started cracking up in the background. By the time the girls had finally fallen asleep, it was almost four in the morning. They awoke to the smell of frying bacon and eggs, cinnamon bagels, and hot chocolate. Spencer Jr. had beaten them to the punch and was already downstairs under the tree shaking and rattling the gift-wrapped boxes that he knew better than to try and open.

With Spencer Jr. prodding them on, the girls had rushed through breakfast, just as eager to get to the presents. They hadn't been disappointed, either. Mya and Ebony had received some lovely gifts from Blake and Lisa—several books, two CDs, two sweaters, and a pair of jeans each.

Tiara had gone shopping with her mom, so she knew exactly what was in each box... except for the last one the girls had been handed. That box had been huge and had both Mya's and Ebony's names on the top. Both girls pulled tissue after tissue from the box before finally getting to the bottom, where they found a plain manilla envelope. Ebony hadn't been able to wait any longer and had grabbed it from Mya's hand. Flipping it open, she'd let out a scream after pulling out two plane tickets to one of the major tennis camps in Bradenton, Florida. The dates on the tickets were during summer vacation. There were also two open-ended return tickets to Washington, DC.

"Oh, Ms. Johnson, Mr. Johnson. Thank you so much! This is super! We get to go to tennis camp in Florida and we also get to come back to DC," Mya enthused.

"Tiara, I'm so glad you moved to Washington, DC," Ebony repeated for the hundredth time since the day before. They were standing by the check-in desk waiting for the Boston flight to be announced. The girls had been talking together quietly, knowing that their grand vacation would soon be over.

"Mr. Johnson," the flight attendant called out as she approached Blake and the girls. "Which two young ladies will I be escorting back to Boston?"

"These two," Blake replied, pointing to Mya and Ebony.

"Well, we're all set to board," she said, watching with a smile as the three girls joined together for a group hug.

"We'll miss you, Tiara," Mya and Ebony called back as they were escorted down the corridor to board the aircraft.

"Call us! Don't forget, Tiara . . . call us!"

"I will," Tiara yelled back. "See you in May for summer vacation!"

Chapter 32

Tiara slammed her locker shut, pulling on the combination lock to make sure it was really closed. The fourth-floor corridor of Skidmore Prep was empty. It was eight o'clock, and by now all the other ninth-graders were in their homeroom class, exactly where they were supposed to be. Tiara was late for school. Blake had received an early-morning page: some emergency had occurred at the hospital and every anesthesiologist on staff, including the director of the department, had been called in. Blake had shot out of the house before seven o'clock, leaving Lisa to handle both drop-offs. Lisa had driven Spencer Jr. to his school first and then circled around to Skidmore Prep to drop Tiara off.

Tiara had taken only a moment to say a brief good-bye to Lisa before jumping out of the car, running up the walkway, and entering the building. She made a quick stop at the front office to pick up a late pass and flew up the stairs to the fourth floor. Now, after dumping her books into her locker and pulling out her binder, Tiara pushed open the door to her homeroom and walked in. Of course, all eyes swiveled around to look at her.

"Good morning, Ms. Johnson," Mrs. Donovan said, interrupting her monologue to the rest of the class in order to turn and greet Tiara. "Do you have a late pass?"

"Yes, I do," Tiara replied, passing it to her teacher before walking to the second row to take her seat. Mrs. Donovan returned to her presentation, outlining the agenda for the day.

"Where have you been?" Amanda whispered to Tiara.

"My dad had an emergency at the hospital. My mom had to drive my brother to school first before she could drop me off," Tiara replied. "What's up?"

"The Valentine's Day dance. It's next Saturday night on the thirteenth of February, from seven o'clock until midnight. And guess what?" Amanda's voice rose a notch higher.

"What?" Tiara asked, trying hard to keep her voice to a whisper.

"We can invite 'outside friends,' other students who don't attend Skidmore. I'm going to invite a friend from Georgetown Prep. Who are you inviting?"

"I'm not sure," Tiara replied before she glanced up and caught Mrs. Donovan staring directly at her.

"Ms. Johnson, did you have something you wanted to share with the rest of the class?"

"No, Mrs. Donovan. Not right now," Tiara responded with a smile. Tiara liked Mrs. Donovan and knew her teacher was really teasing her. Since her meeting with Tiara's mother, Mrs. Donovan had been keeping an eye on

Tiara, quietly making sure that the foolishness from Alicia was finished. In fact, she was keeping an eye on Alicia and her little cronies as well.

Following her conversation with Lisa about Tiara and Alicia, things had improved a little. Although Mrs. Donovan and the rest of the faculty had voted to suspend Alicia and her "ladies in waiting," Lisa and Blake had vetoed the suggestion. They didn't agree with that tactic. Lisa and Blake knew firsthand that bullying came in all sizes. It happened with adults as well as with kids. Bullying was a fact of life and Lisa and Blake knew Tiara was going to have to learn how to handle this emotional abuse sooner or later. Sooner was better.

Alicia and her gang had not been suspended, but their parents had been called in to meet with the head of the school and the disciplinary board. Alicia and her crowd, along with their parents, had been informed that one more incident and all the girls would be invited to leave Skidmore Prep.

Alicia's father had been livid. A suspension from Skidmore would kill his plan for her to attend Yale. He had grounded her until the end of the school year. When this had gotten around the school, Alicia had been humiliated.

Tiara knew Alicia was biding her time, waiting for revenge, but in the meantime, she had been keeping her distance. Tiara knew the immediate battle was over between them, but she wasn't sure if it was leading to a full-fledged war. In any case, Tiara had more important things to think about, namely, the Valentine's Day dance.

Actually, Tiara had already heard about the Valentine's

Day dance. She'd walked past the art room last week and had seen the new posters the art students were making. They were real cutesy with cupids and hearts all over the place. Tiara, however, was not as thrilled as Amanda about attending the dance. As usual, Amanda had someone who very much wanted to go with her. Brooke and Karen probably did as well. Tiara still didn't know anyone at Skidmore well enough to invite her. And she didn't know anyone she felt comfortable enough to invite.

Tiara's mind did an instant replay of the homecoming dance in October. She had visions of the same thing happening all over again. She was sure she couldn't go through another episode like that. Tiara knew she was going to have to come up with some excuse not to attend the Valentine's Day dance . . . something her friends would believe.

Chapter 33

Tiara was abruptly brought back to reality by the homeroom bell. Packing up her books, she stood up and waited for Karen and Brooke to catch up to her and Amanda. The four girls walked down the hallway to their first-period class. With the exception of Tiara, the girls were deep in conversation about the dance. None of them seemed to notice the lack of contribution from her. After about five minutes, Tiara had heard enough and decided it was time to change the subject. "We have tennis practice today, don't we?' she asked, looking at the three other teenagers.

"Yes, we do," Brooke replied after a brief pause, surprised at the interruption. "Right after school. Coach Bob said he expected everyone to attend and to be on time."

"You know why, don't you?" Karen asked the group.

"Of course!" Amanda said. "We're going up against George Mason Prep in a couple of weeks. Those girls are tough. They're the ones to beat!"

"They're tougher than the Jefferson High team. That's the team we tackle next," Karen joined in. "Jefferson High was awesome last year. They destroyed us. This year, we're going to get our revenge. With Tiara on our team, they'll be begging for mercy."

"When do we play George Mason Prep?" Tiara asked.

"Last," Amanda replied. "They're the last team on our schedule. We play them at the end of April, and this year we're definitely going to be ready!"

The four girls walked into their first-period class—algebra. It was obvious the other students were also pumped up. There was a feeling of excitement in the classroom. While everyone appeared to be focused on the math assignment, in reality, most of their minds were churning with thoughts of the Valentine's Day dance, and of course, who would be going with whom.

Chapter 34

It was Friday at midnight. Blake turned the key in the front-door lock, pushed it open, and walked inside. This was his first time home since leaving for the hospital four days earlier. The emergency he'd rushed off to handle had turned into a full-scale disaster. Fifteen tractor trailers had slammed into each other on the Beltway. The unexpected snowfall and cold weather that had suddenly hit the district was the cause.

Snow in DC was a novelty. DC residents had no idea how to drive in it. The typical joke around town was "two inches of snow and the entire city shuts down." Well, they'd had a lot more than two inches. They'd had almost eight inches of snow, and as usual, no one in DC had been prepared. The city didn't have the capability of handling that amount of the white stuff. For sure, the residents of the district didn't have a clue about driving in it. Over eighty people had been rushed to surrounding hospitals. The Greater Northeast Hospital's emergency wards had received the bulk of them, and as a result, all non-life-threatening surgery had been postponed to accommodate the onslaught of new patients.

Blake had been in the midst of everything. As the new director of the anesthesiology department, it had been his responsibility to coordinate everything. He'd been forced to find rooms, set up makeshift surgery units, and the hardest part of all, handle all the surgery schedules. Although the surgeons at the hospital liked to believe they were the head honchos, the "rainmakers" in the hospital, the reality was that no surgery could take place unless an anesthesiologist was present. There was no way any surgeon could even think about cutting into a patient unless they had an anesthesiologist right there to knock the patient out, and on Monday, there hadn't been nearly enough anesthesiologists to handle the number of cases.

For the last four days, all of this had been Blake's responsibility. He'd had to locate anesthesiologists from other hospitals all over the city and from neighboring Maryland and Virginia to come in and assist with the high volume of cases. He'd barely slept during the last four days. He couldn't remember what he'd eaten, or if he'd actually eaten anything at all. He'd been so wrapped up with the emergency cases that he'd completely forgotten to call home. Completely forgotten! As hard as that was to believe, he had.

Yesterday, as everything started to come under control, Blake had finally thought about calling Lisa. He still hadn't made the call, though, because he knew she was going to give him hell. She was definitely going to let him have it, and rightfully so. Blake didn't want to deal with her anger, definitely not while he was still at the hospital, where privacy was a foreign word. He decided to wait, wrapping things up at the hospital before going home to deal with that issue.

An hour later, Blake entered the house on Kennedy Street for the first time in four days. As he walked through the foyer, he heard the sound of soft music coming from the family room. He paused at the entrance to the room and saw Lisa stretched out on the oversized couch. It was almost midnight, so he knew Tiara and Spencer Jr. had to be upstairs, fast asleep. Lisa apparently had lit the fireplace before she herself had fallen asleep in the family room. The fire had long since died down, leaving only the embers smoldering in the hearth.

"You're home!" Lisa said, waking up abruptly at the sound of his footsteps on the hardwood floors.

Blake heard the icy tone in her voice. He knew she was angry. Actually, he knew she was livid. Oh well, he thought to himself, there is no getting around this. There was no denying the fact that he should have called home long before this. It was hard to explain to anyone who wasn't in his position how someone could forget to call home . . . for four days! He knew he had no choice but to accept what she was about to dish out.

"Yes," Blake responded to her statement. "I'm home . . . and I'm beat," he added, fishing for a little sympathy instead of the cold treatment he knew he was about to get.

"Well, I'm glad to see you're okay," Lisa replied, getting up from the couch. "Good night!" she added, her tone as cold as ice as she walked straight past him, out the door, slamming it shut behind her as she made her way upstairs to their bedroom.

"Damn!" Blake muttered as he watched her leave. "Damn!"

Chapter 35

Tiara glanced over at the indoor bleachers before stepping onto the tennis court. Her mom, dad, and Spencer Jr. were sitting in the middle row, close to the baseline, in the huge enclosed tennis center where the Skidmore students played their winter tennis matches. Tiara knew her mom and dad were angry and not speaking to each other. Before they'd left the house to attend the tennis tournament, Tiara's parents had been downstairs in the kitchen. Tiara had quietly taken a seat at the breakfast table. Marilyn was off for the day and Lisa had been at the kitchen counter slamming pots and pans and making the kind of noise women make when they're mad as hell and want everyone within a five hundred mile radius to know.

Tiara knew her dad had been at the hospital the last four days. She also knew he hadn't called home. He'd forgotten, of all things. Lisa had called the hospital several times during the week and had talked to different members of the administrative staff. She'd received detailed information about what was taking place there, but not once had she received a call from Blake. That was the reason for the banging of the pots and pans. It was obvious to Tiara and Spencer Jr. that whatever their dad had said to their mom had not been sufficient for her to forgive him.

"Good morning, Dad. Good morning, Mom," Tiara hesitantly greeted her parents.

Lisa simply nodded.

"Good morning, princess," Blake responded, giving her a kiss on the cheek.

"I thought you'd run away from home," Tiara whispered so only her dad could hear.

Blake gave his daughter a wink, maintaining a silent stance as he poured cereal into a bowl. He really didn't want Lisa to start squaring off with him at the breakfast table, so as far as he was concerned, the less he said for the moment, the better for everyone.

Amanda's mom arrived shortly after breakfast to pick Tiara up. Karen and Brooke were already seated on the last row of the minivan when Tiara joined them. The girls had to be dropped off early at the school so they could warm up before the big match between Skidmore and George Mason Prep. Tiara had eagerly left the house, not wanting to hear what her parents' dispute was all about. She really didn't want to have to take sides against either one.

The competition between Skidmore and George Mason Prep was notoriously fierce, and today was no exception. Joy Goldman had just lost her match. The teams were now tied. Tiara's was the last match of the day. She was going up against Gretchen Moore, otherwise known as "Killer," a senior at George Mason Prep. At almost six feet, one inch, the blond-haired, blue-eyed Amazon looked like she was ready to take Tiara out.

Tiara glanced at the bleachers once more. Spencer Jr. was sitting in between her mom and dad but bending over to speak to someone on the bench below him. Tiara's eyes traveled down. "Oh my God!" she cried out. Landon Andrews! She couldn't believe it. Kamilla was sitting next to her brother on the metal bench. Gosh! What are they doing here? Tiara wondered. Talk about performing under pressure. It was already going to be tough enough having to play against Killer, but with Landon sitting right at the baseline watching her every move, Tiara didn't think she could do it.

"Ladies, are we ready to start?" Tiara heard the referee call out.

Nodding her head, she walked to the serving line and prepared to make her first serve. She already knew the only way she was going to get the advantage over Killer was to jump out and make as many points as she could during the first game. That was her game plan. She had to focus... forget about everyone in the stands... forget about Landon Andrews.

Tiara walked to the baseline and prepared to make her first serve. Reaching back with her racket, she took her serve, sending the ball flying, sharp and fast.

Before she'd walked onto center court, Coach Bob had taken her aside and given her a little pep talk.

"You know, Killer is just that," he'd stated. "She's a

real killer! She's George Mason's ace in the hole and she's coming after you! She's strong and she's good, but you can take her. I've seen your game, Tiara. You can do this if you focus on winning."

Tiara hadn't said a word. She'd simply looked over at the six-foot Amazon and wondered what she could do to outmaneuver the giant.

"This is your house. We're playing at Skidmore, so you're on your own turf. It's your court... you call the shots."

"Okay, Coach. I get the message," Tiara had replied. "I'll try not to lose the keys to the house."

Tiara was now trying hard to hold on to those keys. She was well aware how important this match was to the Skidmore team. If she lost, the tie would be broken and Skidmore Prep would lose the entire tournament. Killer was ranked number three in the division, right behind Sierra Morgan and Lindsey Battle. Tiara knew the odds were not in Skidmore's favor; nevertheless, she intended to give it her best shot.

A lot of things separated Tiara from the rest of the Skidmore players. Her hook of a left-handed forehand and her movements that the coaches at Boston Middle School had always declared were superb. Those were Tiara's secret weapons. By the end of the first set, Tiara was serving. The score was thirty to forty. Killer responded to Tiara's serve with a phenomenal crosscourt forehand passing shot. Tiara was waiting for it, coming back with speed and a two-handed backhand, straight down the line. Facing the first break point of the set, Killer moved in on a short return and hit a forehand that landed really wide. The crowd in the stands went crazy. Tiara had won the first set. This was unheard of. Running up to Tiara during the break, Coach Bob was almost jumping out of his skin with excitement.

"Wow, Tiara! I can't believe it! You're taking Killer down!" he shouted. "Can you keep this up?"

"I'm not sure," Tiara replied. "I'll try."

"You go, girl! At least you're keeping us in the game. Give it your best shot." Coach Bob managed to get the words out before Tiara ran back on to center court. She was pumped up now. Playing the first match had given her a chance to see Killer's game, to evaluate her style. Now she knew what strategy to use. They were playing for the best two sets out of three. Tiara knew if she could take the next set, there would be no need for a third. That was her game plan.

Tiara had the first serve but lost it when Killer returned the balls with a vengeance. Killer won the point on her serve and maintained her edge until she served for the set at five to four. She had started out well enough, winning the first point, but lost the next four with three unforced errors and a double fault. The home crowd was going wild knowing that Tiara had a chance to win, but Killer wasn't giving up that easily, fighting back from a six–three deficit in the tiebreaker to six to five.

Tiara knew this was it—do or die! She took a quick glance at the stands before running back to the service line. Spencer Jr. was standing up in the bleachers. So was Landon Andrews. He was also giving Tiara the thumbs up.

Tiara threw a quick smile at the stands before taking her position. On the next shot, she hit a second serve to Killer's forehand, producing a short ball. Moving forward, Tiara ripped it deep, if not to the ideal spot. Killer returned the shot with a forehand. It fell short and went into the net. The stands went berserk. Skidmore Prep had won! Everyone was shouting, "Tiara . . . Tiara . . . Tiara!"

Before the last rumble of applause had reverberated throughout the courtyard, Tiara had already run to the net, given the six-foot Amazon a handshake, and rushed off to join Amanda, Brooke, Karen, and a group of other spectators who had jumped down from the stands. From the corner of her eye, Tiara caught sight of Landon right about the same time Max Blackstone caught up to her.

"That was awesome, Tiara," Max enthused, moving to stand in front of her.

"Thanks, Max," Tiara replied.

"Are you going to the Valentine's Day dance next weekend?" he asked, smiling as he remembered that he'd asked the same question about the homecoming dance.

Landon and Kamilla joined the group before Tiara could respond.

"Great game, Tiara!" Kamilla managed to make her voice heard above the racket.

"Yeah!" Landon agreed. "Your serves were awesome!"

Tiara was flustered but trying hard to remain cool. "Thanks a lot. I didn't know you two were coming to the game," she said.

"It's only the biggest game of the season. George Mason

Prep and Skidmore Prep are fierce rivals," Kamilla pointed out.

Max had had enough. He wasn't used to being in the background or being ignored. "Tiara, about the Valentine's Day dance. Do you intend to go?" he piped up once again.

"Oh, Tiara," Landon interrupted, deliberately cutting Max off. "I saw the posters around your school for a Valentine's Day dance. I'd really like to take you."

"What?" Tiara asked, startled out of her wits. Had she heard correctly?

"Can I take you to your Valentine's Day dance next week?" Landon repeated, a grin spreading across his face.

"I'd love to go with you," Tiara replied, still in shock.

As more bystanders came up to congratulate her, Tiara stood beaming. Could this day get any better, she wondered.

Chapter 36

Blake glanced at the watch on his right wrist. It was almost four o'clock and he was still sitting behind the large walnut desk in his spacious office at Greater Northeast Hospital. He should have left the office over an hour ago, but a few folders still remained for him to review before he could call it a day.

It had been a hellish week, and as a result, Blake had not been able to go to the gym for his daily workout, not even once. He promised himself that starting today, he'd return to the hospital's workout room and treat himself to a hard, sweaty workout.

Blake had arrived at the hospital at seven-thirty this morning and had been here ever since. Ten days had passed since last Monday's massive traffic accident on the Beltway and only now was the hospital starting to return to normal. Blake wished he could say the same about his marriage. Unfortunately, Lisa was taking this silent treatment thing to new heights. Blake could feel the tension between them the minute he walked through the door each evening. Lisa had barely spoken to him all week and had made almost no eye contact unless it was absolutely necessary. Her silence was beginning to grate on his nerves. If she had a problem with him, he wished she'd just come out and say what it was rather than give him the old silent treatment. Now he knew exactly where Tiara had acquired that extremely aggravating habit of blocking people out. Tiara had only recently started to get over this problem, but now her mother seemed to have found it. This silent treatment was hell!

Last night, Blake had just about had enough. The kids had already eaten and were upstairs studying when he'd decided to confront his wife.

"Okay, Lisa," Blake said as he'd entered their fourth-floor bedroom suite. "Enough of this silent treatment. We need to talk."

"Talk? About what, Blake?" Lisa had innocently asked.

"About why you're giving me the cold shoulder . . . the silent treatment."

"Are you telling me that it bothers you when the person who's supposed to be closest to you doesn't speak to you, doesn't even think about calling home, for a whole week? Blake! For a whole week!"

They'd both remained standing in the middle of the room, fuming and glaring at each other, but Blake hadn't been able to think of one intelligent thing to say. Lisa stood there with her arms akimbo and her hands balled into fists. How could he have done this to her, to Tiara and Spencer Jr., and then declare that they were the most important people in his life?

Blake didn't have any answers, and judging from the

rigid set of Lisa's back, she wasn't going to be any help either.

Blake returned two of the files to his outbox as he heard the knock on his office door. "Come in," he called out.

"Mr. Johnson, I'm so glad you're still here," his secretary, Rita, said as she opened the door.

Yes," Blake replied. "I'm still here. What's up?" Rita usually left at exactly three o'clock in order to pick up her six-month-old baby boy from the hospital's day-care center located on the first floor of the main building. It was unusual to find her still in the office after three o'clock since she would be expected to pay double for each hour her son remained at the facility beyond his usual time. Rita and her husband had only been married two months when she'd discovered that she was expecting a baby. Blake knew money was real tight with them.

"I was talking to John this afternoon. By mistake he spilled the beans and told me he'd purchased two tickets for us to see the new Broadway play that's showing at the Kennedy Center Saturday evening . . . as a Valentine's Day treat."

"That's great, Rita. I'm sure you'll enjoy it."

"I'm sure I will too, Mr. Johnson. The problem is, I already bought two tickets to the show. I was going to surprise John as well. I was wondering if you'd like to have my two tickets and possibly take your wife to see the show?"

Blake was sure Rita wasn't in a position to give away two Broadway tickets, but he thought it would be nice to surprise Lisa and take her to the show on Valentine's Day.

Blake had not thought about getting anything for Lisa. The fact that she wasn't speaking to him had forced all rational thought from his head, and again, he had simply forgotten to get her anything. He knew that could be a real big mistake, like adding fuel to the fire.

"Rita, you're a lifesaver!" Blake announced, jumping up and moving from behind his desk. "I was wondering what I should give Lisa for Valentine's Day. This is the perfect solution. I'd love to buy them from you."

"Oh, Mr. Johnson, you don't have to pay me for them," Rita politely replied.

"I insist, Rita. That's the only way I'll take them off your hands. Is it all right if I write you a check?"

"Ah, yes... yes, certainly," Rita happily replied, thrilled that she was going to be reimbursed for the expensive tickets. "They're really good seats... in the orchestra section. I really wanted to splurge this weekend. It's also our anniversary."

"Well then, I really did luck out, didn't I?"

"I guess you did," Rita echoed.

Chapter 37

Lisa pulled into the faculty parking lot of Skidmore Prep. It was almost two o'clock. She was early. Today was the day she had committed to giving a presentation to Tiara's homeroom class as part of their Future Careers series. Tiara had volunteered Lisa to come in and speak on different careers in the legal field. Lisa had wanted to participate in this event for more reasons than just giving out career information. Although things seemed to be going well with Tiara and her classmates, Lisa wanted them to see another part of Tiara . . . her home life, her family. Lisa wanted to let them know that Tiara was not too different from any of them.

She sat behind the wheel of her BMW and took a moment to catch her breath. She'd been on the go all morning, stopping at DC Jail first to meet with two new clients. Although she'd stayed there longer than initially planned and was running late, she'd still asked the US marshals to bring Kyra Davis up to the attorney/client room for a brief visit.

Kyra was holding up well. Lisa hoped she could hang

on for a few more weeks until their scheduled hearing. The prosecutors were still trying to negotiate a settlement, but Kyra was adamant about wanting to go to trial.

Lisa gave a loud sigh as she parked the car in a visitor spot. There was no doubt she was happy about their move to Washington, DC, but her job at McKenzie, Kennedy, and McKenzie was intense and time-consuming. Blake's new position at Greater Northeast Hospital was also taking up a lot of his time, but it was evident he was enjoying the challenge.

Lisa was still giving him the silent treatment. She knew she should cut him some slack, but just the thought of him going four days without even *thinking* about calling his family was more than she could deal with, so here it was, three days before Valentine's Day and they still weren't talking to each other.

Opening the car door, Lisa stepped out of the parked BMW and walked through the front door of the main building. Checking into the office, she was warmly greeted by Ms. Collins, the administrative assistant to Ms. Block, the headmistress.

"Ms. Johnson, give me a moment and I'll escort you to your daughter's homeroom class. We're so happy you could make it today," Ms. Collins said as she gathered the papers and folders on her desk and clicked Save on her computer. "All set," she said as the computer screen went blank. "This way."

The two women chatted as they left the administration building and headed over to the high school.

"Here we are, Ms. Johnson. Room 401." Ms. Collins

pushed open the door. Lisa followed the administrative assistant into the classroom. The students had been chatting amongst themselves but allowed their voices to die down as they saw Tiara's mother enter the room.

"Ms. Johnson, it's so good of you to come and join us today." Mrs. Donovan reached out to greet Lisa warmly. "Come in... come in. Class, I'd like to introduce Ms. Johnson, Tiara's mom. She's been kind enough to join us today to tell us about the legal field and how to become an attorney. Would you welcome Ms. Johnson?"

The entire class applauded and glanced over at Tiara with a smile, everyone except Alicia Blackstone and her crew. This was the first time most of the students had met Tiara's mother.

"Your mom's very pretty," Jessica Harden, who was sitting behind Karen, whispered to Tiara as Lisa walked over to the podium Mrs. Donovan had moved to the front of the classroom.

"Thank you, Mrs. Donovan, for that wonderful introduction," Lisa said as she settled herself at the podium. "Also, thank you for inviting me to come and speak to you today. Now let me ask a general question—what type of law are you familiar with?" Lisa asked, directing her question to the entire class.

"Criminal law!"

"Trial law!"

"Corporate law!"

"Great... great!" Lisa responded as the students shouted out the different bodies of law they were familiar with. "Those are some of the popular areas of law people generally think of. Popular television shows might lead you to believe a lawyer's job revolves around dramatics, that law is all about litigation . . . trial work. Nothing can be further from the truth.

"Most of a lawyer's job is done outside the courtroom. Many lawyers never litigate at all and, really, the goal of a good attorney is to keep the client out of the kind of trouble that may actually bring them into the courtroom. To the extent the courtroom can be avoided, a lawyer has successfully done his or her job."

"Ms. Johnson?" The young man seated behind Tiara raised his hand to get her attention.

"Yes? And what is your name?"

"I'm Aaron. I was wondering . . . how do you keep your clients out of court? What do you have to do?"

"Well, a lawyer should always be more concerned with securing harmonious and orderly arrangements and avoiding and settling controversy, especially in regard to the drafting of contracts, wills, and other such documents. An attorney who can negotiate a great contract for you will oftentimes save you the hassle of going to court."

"How long does it take to become an attorney?" Amanda asked.

"Generally, a student will attend college for four years. After that, there's three years of law school."

"Do you specialize while you're in law school?" a girl wanted to know.

"No. Law school does not make you an expert in any particular kind of law. It trains you to be a generalist, but it is a springboard into various professional opportunities.

It's up to you to seek out opportunities for yourself and make the most of them as they come along. The practice of law is multifaceted, and the more you explore the particulars of each setting and how it suits your own needs and goals, the more likely you are to find a good match.

"Certain legal positions involve you more directly with clients. Others focus on research, meaning you'll work mostly on your own. Remember that lawyers can be found just about everywhere in a society as complex as ours. The legal arena is a fun and exciting place . . ."

After the presentation, as Lisa left the classroom, Tiara couldn't help but smile at the look on Alicia's face. No doubt about it. Tiara's mom had left a lasting impression on Alicia and her "ladies in waiting."

Brooke turned toward Tiara. "Your mother is great!" she whispered loudly. "She's really smart. I think I might want to go to law school after all."

"She is pretty smart," Tiara agreed. "We're going to pick up my outfit from Saks when we leave here today."

"My mom picked mine up yesterday. It's gorgeous," Brooke returned. "I'm so excited about the dance . . . aren't you?"

Tiara nodded. Frankly, she still couldn't believe she was actually going . . . and with Landon Andrews no less.

Chapter 38

Tiara checked the clock on the living room mantle for the third time in ten minutes.

"Tiara, are you okay?" Amanda asked from her seat on the couch. "You look a little nervous."

Silently chastising herself for being so anxious, Tiara shook her head in an attempt to assure her friend that she was fine. Taking another look at herself in the full-length mirror in the corner of the living room, she wondered again why she'd gotten a tube-top dress. While the dress was perfect, silky black material with pink and red flowers winding down the side, it was probably more perfect for someone else. She hardly had the boobs to keep the thing up.

"You look great, Tiara," Amanda repeated, crossing her legs casually. "Don't be so self-conscious."

"Sorry, you're right," Tiara said, sighing and walking over to join Amanda on the couch.

"The usual response to a compliment is thank you. But I'll let you have that one."

"Sorry," Tiara said, giving Amanda a hug. "Thank you

is what I meant. I just haven't really talked to Landon much since he asked me to go to the dance . . . or asked me if he could go to the dance . . . or . . . well, I don't really know how to say it."

"It was pretty bold that he asked you to your dance. But then, the way he cut in front of Max Blackstone and asked you out . . . well . . . wow."

"That's a good point," Tiara replied, trying to cross her legs and then deciding against it. "I really didn't expect that from him."

"Well, let's not forget the spontaneous Christmas kiss," Amanda reminded her. Turning her head to the side thoughtfully she added, "Come to think of it, he really is a box of chocolates."

"You never know what you're gonna get."

"Exactly." The doorbell cut their conversation short. The girls looked at each other with excitement that was impossible to disguise. Tiara was about to go open the door when her father appeared from nowhere.

"Ah, ah, ah, ladies," he said, waving a finger. "Let me get the door. Just sit and look pretty."

"It's not the fifties, Dad," Tiara mumbled. Her parents had agreed not to embarrass her, which, in her mind, required that they stay far, far away. Until that point they had been milling around silently in the kitchen. She should have figured that wouldn't last.

"The fifties have nothing to do with it," Tiara's mother said, sounding shocked as she appeared from the kitchen.

Tiara's dad opened the door to reveal Amanda's date, Walter Wiseman. Walter was a lanky, freckle-faced sophomore that Amanda had known since middle school. Tiara knew it wasn't exactly Amanda's idea of a hot date. She had been hoping to be asked by a hot upperclassman but Walter had beaten them all to the punch. As Amanda informed her, saying no to one date could mean never getting asked to another dance, which wasn't a risk she was willing to take.

Tiara's dad led Walter to the living room where he and Amanda exchanged an awkward hug. Tiara hoped that, for Walter's sake, Amanda would not be too hard on the poor guy. After all, he did pay for the expensive tickets to the dance and he would pay for her dinner at the great restaurant they were going to.

Landon arrived within minutes of Walter. He was dressed in a sharp black suit that made him look about five years older than he was. His red tie matched the red corsage he pinned on Tiara's dress. As cheesy as it was, Tiara was pleased that they matched.

Tiara was ready to go as soon as greetings were exchanged and introductions made. But her mother had different plans. Whipping her digital camera from the back pocket of her jeans, Lisa held it up as though it were a Grammy.

"A couple shots before you guys go!" she exclaimed. Noticing the frown quickly form on Tiara's face, she sighed. "Just a few! C'mon, gang."

"Oh, jeez," Tiara mumbled, wincing at the *gang*.

"Oh, I'm sorry," Lisa said, laughing. "I meant c'mon, homies, the posse, can you dig that?"

"Just take the pictures!" Tiara laughed, throwing her

hands up in defeat. Her father arranged them and her mother snapped the camera.

"Okay, I'm done," she said when she saw Tiara getting a little restless.

"Posse out," Landon joked, causing the whole group to erupt in laughter.

Chapter 39

Lisa stood by the beveled glass door and watched as Judge Andrews drove off with Tiara and Landon seated on the second row of the Andrews' SUV and Amanda and Walter on the row behind. This was Tiara's first formal affair and she really looked beautiful. As the car rolled out of sight, Lisa turned around, almost walking smack into Blake, who was standing behind her.

"She really looked wonderful, didn't she?" Blake said the exact thing Lisa had been thinking. It was obvious to Lisa that her husband was attempting to force a response from her. Lisa sidestepped him, walking past him toward the kitchen. She obviously wasn't ready to forgive him. Although he really couldn't blame her, enough was enough. One of them had to put an end to this in-house battle. If it had to be him, so be it.

Catching up with her, Blake reached out and put a hand on her upper arm. "Lisa . . . wait! We have to talk."

"Again?" she asked sarcastically.

"Yes . . . again," Blake replied in all seriousness. "I made a mistake . . . a big mistake. I should have called you . . . every day for that matter. I should have called you every day and let you know what was going on at the hospital. I didn't and I'm very sorry! What else can I do? What else can I say?" He stopped talking and stared down at her, silently begging for forgiveness.

Lisa returned his stare and saw the total despair lurking in his eyes. It had to be the longest moment of his life. Finally, she caved in, giving him a one-sided smile. "Please don't do it again, Blake. It really drives me crazy."

Blake let out a deep sigh of relief. "I won't, honey. Trust me, I promise I won't. You'll be the first person I call if I'm even going to be at the hospital overnight," he said, ducking his head to give her a kiss on the earlobe before moving lower to reach her lips. When he lifted his head, the two Broadway tickets were in his right hand, straight under her nose.

"What's that?" Lisa asked, squinting her eyes to see the print on the tickets. As she read the small letters, a shriek came out of her mouth. "Where did you get those? How did you get them?" she asked excitedly, not able to contain herself. "I've been dying to see this show."

"Oh, I have my ways," Blake said, executing a great imitation of Bela Lagosi.

"What night are they for?"

"Tonight . . . curtain call is at eight o'clock. Should we have dinner before or after the show?" he asked nonchalantly, now that he knew he was back in her good graces.

"Eight!" Lisa shrieked. "Blake, that doesn't give us any time to get ready."

"More than an hour," he calmly replied.

"An hour! I'll never make it," Lisa threw over her shoulder as she flew up the stairs.

"I bet you will," Blake softly replied, relieved that he'd been forgiven. He had no doubts about his wife's ability to be ready before curtain call.

Chapter 40

Lisa and Blake joined the huge crowd leaving the John F. Kennedy Center for the Performing Arts. Lisa loved going there, although she hadn't been able to do so as often as she'd like. The famed building provided Washington with a theatre, concert hall, and opera house, all under one roof. It was also the home of the National Symphony Orchestra and the American Ballet Theatre.

Lisa and Blake had been seated in the orchestra section of the opera house. "You must have paid a fortune for these seats," Lisa had whispered to him just before the play started.

"Not really."

"But these tickets have been sold out for weeks. Several of the senior partners at the firm have been trying to get some, especially for this weekend, but they weren't able to. How did you achieve the impossible?"

"I have my ways," Blake replied. "Trust me!"

The show had lasted two hours. Now, following the theatre crowd to the underground parking lot, they found their car, which Blake had parked close to the exit.

"That was smart of you to park over here," Lisa commented as she eased into the passenger seat.

"It's always easier to walk a little further to enter the building than to have to wait forever to exit the parking lot," Blake replied as they cruised out of the lot ahead of the line of cars forming behind them.

Lisa stared out the passenger window of the BMW as Blake's voice filled the car. He was singing along with an old Lionel Richie CD. The man had eclectic taste in music but always seemed to know all the words to the songs.

Downtown DC came into view as Blake drove past the Mall and the reflecting pool, toward the northeast section of town. Lisa tore her gaze away from the passing scenery to focus on Blake. "We're not going home?" she asked.

"No, I thought you might enjoy hearing a little music at the club. I owe you a special evening," he said by way of explanation.

She could always depend on Blake's honesty. He never kept his true feelings hidden from her, regardless of what those feelings were. If she didn't like what he had to say . . . oh well, that was another story, but he was still going to let her know what was on his mind.

Blake pulled up to the entrance of Love, one of the hottest clubs in the DC area. Pushing open the car door on the driver's side, Blake got out of the vehicle just as a smartly dressed valet came up on the passenger side of the vehicle to hold that door open for Lisa. There was no waiting to enter the building as the rest of the people in line were doing. The striking couple were whipped through the front door and immediately escorted upstairs to one of the VIP lounges even though the waiting area near the bar they walked through was jam-packed with a Saturday-night crowd waiting to get to one of the main lounges.

"Well, do you have connections or what?" Lisa asked Blake as they settled into one of the decorated tables in the reserved space. The room had been decorated in a Valentine's Day motif. Everything spelled love . . . cupids . . . arrows.

"One or two connections in high places," Blake responded. Getting into Love on a Saturday night was generally impossible. Getting into one of the VIP lounges was virtually unheard of, so Lisa knew that Blake had to know someone.

"One of the doctors on staff has a cousin who is part owner of the club," Blake informed her as a waiter came to take their orders. "What would you like?" he asked, glancing at the menu.

"It really is a little late to eat a full-course meal, but the stuffed shrimp sounds good."

A short while later, Lisa and Blake were feasting on plump shrimps and watching the dancers through the glass pane window on the dance floor below. The music coming through the sound system was great.

"This really is a lot of fun," Lisa threw out, watching the intricate steps of the dancers down below. "We haven't done anything like this in ages. Why not?" she asked in a puzzled voice.

Blake knew exactly what she meant. Before Tiara and Spencer Jr. had entered the picture, they'd done this sort of thing all the time. Even though he'd been in medical school and money had been tight, they'd always spent time together discovering and dabbling in all the fine events Boston had to offer. It really hadn't mattered so much what they were doing, they had just wanted to be together. Now that they had the money and were more comfortable financially, they never seemed to have enough time to spend together. Blake preferred the old way better; he wanted them to be together more often.

Jumping up from the table, Blake spontaneously grabbed Lisa by the hand. "Come on, let's dance!"

"Dance! Are you kidding? Blake, stop!" Lisa called out as her husband dragged her to her feet, pulling her along beside him out of the VIP room and down one level to the dance floor below. By the time they got there, Lisa was laughing hysterically, totally unsure of whether or not her legs would keep her upright to carry out the wild movements the other couples were maneuvering on the dance floor.

"Feet don't fail me now!" Lisa exclaimed as she started moving to the music.

They had a blast, gyrating and moving to the loud rhythms of the music as song after song came on until finally they were too exhausted to take another step.

Falling into their seats back in the VIP suite, Lisa was all smiles. "I really enjoyed that, Blake."

"I did too . . . a lot!" he replied as he signaled to the waiter. "A bottle of Moet champagne and some of your Valentine's Day dessert."

"What is it?" Lisa asked, referring to the dessert.

"A surprise! You'll see."

Lisa patiently waited, sipping the ice-cold water that had been left on their table. She continued to look down at the dancers one level below. "We used to be able to dance like that," she remarked, "all night long."

"Is that before we got old?" Blake asked with a laugh.

"Yes, I guess it was," Lisa replied as the waiter returned.

"Here you are, madam, sir." The waiter laid a silver tray loaded with strawberries in front of them. Beside the tray, he placed a deep fondue bowl filled with chocolate sitting on top of a warmer.

"Oh . . ." Lisa sighed happily "This really couldn't get any better."

Blake picked up a strawberry, dipped it into the hot chocolate, and held it to her lips.

"Ummm . . . this is heavenly," Lisa said, talking around a mouthful of tart berry and sweet chocolate.

"Well, maybe it could get a little better," Blake replied, then opened his mouth to accept the chocolate-covered strawberry Lisa was holding out to him.

"How?" she asked.

Blake didn't reply. Instead, he reached into his jacket pocket and held out a long flat navy-blue jewelry box, placing it on the table directly in front of her. Lisa glanced up at him but didn't say a word. Instead, she picked up the box and gently pulled it open. Inside on a white satin bed was a beautiful gold bracelet encrusted with four diamonds, each about one caret in size.

"Four diamonds to represent the four of us . . . you, Tiara, Spencer Jr., and myself. A diamond to symbolize all of the people we both hold dear to our hearts," Blake said softly. "People who should never forget about each other no matter what."

"Blake... what can I say? It's beautiful and so unexpected," Lisa managed to get out.

"Maybe you can say I'm forgiven... completely," Blake suggested.

Lisa stared at the man she had married over fifteen years earlier. He was so competent, always serious, always so thoughtful... well, almost always.

"You're completely forgiven, Blake. Happy Valentine's Day... and thank you for everything," she whispered across the table.

Chapter 41

The plan for the evening was simple: dinner, dance, home. This is what Tiara thought as Judge Andrews pulled up in front of Skidmore Prep. She had already made it through dinner without embarrassing herself and she was quite proud of that.

They had eaten at a French restaurant called La Rive Gauche, which had been Amanda's suggestion. Tiara, who was only vaguely familiar with some French dishes, had been privately apprehensive, but as it turned out, Landon surprised her by being familiar with most of the food on the menu.

"My mom received a gift to study French cuisine in France the summer after she finished college," Landon breezily explained. "We eat French food all the time at home . . . either that or takeout!"

It was Landon's charismatic personality that kept the dinner conversation afloat, and Tiara had been grateful for that.

Now at the dance, Tiara had mellowed out somewhat. She was still nervous, but it was different from the nervousness she'd felt at homecoming. It was an excited kind of nervousness that came from being around a boy you liked. By the time they had put their coats in the coatroom and hit the dance floor, Tiara was relaxed and ready to have fun.

They danced for a good forty-five minutes before stopping for water. Amanda and Walter also chose that moment to come over and take a break.

"This party is so cool," Walter announced.

"Yeah, I'm having the best time," Amanda agreed.

Tiara took a close look at her to see if she meant it. She did. Amanda was having a super time with Walter.

"This place is so crowded. There are tons of people here from a lot of different schools," Walter said just as Karen and Brooke showed up with their dates.

"Hi, you guys. Isn't this great?" Brooke asked the group as a whole.

"Yeah . . . super," Tiara replied. "This is so much better than homecoming."

"I guess so," Karen agreed. "For one thing, you don't see Alicia and her gang anywhere around do you? So much for being grounded."

"Tough break," Brooke said; they all laughed.

"Hey, this DJ is pretty good, right?" Tiara asked breathlessly as they grabbed prefilled cups of water from a table at the side of the cafeteria.

"Yeah, he's all right." Landon shrugged. Tiara glanced at him uneasily, causing him to add, "I mean, I'm having a good time, don't get me wrong. But he's just playing pop hits, you know?"

"Oh, yeah." Tiara nodded. "You're right."

"Do you think if I made some suggestions he would play them?" Landon asked.

"Yeah, why not?" Karen replied. "Never hurts to try."

Landon agreed and set off to the DJ booth. Tiara took another swig of water as she watched him make his way across the cafeteria. There was no debating it, Tiara thought to herself, she really had the best-looking date in the place.

"Hey, Tiara," a voice said from behind her, wrenching her from her thoughts. "You look . . . amazing."

Tiara turned to see who was speaking. "Oh, thank you, Max. You look good too."

"Thanks." Max self-consciously straightened his pink button-down shirt. "Where's your date?"

Tiara gestured toward the DJ booth where Landon was talking and laughing with the DJ.

"Seems like a cool guy."

"Yeah, he's pretty cool," Tiara agreed, although she was unsure where the conversation was going.

"You know, Tiara, I had planned to ask you to this dance," Max blurted out, finally revealing what was on his mind. Both Karen and Brooke just stared speechless. This was Alicia Blackstone's cousin, for heaven's sake. Was he serious? Had he really wanted to take Tiara to the dance?

"Really?" Tiara voiced her surprise. She never would have thought Max or anyone else from Skidmore would be seriously interested in asking her out. "I had no idea."

"Obviously I should have acted on it faster," Max said wearily. "I'm not saying it to make you feel bad or anything. I just . . . well, I guess I just wanted you to know."

Tiara was trying to think of something to say but Max cut the conversation short.

"Anyway, here comes your date," he said, nodding in Landon's direction. "Have a good night, Tiara."

"Thanks, " she said, but Max was already walking away.

"Mission accomplished," Landon reported proudly upon his return. "He said he's gonna play some hip-hop. Now to really get this party started!"

"Sounds good," Tiara mumbled absentmindedly. She was still thinking about her brief conversation with Max and whether it was something that would be discussed again or forgotten as though it never happened.

When the dance was over, Judge Andrews was waiting outside for them. It seemed that everyone had had a good time. Amanda and Walter were talking as though they were best friends, which was a vast improvement from his awkward comments at dinner and her courtesy smiles and laughs. Tiara was also happy that her own date had gone well. She had had fun with Landon. As he had predicted, the party really did start jumping once the DJ switched to a different genre of music. It was funny how practically every kid at Skidmore knew the words to every hip hop song he played. Tiara was proud that her date was the one responsible for making the party better. Several people even came over to thank him for getting the new sound going.

Walter was the first of the crew to be dropped off,

followed by Amanda. Left alone with Landon, the nervousness Tiara had felt at the beginning of the evening immediately returned. Suddenly she was very aware of her entire body, her hands folded cautiously in her lap, her long legs forcibly crossed, and her face looking forward rigidly. All her efforts at playing it cool went immediately out the window.

"I really had a good time tonight, Tiara," Landon said as they pulled out of Amanda's driveway.

"Me too," Tiara replied quickly. Then, realizing she might have sounded too curt, she repeated it. "Me too."

"That's good. Maybe we can spend some time together then, in the future."

"Sure," Tiara replied, smoothing the bottom of her dress.

"Are you nervous?" Landon asked, sounding amused and speaking softly so his dad couldn't hear the conversation. He reached for one of her hands. "You shouldn't be."

"I'm . . . I'm not," Tiara replied, turning to face him.

"Oh good," he said as he leaned in to kiss her. This, Tiara thought to herself, felt even better than Christmas.

Chapter 42

It was Wednesday afternoon, February twenty-fourth. Four days remained before Kyra's scheduled trial and Lisa was trying hard to pull the loose ends together. Sitting behind her desk, she swiveled her chair around to gaze out the large picture window directly behind her. She'd just returned from meeting with Kyra at DC Jail. Lisa's client was adamant about going to trial; she didn't care that all the evidence pointed toward her guilt. She was determined to go into that courtroom and prove her innocence. Lisa knew the odds were against her client winning her case. She also realized a loss could mean a life sentence for Kyra, but right now, she had very little choice in the matter. She had explained to both Kyra and her parents, several times, in fact, what the outcome of a loss would mean for Kyra. She'd sensed that the senator and his wife had wanted to back down—to go ahead and negotiate a plea agreement—but Kyra had the final say... and she'd wanted to go forward with the trial.

Lisa pulled her thoughts back to the present as she heard the buzz of the intercom on her desk. "Yes?"

"Ms. Johnson, Mike O'Leary is on line two for you. Would you like me to take a message?"

"No . . . no, Ellen. I'm free right now. I'll take it." She reached over to pick up her phone. "Hello. Lisa Johnson speaking."

"Hi, Lisa. It's Mike. How's everything going?"

"Fine. What's up?" Although a number of her cases were being prosecuted by the district attorney's office, Lisa hadn't been in contact with Mike for at least a week.

"The Kyra Davis case," Mike replied.

"What about it? We're set to go to trial."

"I'm not sure about that. We just received a call from our investigative department. As you know, the Davis family has been under constant surveillance . . . their phone lines have been tapped."

"Yes, I've known that for quite some time." Senator Davis and his wife were also fully aware that their every move was being monitored. "What's the problem?"

"We received word that a phone call came in about three hours ago. Part of the call was recorded, but we couldn't trace it."

"What did the person say?"

"It was a threatening call. We think it was from a member of the Heats street gang. It was a male voice. The person threatened to kill Whitman High School's class president. You know who that is, don't you?" Mike asked.

"Yes . . . Desmond Davis," Lisa replied in shock. "Kyra's younger brother."

"Right."

"That confirms a lot of what Kyra has been saying all

along," Lisa replied. It also explained why the senator and his wife had been pushing Kyra to accept a plea agreement. Desmond Davis was not only Whitman High's class president, he was also their star athlete and an honor student. He would never voluntarily be involved with a group like the Heats, in the same way that Kyra would never voluntarily have joined up with that group.

"Talk to me, Mike. What are you thinking?"

"More and more, my office is leaning toward the conclusion that Kyra Davis may in fact have been forced to drive that getaway car . . . very much like she's been alleging all along. This is the first concrete piece of evidence we have to support that."

"What do you intend to do now?" Lisa asked, actually seeing a light for Kyra at the end of this very dark tunnel.

"Well, with this tape, we may be able to work out some kind of deal. My office wants to nail this case shut . . . tight. These gangs are taking over. Most of them used to be on the west coast and in New York City, but recently they've expanded their operations from poor neighborhoods in major cities to small towns and affluent communities. They're now threatening countless teenagers like Desmond Davis whose status as a gifted student, an accomplished athlete, and a popular member of the school community has sheltered him from violence. They've managed to really get a niche into certain communities and they just won't lighten up. These gangs have become more mobile, allowing them to move into areas once considered immune from this sort of thing. They've found their way into the Washington, DC, area. They're running into other gangs and now all hell is breaking loose. We gotta shut them down before they explode."

"I agree. So what do you want me to do?" Lisa asked.

"We would like you to talk to Kyra. See if she'll work out a deal with us. See if she's willing to testify against the person who made the call, once we identify him. I'm certain he's the one who's behind a lot of this."

Chapter 43

Skidmore Prep wasn't necessarily known for its sports teams. One hundred percent college acceptance rates and outstanding SAT scores were areas where the school could boast. But one thing Tiara quickly noticed at the beginning of basketball season was the incredible school spirit Skidmore students granted the team.

There was a lot of hype about the upcoming tournament that would open Skidmore's basketball season. The games would be taking place in Skidmore's state-of-the-art gymnasium.

Tiara was not a huge basketball fan. At her old school in Boston, football and hockey had been the sports that drew crowds. Because of this, Tiara had been attending football and hockey games since she was in elementary school. She was almost embarrassed to admit to her Skidmore friends that she had never even watched a full basketball game.

"Are you serious?" Karen exclaimed. Her dark eyes popped behind her thick lashes as though Tiara had just admitted to committing a crime.

Tiara, Karen, and Amanda had arrived at homeroom

within minutes of each other. As usual, Brooke and Aaron had not yet arrived. They were always the latest of the bunch.

Tiara laughed. "It was just never the thing to do," she said in her own defense.

"Well, it is here," Amanda replied. "I don't even think most of the school knows the difference between an alley-oop and a layup but everyone gets excited for basketball season."

"You only know the difference because I told you," Karen quickly reminded her. Amanda shrugged and smirked.

"Anyway, you've got to come to the game."

"It's a chance to see some good basketball," Karen said, then quickly added, "Not Skidmore, but the other teams." Karen explained that Skidmore invited several surrounding schools to their tournament every year, including Woodson High, which had one of the best teams in the city. Tiara recognized Woodson as the school that Kamilla and Landon attended. She wondered if either of them would be at the game.

"The game starts at five," Karen told Tiara.

"I'll call my parents," she replied. She usually got picked up at five. "I'm pretty sure it won't be a problem." Tiara used the main office phone to call her dad before lunch. As she suspected, he not only gave her permission to stay for the game, but also said that he was interested in seeing for himself if Skidmore could hold its own on the court.

Tiara told her friends excitedly as she joined them at their cafeteria table, but they did not share in her enthusiasm. As soon as the statement "My father's coming too" escaped her mouth, Karen, Amanda, and Aaron exchanged questioning glances.

"What?" Tiara asked. She looked at Brooke to see if she had picked up on her other friends' skepticism. True to her usual clueless state, Brooke was stuffing her mouth with a bacon burger, strands of blond hair being shoveled in as well. Trying not to let her disgust show, Tiara gestured to her to take care of the hair situation.

"It's just that . . . games are drinking events," Amanda began.

"I've never invited my parents to a game," Karen informed her as though it was law. "It's almost worse than having them chaperone a dance because the lights are on."

"That's a good point." Aaron nodded in agreement while putting ketchup on his fries and burger.

"So people drink at the games?" Tiara asked, wondering if every event at Skidmore was simply an opportunity for these kids to throw a couple back.

"Not at the games," Karen replied. "But before the games most people get a little tipsy."

"Why?" Tiara asked. She had seen people drink at sports events she had attended with her parents, older men guzzling beers while yelling at the referees . . . but they always seemed to be there for the game first, beer second. Karen and Amanda were making it seem as though the excitement of the Skidmore tournament revolved around alcohol, to the point that parents were intentionally kept away.

"It's just a thing," Amanda said.

"Tradition," Karen added.

"Everyone pregames," Aaron admitted.

"It's like, a rite of passage, you know?" Amanda told her.

Brooke was still stuffing her face absentmindedly. As usual she seemed to have no interest in the topic at hand.

"I see," Tiara replied, realizing they were waiting for her understanding. But she didn't really see, nor did she understand. In fact, Tiara was pretty sure that Amanda was not using the term "rite of passage" correctly.

Tiara's understanding was that a rite of passage was an act that, once completed, signified the transition from the blamelessness of childhood to the responsibilities of adulthood. A bar mitzvah was a rite of passage. A girl's first period was a rite of passage. Downing a crude selection of your parents' liquor before attending a high school basketball game was an asinine imitation of what an ill-informed teenager considered the cooler side of adulthood.

"Well, I'll be with my dad," Tiara replied. "But I'm sure I'll see you guys there."

Amanda and Karen nodded apathetically. It was an innocent enough interaction, but Tiara noticed Aaron wince, the only acknowledgment of the tension that befell the group. The subject was promptly changed to the quality of the day's lunch and Brooke finally had something to add to the conversation.

Chapter 44

Karen's word was true, Tiara thought as she entered the gym with her father. The place was as packed as her friends had predicted. Most of the students had found a spot in the far section of the gym, which Tiara noticed was separated into sections by class year, with the seniors all the way at the top and the freshmen all the way at the bottom.

In addition to pregaming, it was also a tradition at Skidmore for students to dress according to theme. The theme for this first game, which was Skidmore versus Woodson High, was camouflage. Every student in the gym, except for Tiara, was decked out in camo print. Most had on camo T-shirts, but some kids, specifically a group of obnoxious but popular seniors that entered the gym moments after Tiara and her father, were clad in full army uniform, including authentic-looking army boots and face paint.

"What is that? The ROTC program?" Tiara's dad joked, knowing full well Skidmore had no such program.

"That would be the student cheering section." Tiara

laughed as they trudged up the bleachers. "I guess I missed the memo."

"I guess," Tiara's dad agreed lightheartedly. He gestured to a couple of empty seats and Tiara nodded. "What school is Skidmore playing?"

"Woodson," Tiara informed him, following him to the empty space on the bleachers. "You know, the school Landon and Kamilla go to. It's not too far from here actually."

"Oh, right. You should have asked them if they were coming to the game."

"I would have if I had known about it in advance."

"You know, you're welcome to go sit with your friends," Blake said lightly. "I wouldn't want to cramp your style."

"Nonsense," Tiara said quickly. "These are good seats. We can see everything from here."

"Suit yourself." Her dad shrugged. Taking a seat, he unwrapped one of the hotdogs they'd bought at the concession stand in the lobby.

"Plus, I don't see my friends," Tiara added, following suit with her own hotdog. "And there's not that much space left in the student section."

"Hey, you ain't got to make no speech," her dad teased, quoting one of his favorite movies, *Cooley High*. "I'm more than happy to share your first b-ball experience with you. I can't believe we never took you to a single game, although I've never been a huge basketball fanatic myself."

Tiara nodded, only half listening. While her father talked, she scanned the student crowd. Her eyes fell on Alicia and her posse. They were positioned on the lowest benches of the freshman section, clearly trying hard to appear cool. They had on shades and matching cropped camo tank tops. Tiara chuckled to herself as she dressed her hotdog in some ketchup and mustard. They had gotten pretty good seats despite the growing number of sweaty, obnoxiously intoxicated freshmen that were spilling over into their section. If Tiara's dad had noticed the particularly nonsensical behavior of the students, he didn't comment. Instead he saved his remarks for the arrival of the Woodson High cheerleading squad.

A catchy hip-hop beat boomed over the loudspeakers as the cheerleaders from the rival school made their way sassily onto the court in their blue-and-white uniforms. Their routine was short but packed with attitude, an indication of what Woodson High had to bring to the table. They were almost as good as the cheerleaders from her old school, Tiara and her father agreed.

When the routine was over, the girls left the court with as much admirable arrogance as they had had on arrival. As the last cheerleader exited the court, Woodson's noticeably all-black team filed out of the guest locker room. The Skidmore crowd clapped politely while the Woodson fans on the opposite side of the gym hooted and hollered. Tiara took a good look at the crowd, trying to spot Kamilla or Landon, but she had no luck. Woodson's starting five was announced and the rest of the team took the bench.

It was then that the lights dimmed and the spotlights flashed. Skidmore had no cheerleaders, but Tiara had to admit they did not allow Woodson to outshine them. Each player was announced as he came running in from the locker room, and the Skidmore crowd loved every moment of it, especially the entrance of Ahmed Randolph.

"He must be the star," Tiara's father commented. Tiara chuckled, rolling her eyes. She didn't know if Ahmed was a star, but she was certain he brightened the eyes of Skidmore students, especially the female ones. Not that she was above it; she definitely saw what made him appealing. He had smooth dark skin, bright brown eyes, and a pleasant laugh. He was a rare aesthetic in the halls of Skidmore, and she appreciated his presence just because there were so few good-looking guys to look at. At the same time, he was aware that his presence was appreciated by the deprived female population, so his arrogance overpowered his physical appeal, at least in Tiara's eyes.

Chapter 45

The first half of the game was practically a wipeout. Skidmore was down by over thirty points with seemingly no potential for a comeback. Had this been her old school, Tiara would have been embarrassed, but she had already been prepped on what to expect from Skidmore's b-ball team, and while it was somewhat disheartening, she had no hard feelings about it.

Not everyone in Skidmore's crowd felt this way, however. In retrospect, Tiara thought to herself, she could have seen the catastrophe coming. While she didn't see when the first Skidmore student held up that first dollar bill, she had seen the expressions on the Woodson High students begin to change, from pride to confusion to anger. It was this change of expressions that caused Tiara to look to her right at the Skidmore student section. There she saw a mass of students holding up various bills, some twenties, some tens, some fives.

"What's that about?" her father asked, taking in the scene for himself. Tiara shrugged, keeping her eye on the bills, waiting to see what would happen next. Perhaps this was another one of Skidmore's many traditions, she thought. But she noticed the players of both teams were looking toward Skidmore in confusion as they filed to their respective locker rooms.

When the teams were gone the Woodson cheerleaders began to make their way back onto the court. It was then that the chant began. Tiara could not be sure where it started, but the entire Skidmore student crowd picked up on it very quickly.

"Yeah, your players can make a score, but have you ever seen these before?"

"I don't get it," Tiara mumbled to her father, wondering if he could offer an explanation.

"I guess since Woodson is a public school, they're making fun of them for not having money," Tiara's father replied, looking disgusted. "I would expect more class from Skidmore, but I guess that can't be bought, no matter how much the tuition costs."

Tiara said nothing as the Skidmore bills flapped higher. A part of her, the larger part really, wanted to cross the gym and join the Woodson crowd, but they were starting to get rowdy themselves. They had caught on to what the Skidmore students were cheering and had started a chant of their own: "Scoreboard, Scoreboard."

The Woodson cheerleaders looked confused, but it seemed they didn't know what else to do so they started their routine. They managed to gain the attention of the crowd for a total of thirty seconds before they lost it again.

There was a shrill female scream from the Skidmore student crowd. Within seconds the freshman section of

Skidmore students was running onto the court or out of the gym, though what they were trying to get away from remained unclear.

"What the hell?" Tiara's father mumbled as they both tried to get a better look. A couple of seniors from the top bleachers ran down to the floor level, fists cocked, ready to swing. As the freshman section disappeared out of the gym, three members of Skidmore security finally picked up on the situation and ran toward the chaos. A few other security guards were over by the Woodson section, trying to calm down that crowd. Seconds later everyone's question was answered as security grabbed five students, three from Woodson and two from Skidmore.

Tiara gasped as she recognized one of the Woodson students flailing to get out of the security guard's grip. "I guess now we know Landon made it to the game," her father said, voicing Tiara's own realization.

Chapter 46

The security guard had let Landon leave with the Johnsons, although he didn't restrain his skepticism when Tiara's dad claimed Landon was his son.

"So you got one at Skidmore and one at Woodson?" the security guard asked, eyeing Tiara's Skidmore Athletics T-shirt that she hadn't bothered to change out of. Tiara's dad shrugged. "Looks like you've got a war on your hands."

"Just call me the general." Tiara's dad shook hands with the guard before steering the two teenagers away.

It wasn't until they were in her dad's car that Landon decided to speak up. He had looked embarrassed from the moment Tiara's dad had run out of the gym, caught up with security, and claimed Landon as his own, apologizing on his behalf.

"Thanks for that back there, Mr. Johnson," Landon mumbled. He was sitting in the passenger seat and Tiara couldn't make out his face, but he sounded upset.

"I have to admit I was shocked to look down and see that one of the students starting trouble was you," her dad replied calmly, pulling out of Skidmore's parking lot and onto the road.

"We didn't start it!" Landon exclaimed, then catching himself, he added, "I mean, it shouldn't have come to violence. That was our fault. But we didn't start it."

"Fair enough," Tiara's dad said. "I'm not going to judge you on it. That's for your parents to do."

"Yeah, I'm sure they'll be pleased."

"What exactly happened?" Tiara asked from the backseat, curiosity finally getting the best of her.

"We heard the chant, didn't like it, and went over to handle business," Landon replied curtly. Turning to look at her, he added, "Simple as that."

"Oh," was all Tiara could manage. There was something about seeing Landon angry that made him even more attractive than before.

"Simple as that, huh?" Tiara's dad asked. He seemed amused and disappointed at the same time.

"Mr. Johnson, I know what we did wasn't right, I get that." He sighed. "But you have to understand where Woodson is coming from. Most of the black kids in that school are coming from the other side of town. Like, the other side. One of my best friends is on the team and he's coming from the other side, you know? It's not fair that he's working so hard and still has to hear chants like that when he's just trying to be a better person."

"Landon, the team was in the locker room," Tiara's dad reminded him. "They couldn't hear the chants."

"I don't know, it's the principle of it, Mr. Johnson," Landon mumbled. "It's just the principle."

"This seems like a classic case of not knowing when to pick your battles. And I don't mean to lecture you. I'm sure you'll get enough of that at home."

"You're probably right. I know that you are. I'm not the best at picking battles, that's for sure."

That's for sure... Tiara wondered at that final comment. Landon was definitely an interesting guy. First there was the unexpected kiss at Christmas, then the charming guy at the Valentine's Day dance, and now this fight.

Never a dull moment....

Chapter 47

"Miguel circled around the block for a while. I was too nervous to try and figure out where we were going. The two men in the backseat were yelling at each other. One of them, Victor, kept saying that he wanted to make the hit right away. The other guy, Ricardo, he wanted to wait. They both had guns and I was really afraid of what they were planning to do and what they were going to do to me," Kyra said, trying hard not to break down.

"We left Georgetown and drove uptown toward Spring Valley, another very ritzy section of town. We were getting real close to American University when Miguel stopped the car in front of a Starbucks and got out. He ordered me to slide over to the driver's seat."

"What did you do then?" Mike asked.

"With the two guys behind me holding guns to my head, I didn't have much choice. I did what Miguel told me to do. I slid over behind the wheel of the Cutlass and waited for him to get back in on the passenger side. Once Miguel was back inside, he told me to drive straight down the road. He kept telling me which streets to take until suddenly he ordered me to slow down. I did exactly what he said because Victor and Ricardo still had their guns pointed at my head.

"After I slowed down, they waited a minute or two. Then the next thing I knew, all hell broke loose. They opened fire. I had no clue who they were aiming at or what to do. I jammed my foot on the brakes and started screaming. The next thing I knew, all three men jumped out of the car. I heard the screeching of police sirens and before I knew it, I was being surrounded by at least twenty police officers. I was arrested on the spot. Miguel and the other members of the Heat gang had opened fire on a rival drug dealer's gang. It was only after I was taken to DC Jail that I discovered that Tony Linwood, an innocent bystander, had been shot in the crossfire."

Lisa glanced at each member of the grand jury. She could tell that it was a wrap. It was obvious that every juror believed every word Kyra had said. Lisa took a second glance, this time looking over at Mike O'Leary. Mike gave her a slight nod and mouthed the words, "Good job."

Lisa stood in the conference room of McKenzie, Kennedy, and McKenzie. It seemed like she was surrounded by every member of the law firm and all of Kyra's family . . . the senator, Mrs. Davis, and their son, Desmond. Kyra was still at DC Jail. Lisa and Mike had worked out a deal. Kyra was going to be relocated and placed in protective custody.

Chapter 48

Tiara opened her locker and as usual braced herself for the potential downpour of textbooks and knickknacks. Over the past eight months, her locker had become the holding ground for a lot of things she didn't have the heart to throw away but hadn't been so attached to as to take home.

There were tennis balls and extra sneakers from the fall and winter tennis season, a schedule of the matches for the Skidmore basketball tournament, and a deflated red balloon from the Valentine's Day dance. This was in addition to folders of old homework assignments, sweatshirts, scarves, and hats that she had been meaning to take home or give back to the friends she had borrowed them from.

In retrospect her first year in Washington, DC, had gone by very quickly. There had been both ups and downs, of course, but that was always how things went. She had started off desperately missing her buddies from Boston, but her parents had helped by bringing Mya and Ebony to DC for the Christmas break. It had been nice to have her friends there when she needed them the most, to show her the positive side of the new city. Oh, there was no doubt that the troublesome run-ins with Alicia had been extremely hard to deal with, but it was clear in Tiara's mind that she had gotten the upper hand in that situation.

Yes, the positives certainly outweighed the negatives, which had made the year go by very quickly, especially the spring. Tiara had joined Skidmore's track team, so between school, track practice, tennis at the Arthur Ashe Foundation, family commitments, and spending time with her new friends, Tiara was usually exhausted by the end of the week. Now, here it was, the last week of school before summer vacation, and although she would be going to Boston for part of the summer, Tiara was sad. She knew she was going to miss Amanda, Karen, Aaron, Max, and Brooke. She was going to miss all her new friends at Skidmore Prep.

"Hey, Tiara, aren't you gonna get ready for the meet?" This was from Brooke, who had joined the track team as a discus and shot-putter.

"I'll be on my way in a minute," Tiara answered her. "I just wanted to start taking some of my things home."

"Why?" Brooke asked. "We've still got another week before school ends."

"Yeah, but I've got a lot of stuff in here." Tiara gestured to her overstuffed locker. "I want to be able to bring it all home."

"That's a good idea. My locker's pretty full too."

"A lot has happened this year," Tiara said, stuffing one of her sweaters into her backpack and zipping it up.

FRESHMAN YEAR

"And it's only freshman year. Imagine what sophomore year is gonna be like!"

"Probably just as great," Tiara replied thoughtfully, slinging her backpack on her back and picking up her sports bag. "Just as great if not better." Slamming her locker shut, Tiara walked side by side with her friend . . . on to the next adventure: sophomore year.

If you enjoyed *Freshman Year*, look for Tiara and her friends soon when they return for *Sophomore Year*.

SOPHOMORE YEAR

"You have a nice year, Tiara. Sophomore year is going to be just so sweet!"

"I'm counting on it, Ray. See you later," Tiara replied walking off deep in thought. Yup...she was really looking forward to some fun and excitement this year. She now had her own circle of friends at Skidmore Prep who seemed to like her for just who she was. Granted, a few bullies who were determine to make her life miserable still remained, but for the most part, Tiara had figured out how to get around them.

Tiara raised her right foot to step off the curb when the madness began. A rush of black SUV's with flashing lights whipped into the Skidmore parking lot shooting past, right in front of Tiara. There had to be at least six vehicles, the first one missing Tiara by less than a foot.

Tiara stood still in shock as the line of black Cadillac

Escalades zipped past her. Red and blue police lights flashed from each vehicle, some lights were spinning from above the front windows, while others were flashing above the rear windows. That wasn't all. Even more lights were flashing on the floorboards of the black Escalades. Tiara never heard Ray approach her but almost magically, he was standing beside her, concern written all over his face.

"Tiara...you okay?" Ray quickly asked, not even trying to hide the fear in his voice. One of his favorite students had almost been run over, right before his eyes...and by the president of the United States Secret Service motorcade.

"Yyy...yes. I think so," Tiara stuttered in response to his question. "I'm okay. What was that all about?"

"It's our new student...Cameron Woodson...President Woodson's son. He's starting Skidmore Prep today," Ray informed her, surprised that she was unaware that the president's children would be attending Skidmore. For the last few months, this bit of news was the only thing on the radio, TV, internet, you name it. Anyone who lived in DC knew about it...in fact, everyone in the world knew about it.

"Yes. Yes. I knew they were coming to Skidmore but for some reason, I didn't expect all this noise and flashing lights and everything. There are at least six cars here. How many kids are they bringing? I thought there were only two boys," Tiara replied, still staring at the line of cars pulling into the parking spaces obviously reserved just for them.

"There are only two kids. The younger son Conner is thirteen. He'll be attending the middle school in the eighth grade. The older one is eighteen. He's the one coming here," Ray informed her.

"Are you telling me they really need six huge SUVs to get one kid here?" Tiara questioned, still watching as the line of cars settled into the parking spots. As she spoke, eleven clean shaven men all dressed in dark suits exited the SUVs and took their positions in front of each Cadillac Escalade. Each officer stood at attention, observing any and everything in the parking lot. What they were looking for Tiara had no idea, but they stood on alert as if waiting for something to happen.

Tiara noticed that each man was wired. Sneaking up through the collars of their starched white shirts and wrapping around the outer part of each of their left ears were spiral cream colored wires and earplugs. Wow... was this something? And to think she was the first one at Skidmore to see it.

With the exception of the driver in the third vehicle, all the other drivers of the fleet of SUVs stepped out of their respective cars. The driver of the third Escalade remained seated behind the steering wheel. No one said anything, not the Secret Service men, not Ray, and certainly not Tiara.

There was dead silence for about sixty seconds, then almost on cue, one of the dark suited men approached the passenger door of the third SUV and opened it. Stepping aside, he held it open, waiting at attention for its occupant to step out.

"I sincerely hope this isn't the way they plan to bring this young man to school every day," Ray commented loud enough for several of the suited men to hear. "Because if that's the case, I'm definitely going to have to talk to them. They're certainly going to have to do a lot better than this."

At this point, Tiara was clueless to what Ray was saying. She'd stopped listening. Tiara's eyes were glued to the young man stepping out of the third Cadillac Escalade. Tiara had previously seen pictures of President Woodson's sons. After the inauguration, she had read an article explaining how only the president and his wife would be moving into the White House in January leaving their two boys with their grandparents in Antigua until the start of the new school year. The newspaper article had indicated that even though both boys were home schooled, the move to the White House in the middle of the school year would just be too disruptive. Instead, the president and the first lady had decided their boys would come to Washington, DC at the start of the school year and join their peers at one of the local schools. The school of choice…Skidmore Prep.

Normally, it would have been virtually impossible for just anyone to move to DC and corner one of the coveted spots at Skidmore Prep. Skidmore was notorious for being one of the oldest prep schools in the country. It was definitely the oldest one on the East Coast and often referred to as "the Harvard" of all prep schools. As a result, the average human being was never going to just get in like that. Everyone knew without asking that "not just anyone" got accepted here. As Tiara had been informed last year on her first day of school, there where two basic criteria for gaining admission: One…you definitely had to be smart to

SOPHOMORE YEAR

get into Skidmore. Two, you'd better know someone! Obviously, being the president's son would qualify you on both counts.

Like every other female student at Skidmore, Tiara had been excited when she'd heard that the president's son would be completing his senior year at Skidmore Prep. Just like everyone else, Tiara had gazed at pictures of the president's oldest son and concluded that he would make a wonderful addition to the male population at Skidmore. Now that she was seeing him in the flesh, Tiara realized only too well that none of the pictures had done him justice. The person who stepped out of the black Cadillac Escalade SUV...the image standing no more than ten feet away from her...was a picture of sheer beauty. The oldest son of President Woodson was to die for!

The young man who'd stepped out of the car was no less than six-feet two-inches tall with the body of a quarterback. His pale blue jeans fit like a second skin. His white button-down shirt neatly tucked into those pants was held up by a belt, an almost foreign object in this day and age. On anyone else, the Navy blue blazer which fell midway to his thighs would have looked geeky, but on him, it looked oh so sophisticated. His hair had obviously just been cut for the first day of classes and made him look polished and well... preppy. Tiara wondered what he looked like behind the dark shades he was sporting. They fit him perfectly and looked just so cool.

"We go this way Sir," one of the dark suited Secret Service men instructed the first son. "Your homeroom is in that building over there on the first floor," the agent explained, waiting for the young man to make a move and follow the other four Secret Service men who had already started walking towards the high school's main building.

"I think we should check and see if the young lady we almost ran over is okay... don't you?" the first son questioned.

The agent he spoke to didn't miss a beat. "Someone will address that matter, sir. Right now, we have to get you inside the building."

"Somehow that doesn't seem right," the young man replied walking over to where Tiara and Ray were standing. The agent who had spoken jumped in front of him in an attempt to block his way.

"Sir, we cannot deviate from the plan. Our men have been over here several times and practiced your arrival and departure down to every last detail. As you know, we have gone through the route and checked every detail to ensure your safety. Our command posts are inside the building to the left. That is where we will be stationed all day while you are in school. We will have one guard that will follow you throughout the building and we will be monitoring everything from our command posts. We therefore need to follow procedures and gain access to the building now before the other students start arriving."

Tiara listened in complete amazement to everything being said. Had they forgotten she was there? It didn't even dawn on her to make a move. Frankly, she wasn't sure if the Secret Service men at this point would have allowed her to enter the building before the first son. Still in a trance, Tiara watched as the young man circled the Secret Service agent speaking to him and walked the short distance to stand directly in front of her.

"Are you okay?"

Tiara didn't respond. She was still too dumbfounded to say a word. She simply continued to stare even as she heard some of the other agents start to snicker. From somewhere beside her, she thought she heard Ray respond.

"She's fine young man," Ray stated. If nothing else, the sheer politeness of the president's son made Ray want to calm his fears. "She wasn't hurt," Ray continued. "I think she was just surprised by all the commotion...the flashing lights and everything," Ray explained.

"I see," the first son replied, still not making any move to leave. Reaching out, he stretched his hand to formally greet Ray. "My name is Cameron Woodson. I will be starting Skidmore Prep today," he said, speaking to Ray but looking straight at Tiara

"Yes...I know who you are," Ray replied "We've been expecting you. Welcome to Skidmore Prep."

"Thank you. I'm looking forward to being here," Cameron replied, once again speaking to Ray but still looking directly at Tiara.

"You'd better move along now young man before the other students start to arrive. It was very kind of you to stop and check on Ms. Johnson...Ms. Tiara Johnson," Ray willingly supplied the information. By this point, there was no mistaking the fact that all the Secret Service agents were openly snickering. Tiara still had not said a word.

"Sir, we go this way," the agent who had previously done the most talking chimed in. He quickly gave Tiara the once over, memorizing her face before escorting the first son into Skidmore Prep's high school.

CPSIA information can be obtained at www.ICGtesting.com
Printed in the USA
BVOW01s1104100414

349874BV00001B/1/P